Some Girls Like Dragons

ERIKA GIFFORD

ISBN: 1540699315
ISBN-13: 978-1540699312

Published by Teragram, ink,
www.teragram.ink

Edited by Sandra Peoples, Next Step Editing,
www.nextstepediting.com

DEDICATION

To everyone who didn't ask if it was ready for the world
or if the world was ready for it,
but rather:

"When can I read it?!"

CONTENTS

Prologue	1
Chapter One	4
The Beginning of it All	10
Chapter Two	12
The Beginning of the Siege	19
Chapter Three	25
Marja	33
Chapter Four	37
Decisions Must Be Made	47
Chapter Five	53
Being Me	60
Chapter Six	64
The Wall	72
Chapter Seven	75
The First Skirmish	84
Chapter Eight	87
Traitor	96
Chapter Nine	101
Marja and Mother	108
Chapter Ten	113
The Secret Attack	124

Chapter Eleven 129

Wrapping Things Up 137

Chapter Twelve 142

Chapter Thirteen 150

Chapter Fourteen 162

Chapter Fifteen 170

Chapter Sixteen 179

Epilogue 191

SOME GIRLS LIKE DRAGONS

PROLOGUE

"Hear ye, hear ye!" shouted the herald. His voice was hoarse from trying to be heard over the large crowd that had gathered around him and the sound of horses and carts, screaming children and mothers haggling with merchants from far off lands.

Everyone seemed to be out today. Even the schoolboys. But something wasn't right; the horses and carts weren't loaded with goods for peddling or produce for the farmer's market or merchant's stores, they were loaded with mothers and children and were led by fathers with grim haggard faces. You could tell they were leaving town, or were at least trying.

The haggling going on sounded flat and fearful. No one laughed or cracked jokes today. People's faces were sharp with hunger and foxy with fear. Soldiers stood at every street corner.

Four months of combat had left rubble strewn about the street. It was a small city in a small country with few imports and no exports, and really couldn't have defended itself any longer than those long four months. Its enemies were very surprised when it had lasted that long, and needless to say, the residents were frightened.

That is why the hoarse herald had to shout before he could quiet the crowd. The people didn't want to hear what he had to say because they loved their king, queen and princess, and the last they heard, the king had been injured during battle and the rumors that he was dead were already circulating. They had also gotten word the queen was mortally ill. The princess had, perhaps, escaped.

"Hear ye, hear ye!" cried the herald, the crowd quieted and he pulled out his scroll. It was a long one so he stepped back three steps to be in the shadow of the castle that stood higher up the hill, gray and blocking out the sun. "In the nineteenth year of our Lord, Orchalon, King of Fairfalcon, has become ruler of this land!" the soldiers stomped, clashed their swords against their shields and cheered as the village folk began to walk away, disgusted with the proceedings.

The herald raised his voice, "King Orchalon has cast down your rulers: your king and queen. He has conquered your nation, and is even now hunting down the last of the royalty." The villagers stood still, rooted in fear and apprehension.

"So, then the princess still lives!" an elderly man whispered.

"Aye, she's off to Grayhust, like as not. Clever girl," hissed an old hag.

"The king's bound to catch up with her sometime," interjected one of the nearby soldiers. "Now quit talking, the rest of us would like to hear what the man's saying."

"His majesty's army believes it has the former Princess Scarlet Elwen Silvergleam Oreldes cornered in Westfay, a village a little north from here. Where, when found, she will be tried as a war criminal and beheaded for her crimes."

"I don't fancy that kind of a trial," the man whispered again.

"I guarantee it's already cut and dried," the woman shot back. "Why! They've already condemned her!"

"I'd have to do the same in their place," the man said.

"Why?"

"Why not? It was her sneak attack on King Orchalon's army that made us last so long! If it wasn't for her leading our army, we would never have lasted so long!"

"Hush!" cried the soldier. "Do you want to be tried for treason? I could turn both of you over for talking like that! You villagers idolize your princess too much and nothing good will come of it."

The old man left the market and the woman moved away from the soldier.

"King Orchalon's second and youngest son, Prince Konrad Thurindir Starseed Faervel, will be joining his father here before the next moon, and will be king of the country when his father dies. You will be glad to know," the herald began, looking up, "That the kingdom of Fairfalcon and Hedgecliff will remain as two distinct kingdoms. King Orchalon's eldest son will be king of Fairfalcon and his youngest, Prince Konrad will be king of Hedgecliff."

At this proclamation, a murmur ran through the crowd, each person repeating a bit of gossip they had heard about the prince, or a sigh of relief that they would stay as one country and that "Things might not be too bad!" and "A nice young, soft-hearted prince is just what we need after his father, the king."

A girl in servant's garb fingering a simple ring in her hand looked on from the shadows in disgust. "How easily hearts are changed and deceived," she thought as she turned away.

"Perhaps," said one young mother to a man next to her as she tried to keep her young ones close, "They'll spare the princess, and they'll make her marry the prince to secure him on his throne." Her small child finally broke loose and she left the square to catch him and didn't hear his response.

An interesting idea, the man thought as he pulled his hood over his eyes and moved away. *Perhaps when I tell him, the King will reconsider.*

"You will all welcome Prince Konrad Thurindir Starseed Faervel when he enters the village and rides up to the castle. I suggest you at least *try* to make a good impression," the herald hinted, going off script. "Perhaps he will not be altogether too cruel." The herald rolled up his scroll and put it in his saddle bag. "I'm off! I need to make it to three more villages before tonight and then I'm off to join his majesty's army in Westfay up north to bring back news from them." He mounted his horse and galloped off to the west gate, past the patrol keeping anyone from coming in or out, and out to the farm lands shouting. "Hear ye, hear ye!"

The people began to walk away, or finished haggling with merchants as the castle's shadow grew as the sun sank lower and lower into the ground.

Only a year ago the castle had been warm and inviting, and now it was cold and dark, if only because the king was dead and his place filled with a foreign king, the beloved queen dying or perhaps already dead, and the hero, the princess hunted down with a death sentence on her head.

CHAPTER ONE

"His majesty King Orchalon orders you to prepare a feast in honor of his son, Prince Konrad Thurindir Starseed Faervel," the servant began, still out of breath from the long stairs he had descended to get to the kitchen. "You have the rest of the month to prepare it, but it must be done when he comes next moon. You had better make it good or he will dismiss you," he warned.

"My lord," the cook stammered, popping her knee on a curtsy. "If my scullery maid doesn't upset the cake, or burn the roast pig, or add too much salt to the bread, as she is apt to do, I shouldn't see any reason why his majesty should worry."

"Scullery maid?" the upper servant asked.

"Newle," she answered the servant as she turned to the tall thin girl with jet black hair tied up in a green scarf who was kneaded bread. "She's rather clumsy but trainable. She will be an honor to our king's servants if she will learn anything, and a pretty and useful bride when the time comes too."

The cool took a pinch of pallid and sticky dough, put it in her mouth and chewed on it for a second. "Salty," she muttered and spit it out on Newle's sleeve. "Bake it, but feed it to the pigs," she paused to watch Newle follow her orders, but she didn't move. "No need to keep kneading it like that, stupid. Pigs don't mind if the bread's heavy." Newle molded the bread into a pan and put it on the windowsill. "And no need to let it rise either," she hissed.

Newle stood still for a moment before asking in a small voice. "Is the fire ready for it, Cook?"

"Of course not, idiot!"

"Then I might as well let it rise Cook, there's no harm to it. And if some poor beggar comes along we might give it to him because it will be nice and light, even if I put too much salt in it."

The cook slapped her across the face and shooed her out to milk the cows.

"I see you have everything under control," the upper servant said with a knowing smile when she turned back to him. "But take my advice, stay on your toes because if the prince hears of this, you'll be gone."

"What do you know about the prince?" the cook asked as she bustled around the room setting things in order.

"I was one of his lower servants back at Fairfalcon. He rescued me from being a scullery boy under a rather mean Cook," he spoke sharply, but then softened a little. "Take my advice, the girl has more brains than you do. If you just let her think, your kitchen would be much better, if not kinder."

The servant left up the great winding stairs that lead to and from the dining room and the cook was left to simmer her rage in a big pot over the fire.

Why does Cook blame me for everything? Newle wondered. *If the milk won't skim, if she burns the food, if the strawberries are missing, if a half a pie is gone. Anything! It's even a well-known fact that the stableman shares pies with his girlfriend from the village. It's also a well-known fact that he shares strawberries and cream with her,* Newle huffed under her breath. *If I were queen* ... but she stopped herself before she finished her thought.

Newle came back with the pails of milk from the cows, put them in the cellar and went out for a second trip.

She came back in, her slender young back bent under the yoke with two pails of milk. They too went down to the cellar.

Newle knew what she was doing; she had done this a hundred times. After the milk, she took the leftovers from lunch out to the pigs and grain to the chickens. She didn't have to gather eggs because she had done that earlier.

Then she eagerly took Cook's shopping list down to the butcher.

The moment she was out of Cook's sight, she lifted her head, fingered a chain with a ring on it which she had pulled out from under her shift, smiled, and swung her basket. She practically ran to the butcher's.

"One day," she thought, "One day, I'll leave this drudge of a position and I'll head east. I'll see the dwarfs, I'll see the elves and I'll see dragons; the people here don't need me and they don't want me."

As she walked through town she nodded at everyone she went past except the soldiers. As she passed them, she slipped into the shadows and avoided their gaze. She had once had an encounter with them that she did not want to repeat.

When she got to the butcher, she entered through the side door.

How the tides have turned, she thought, searching the room for the familiar face she knew would be there. *One day, when things are right again, I will have my own servants get my order. Or perhaps I'll go with them and let them come in through the front door. Then they'll be treated like normal people. Just think of the change!*

She waited in line as the butcher, who was a hearty old man, gave first a boy then a fine lady their orders.

"And what can I do for you, miss?" he asked when it was her turn.

"I've come for Cook's order. You haven't forgotten it have you?" Newle asked timidly, a little afraid to ask after her true purpose.

"Forgotten it? My best and favorite customer? How could you think it!"

"I'm sorry I doubted you, Cook's been dreadful today," then she thought for a moment. "Or maybe I've been dreadful. There's always a possibility."

"You? Dreadful? Never. The moment Cook lets you out of her sight I'm hiring you to help out here. You're fifteen and that's old enough to join my other apprentices."

"I'm sorry," she teased with a smile, still nervous. "But I'm not allowed to think about deserting like that. Now, Cook's order."

"You're right," he admitted as he pulled out the choice of meat Cook had ordered and wrapped it up in paper with a sigh and a smile. "Mutiny can wait. Is there anything else I can do for you?" he asked, leaning on the counter.

Newle hesitated, but finally revealed the true reason she had practically run here. "Where is Marja?"

"She's outside around back," the butcher gestured and turned to his next customer.

Newle thanked him, left through the side door, and turned to go around back. The small, fifteen-year-old girl that she met there ran to greet her with a tight hug.

"I'm so glad you're alright!" the girl, Marja, finally gasped. "I haven't seen you in weeks."

"I'm sorry," Newle replied. "You haven't been here the last few times that I've been able to come.

"I'm sorry too." Marja replied.

Newle finally revealed her true reason for coming. "How are you? How's life?"

Marja pulled away from the hug. "I can't forget him."

Newle nodded. "Stefan will be missed, everyone will be missed." she pulled Marja into another hug before she turned to run back to the castle.

"Be careful!" Marja called after her, just as she had done many times before.

Dinner was fast approaching, and Newle took care to tuck the chain and ring back underneath her shift before she pushed the large kitchen door open.

"I got the meat for tomorrow," Newle said breathlessly when she got back, careful to leave out any information of her visit.

"But it didn't have to take that long," Cook grouched. "Now unless you hurry, the king won't have anything for dinner!"

"Cook?" Newle asked, anger rising as she took a deep breath. "Don't you think you dote on the new king too much? Don't you feel any responsibility or loyalty to the old king?" Angry tears welled up in her eyes, "Or what about the queen? She's dead! Or the princess!" she hesitated. "They have no idea where she is! Don't you feel any loyalty to the old order?"

"Hush child!" the cook cried. "You don't know what you're talking about. The king is dead. He is no more. Why should I care if someone else is king now? The queen is also dead. And as for the princess, who could care less? We've lived in the same castle for years and years and I have never seen her. Besides, they do know where she is—she's down in Westfay and bound to be hung before the end of the week." she answered matter-of-factly.

Newle's eyes began to well up with tears as she was overwhelmed with emotion for the kingdom that was slipping away.

"Run," the cook said giving her a quick push. "Chop up some herbs for the stew."

Newle was only too glad to obey, if only so her angry tears could vent her emotions privately. She took a small kitchen knife and went out to the garden to cut the herbs.

Why? she thought, angrily kneeling and slashing at the herbs. *Why did there have to be a war? I've lost my father and mother in only a few short months.* Tears slid down her cheeks and splashed on her dress and the herbs she was cutting. *It's nearly winter and there will be no way out of the country for months because the mountain path to the east will be blocked! What have I done?* she cried. *Why have I waited this long?* but as she thought this, she remembered why she couldn't leave—the face of her friend, the girl from the village, haunted her.

When she was done, and had nearly controlled her tears, she stood up and took the herbs back into the kitchen.

From that moment on she didn't have a second to call her own until dinner was served and put away. Then the cook hung up her apron and told Newle to put her bread on with specific instructions not to burn it, and left for home.

When the cook had left, Newle took her bread, which had risen beautifully by now, and put it in the oven.

When that was done, she had nothing else to do till it was baked, so she opened the door to the outside to let some heat out and let the November air in. Then she sat down by the fire with her arms around her knees and fiddled with the chain with the ring on it. The chain and the ring were brighter than silver and the scarlet crystal on the ring shone like a star.

It's been six months now, she thought, twirling the chain around her finger as it flickered in the firelight. *From the moment that the siege began to now. Four months from the beginning of the siege to the end of it. Two months from the end of the siege to now. And in those six months I've lost my country, my father, my mother, and everyone thinks I'm in Westfay cornered by the king's men!* She turned the ring over and held it up to the firelight. *What does it take to be a princess in disguise? How long will it take? Will I ever get my country back? I guess I'll never be Princess Scarlet Elwen Silvergleam Oreldes again! If you think about it, it's not too bad. No one telling me what to do, except Cook. No pressure to marry, no reason to marry, no one to marry—what could be better?* She paused to look at the fire and convince herself it was true. *At least I'm not dead, or in prison. And I'm alive, and still near the castle. I'm a hero to the villagers and perhaps in a little while I can reveal myself to them and overthrow the Fairfalconers.* She sniffed the air and changed the topic. *Even if it has too much salt in it, the bread does smell good.*

"Perfectly heavenly." came a voice from the door. Newle was startled. She frantically shoved the chain back under her dress.

"I didn't mean to surprise you," the person from the door began with a smile in his voice.

"Not at all," Newle assured from the hearth, a little breathless from being startled.

"Do you mind if I come in? It's fairly cold out and I'm hungry," the voice asked.

"Of course not," she answered, scootching away from the fire a bit. A young man came in and sat down next to Newle, but still with a comfortable distance between them. He was tall and handsome. His golden, windswept hair glowed in the firelight and the light flickered in his brown eyes.

"Did you make the bread?" he asked.

"Of course I did," Newle explained, not sure if she could trust this stranger. "Unfortunately Cook didn't think it was good enough. She always says I put too much salt in it, so it's destined for the pigs."

"Well, do you put too much salt in it?" he asked, looking at her sideways.

"We can find out in a minute if you would like to try some," Newle told him.

She stood up, opened the door to the oven, pulled the bread out with a dishcloth, put it on the table, and brought out a knife.

"So what's your name?" Newle asked.

"Konrad, and yours?"

"Newle."

"What do you do here?" he asked, using the knife to cut the bread as Newle brought out butter and two plates.

Newle hesitated, "Scullery maid. What do you do?"

"Nothing," he told her, looking away.

"How does that work for you?" she asked, curious.

"I don't know, it's all about to change though. My father called me over to join him in his ..." he paused, still looking away, "... business."

"What does he do?" Newle asked.

"Things. Look here," he began, putting down the knife with a grin. "We just met, don't you think it's a little early to ask those questions?"

"I let you into my kitchen and am feeding you bread that I made only four hours ago. I think I have a right to know about you." Newle replied indignantly, her hands on her hips.

Konrad laughed, "Right you are! But some things I would rather keep secret. What do you do?"

"Scullery maid, I told you that," she answered looking at him sideways, her hands still on her hips.

"What else do you do?" he persisted.

"Some things I would rather keep secret," Newle told him, setting the two slices of bread on plates and handing one to him.

They both took a bite of the warm, moist bread.

"Not bad, Newle. Not bad," Konrad smiled.

"I must admit I don't know what Cook was talking about with too much salt," Newle began. "It's just bread."

"Wonderful," Konrad exclaimed with a mock bow. "A culinary accomplishment. Now I must be off."

"Where to?"

"Up," he said and slipped out the door.

Well, Newle went back to the fire to finish her slice of bread. *I have no idea who he is, but Cook is going to be mad I gave my bread to a complete stranger. I wonder what Konrad is doing here,* she thought settling herself in a comfortable position. The thought floated through her head as she just sat there looking at the fire, her head slowly nodding as her eyes closed.

THE BEGINNING OF IT ALL

Looking back, I'm not sure what I was really thinking when I heard that cry come out from the city. Something didn't connect in my brain, something didn't compute. Even now as the words "To the gate! Defend the bridge!" echo through my head, I don't have a sinking feeling. To me, a sheltered princess living in a nearly enchanted castle, these words meant adventure, not hardship. They meant a new life, not the universal death that soon would engulf us all.

War. Such a simple little word. One that separates families and friends.

Marja and I were with mother at the time. When the servant came in to tell her, we quietly slipped out the door and ran down the hall.

"Marja!" I cried, "What will we do?"

"Your father will bring his army about," she whispered as her fragile face turned another shade paler. Her black hair cascaded down her white gown of mourning. She had been wearing it since her father and mother, the Duke and Duchess of Vliit Forest, died the year she came to live with us. Marja had been my sister ever since.

"Come on," I told her, "It can't be that bad. I'm sure Father will have the invaders gone within a week."

Slowly we walked down the hall, her faltering steps trailing after mine. We turned at the bottom of the stairs and dashed off to the throne room. Father had been in there most of the day. Even the cry from the city barely moved him. Indeed, he was needed there all the more now that war was upon us. We slowly tiptoed into the room, knowing we would not be welcomed.

"Father?" I whispered. He was seated with his back to us, a semi circle of advisors engulfing him as if to keep the invaders out. The few windows that lit the room had already been covered with wood to keep out the small shards of glass that would eventually rain down upon them.

"Scarlet Elwen Silvergleam Oreldes!" he cried. His deep voice lost in the gloom. "Get out of here!"

I took a step forward, half hesitant, "But Father? It's not that bad … is it?"

"Guards!" he called into the gloom, his voice deepening to a growl, "Get them out! I am not to be disturbed."

Tears in my eyes, I ran. Pushing through doors and slipping out into the garden. There, in the nearly quiet day, the words called up from the city hit home.

"Fairfalcon," I shuddered, looking down on the city with fearful eyes. "Only Fairfalcon could bring such destruction."

I remember that the cold night set in quickly for early autumn. The trees were just beginning to turn and the nights were getting longer and chillier. The full moon was beaming down upon me before Marja came out, her white quivering frame silhouetted against the dark wall of stone.

"Are you coming in?" she asked. I didn't answer.

She sat down next to me, shivering and chattering her teeth. Heedless of invasion and war, I slipped my cloak off and gave it to her. She thanked me with a nod.

"What are you going to do?" she asked me in a quiet voice when she had warmed up a bit.

"Nothing, I guess." I had gone over it in my mind. "I'm a girl, I can't go to war, I can't even rule in my father's absence. Mother will take care of that."

"I felt the same way when my parents died." Marja reminded me. "And yet there were many things I did. I still helped my people. Be there for them, Scarlet Elwen, it will mean the world to them."

I sighed, stood, and helped Marja up. "Come on, they must be looking for me." Shoulder to shoulder, we walked back into the castle.

CHAPTER TWO

The next morning, Newle woke up when Cook came in and kicked her awake. Cook was in a bad mood.

"Wake up, you lazy rascal! We have a long day ahead," Cook snorted.

"Do we have to cook the feast for the prince?" Newle asked groggily as she sat up.

"No, and that's only the worst of it," she began. "He came out last night, he came the moment he heard from his father. He didn't even wait to pack or tell anyone. He rode his horse all the way from Fairfalcon to Hedgecliff and didn't even stop for rest. He's with his father this morning and will be heading out to the lands this afternoon. Then tomorrow he's going out to Westfay to catch the princess, though I wouldn't wonder if they found her before then."

They'll never find her, Newle thought. *She's right under their noses and they'll never find her.* Then aloud, "I'm sorry, Cook. Will you be making anything special for dinner?"

"On my honor!" she cried as she flustered around the room. "The prince doesn't deserve it! He's a scallywag if I ever saw one."

"Well, have you?" Newle asked.

"Have I what? You impertinent fool!"

"Seen him," Newle explained as she gathered the last of the loaf of bread in a basket to feed the pigs.

"We crossed paths last night on my way home," Cook began with rage in her eyes. "He was riding a black horse and his cape was fluttering out behind him. He was impertinent when I asked where he was headed."

Newle got her cloak, opened the door a crack to let herself into the cold and dark morning. She slipped out into the quiet morning air.

"I'll bet anything that it was Cook who was impertinent to the prince," she whispered to the pigs as she fed them. "And that would explain why she's so angry this morning. She knows he was bound to see she was a royal cook and worked at the palace. Now she has made a bad impression and thinks he might send her away. Trust Cook to make a mess of a passing encounter." The hens cackled in agreement.

Newle enjoyed her outdoor chores if only for the fact that she was away from Cook and could think about being a princess while fingering the chain with the ring on it.

"When I'm back in my true place," she told the hens, "I will send the prince and the king out of Hedgecliff and back to Fairfalcon where they belong. Then they'll come begging me forgiveness. Just think of the haughty prince on his knees pleading with me to find favor for him in my eyes, and his evil father imploring me to have pity on him unlike he had on my father." The hens gave little clucks as she gathered the eggs from underneath them.

"But," she said thoughtfully, "I can either show them justice or mercy. I could take their lives or I could grant them. They haven't done anything to me personally. Perhaps the prince didn't think they should do this. Maybe he was fighting on our side the entire time. Suppose we would become good friends if I spare his father's life. Imagine, me as queen, bringing peace to Fairfalcon and Hedgecliff at last!"

Her morning chores done, Newle turned back to the castle and set the buckets outside the door. She brought the eggs in and set them down at the table.

"Newle! You take too long!" Cook blustered, "His majesty will be wanting his breakfast in less than an hour and we still haven't sent up the porridge to the other servants!"

"I'll take it up, Cook," Newle replied,

"Not now, cut some herbs for his omelet." Cook handed her a knife, "I got mushrooms on my way home and I have garlic and sausage all ready."

Newle took the knife and she went back out. She was back in less than a minute with the herbs Cook had asked for. She then put the stack of bowls and spoons on a board, balancing it like that as she picked up the large pot of porridge, and began walking up the spiral stairs that led to the servants' dining hall. They were steep and she had to rest after every five steps, but she eventually made it to the top. Leaning against it, she pushed open the big thick oak door that led to the upper servants dining hall. The cool air in the room smelled like cold, clean, wet stone. It reminded Newle of brisk fall mornings, streams and waterfalls, and just plain old cleanness.

"Good morning!" several servants called out as she entered.

They were all new servants from Fairfalcon who wouldn't recognize her in any way.

"Good morning!" she replied with a tentative smile. "As soon as I put this all down, breakfast is served."

The servants gathered around the table as Newle put her load down and took the lid off the pot. She began dishing the porridge into the small bowls.

Her stomach growled, remembering the small slice of bread she had eaten last night. She knew Cook was in a bad mood and wouldn't let her eat anything but small scraps for lunch and dinner.

I wonder if she'll ever find out if I just eat up here with the servants? she thought considering it for a moment. *Some of them don't like me and they know I'm supposed to eat downstairs, they will probably tell Cook if I don't.* She thought with a sigh as she scraped the bottom of the pot with her ladle and filled the last bowl. She put the lid back on, tucked the board under her arm, and picking up the pot, she went back downstairs.

"Late," said Cook as Newle came back down. "The omelet is done and I wouldn't wonder if his majesty sent me away for it even if it is your fault."

Cook handed Newle the tray with three plates on it and sent her back up.

So back she went. Each step harder than the last.

It was always like this: up, down, up, down. All that delicious and wonderful food passing right before her eyes and not a single bite of it ever came to her.

Newle was a princess and not used to living as scullery maid. She found her tasks hard to learn and the punishments even harder to endure. But Marja urged her to keep close to the castle; perhaps she thought Newle could retake it one day. Newle herself didn't want to leave—perhaps she didn't want to leave her people under the rule of the Fairfalcon king, perhaps she just didn't know where to run. But no matter the cause, she stuck to her duties and did them well.

She went up two flights of stairs this time and then turned to the left. She was making her way through to the heart of the castle where she would hand the platter to the king's servant and he would take it to the king. Newle would wait there while the king ate and she would take the tray with the dishes back down, picking up the upper servant's dishes on the way.

She turned right and went down a long hall that she knew too well. The king's door was on the left and his valet was standing outside. His coat and uniform were immaculate down to every detail.

"The king's breakfast," she murmured with a little curtsy.

"He's been waiting. What took so long?" the valet asked.

"Cook was in a bad mood," she replied.

"Well, wait here," he took the tray into the king's chambers.

Newle sat with her back against the wall and her arms around her knees. The valet had left the door open and for a while she didn't pay any attention to what was being said.

Suddenly one of the voices caught her attention.

"We'll never find the princess in Westfay." It was a young voice she heard. "I suggest that we just stop looking for her. Perhaps she died in the last stand. Perhaps the rumor was started by some poor Hedgecliff villager who needed some hope. Needless to say, I don't think we'll ever find her."

Why does he sound so familiar? she asked herself.

"My son," came an older, wiser voice. *The king,* Newle thought. "Perhaps you are right. But I cannot help thinking she is somehow still alive, and fairly near at that."

"Well, as your advisor, King, I suggest we keep looking." came a third, shrill voice.

"Why?" asked the king.

"Because if she were found, you would have a bargaining tool with the villagers." It was the shrill voice again.

So that's all I am, a bargaining tool, Newle thought.

"Tell me ..." came the prince's voice. Somehow he sounded familiar.

Newle scooted closer to the door.

"Valet," the king interrupted, "Close the door, we don't want anyone overhearing what Lord Grissel has to say."

Newle panicked as she backed away. Had he heard her? The door was pulled shut and the conversation resumed in lower tones while Newle sat back.

What sort of bargaining tool could I give them? she wondered. *Maybe I should have left when I had the chance. Whatever advantage they are talking about, I certainly don't want to bring it to them!*

The voices in the room grew louder. Newle could hear the prince's voice rising above the others but could not make out what he was saying. *Once they catch me, the only thing they can do with me is kill me*, she thought.

The prince's voice rose even louder, "No father!" he shouted, "No! You promised mother you wouldn't do that."

"My son. This would secure your throne. I'm not forcing you to do anything. I'm just saying Lord Grissel has a point."

"My prince," began the shrill voice of the lord.

"No! Speak no more, you filthy varmint!" came the high commanding voice of the prince, "When I am king my first act will be to banish you from my kingdom and brand your cheek so everyone will know to shun you. My other act will be to revoke all titles and lands that belong to you and install some wise officer to your place ..."

"Your majesty!" began Lord Giselle,

"Silence, you fool!" shouted the prince, "What you have proposed is preposterous and wrong! Now leave before I call the guards to make you leave!"

Newle heard a chair scraping against the floor and she scrambled to her feet. The next moment the door was pushed open and a man of about seventy years old with a long haggard face and a crooked nose stormed out as Newle bobbed a curtsy to him. The man didn't even give her a second glance. She sat down again with her back against the wall and her arms around her knees.

She heard the king talking to the prince, trying to make him reconsider. But the king was interrupted almost immediately with a sharp rebuke.

I *wonder what it could be?* Newle was beginning to worry. *What if they know? What if they have a plan? I should have crept up and put my ear to the door when I had my chance. Now they might have a plot to catch me and I'll never know about it until it's too late! Drat it! Now I've ruined my only chance at this all.*

The voices in the other room stopped and the door was pushed open again. Newle scrambled to her feet and bobbed a quick curtsy before she even looked at who it was.

"No need for that," came the indignant voice of the prince. "No one else treats me like I have a choice in my own kingdom. Of all the absurd ..." Newle looked up, surprised. "Why, it's you!" the prince said. Looking straight down at her was the light haired, brown eyed man from last night.

"Prince Konrad?" she asked, recognizing him. "You're the prince?"

She was so confused. Did he come to her last night concealing his identity so he could find out who she was? *But no*, she thought. *That's illogical. He doesn't know anything about me.*

The prince was looking at her rather sheepishly, "Yes, I did leave out that detail last night."

"May I ask why?" said Newle.

"Well I guess it isn't proper for a young prince to go to the kitchen to ask for a midnight snack before going up to his father. Besides, sometimes I like to be treated like just a normal person. No one telling me what to do, no one planning my life for me." At this he stopped angrily and seemed to be deep in thought for a moment.

He should know that being a normal person is not much better than being a prince or princess, Newle thought.

"Anyway," the prince laughed, "I'll be stopping by the kitchen later today. I have some choice words for the cook. You won't tell her, will you?" he begged looking anxious for a moment. "I'd like to keep my visit a surprise." Newle nodded, still stunned.

"Oh," the prince remembered, "I would like you to send up some bread with lunch. Make sure Cook knows you are to make it." Newle nodded again as the prince turned around the corner and she was left alone.

As fate would have it she wasn't to be left alone for long. The immaculate valet came back with the tray. Newle took it from him and went back down the stairs, stopping by at the servants dining hall to pick up the emptied dishes.

"Newle, you brat," Cook bellowed the moment Newle was back, "you've been up gossiping with the other servants again? Don't even try to deny it. Now run down to the miller and tell him I need another fifty-pound sack of flour and one of meal. Remind him to charge it to the king's tax!"

"But Cook ..." Newle began.

"No buts young lady! Out you go!" the Cook interrupted.

"I was just going to say that the prince wants bread with lunch."

"I'll make it while you are gone. Now scat!"

"But he wanted me to make it," Newle began.

"Don't lie to me you rascal. Now move it or I will give you the beating of your life!"

Newle grabbed her cloak and ran out the side door and down into town. Only there did she slow her pace.

Now, Newle was a strong girl—a real princess to the core—but even though, she still let a tear escape from her eye. It rolled down her cheek and made a dark wet spot on her cloak.

She had been a jewel in her country before everything, but now, with all her trials, her hard work, her endurance, and her resolution—her failures even—now she was more than a jewel, more than just a credit to her family. She was becoming stronger, and even if no one noticed, she was becoming more beautiful as more than just the air of a princess shone through. Something deeper, something better than all the jewels and credits could ever become.

"Bother this cold," she muttered. *Perhaps it's time to leave. There is nothing I can do for my country anymore*, she thought while walking a little farther. *That's foolish. There will always be hope. I will never leave my country until it is no more.*

With this resolution she walked down the lane, delivered her message to the miller and walked back to the castle.

When she got there, she stood outside a few moments, screwing up her courage.

"I'm back," she announced when she came back in.

"About time. We only have four hours till the midday meal."

"Have you started the bread?" Newle inquired,

"Of course not, you impertinent simpleton," she answered, cuffing Newle's ear.

"May I do it then?" Newle pleaded, "I won't put too much salt in it."

"I'll make it myself," Cook snapped back, giving her a little slap. "Now stir the stew by the fire. I have birds to pluck before dinner tonight."

Newle sat down by the fire, stirring the stew until the moment Cook was out of the room. Then she stood up, gathered ingredients, and began to mix bread dough. Newle knew from experience that Cook would be outside for a long time plucking birds.

So, pausing every now and then to stir the stew, she kneaded the bread and then set it behind the milk churn. It would get the heat of the fire to make it rise, but Cook wouldn't see it when she came in. Cook was outside for a long time. *Flirting with the soldiers*, Newle thought.

When Cook did come back in she was in a more pleasant mood, "Two hours until we need to be ready."

The rest of the morning Newle was bristling with anticipation. She had managed to slip the bread into the oven unnoticed and it was ready when the rest of lunch was finished. She covertly cut it and put the entire loaf on the tray, not without a sigh—she was starving—and began to take it up.

The moment she picked up the tray, the door opened. "Your majesty!" she cried, startled. Remembering her manners she went down into a deep curtsy.

Cook, in the manner of an uneducated servant, knelt on the floor and kissed the prince's hand.

"I came for the lunch tray," he announced surveying the room with a critical eye.

"Your majesty! Your servant Newle was about to send it up." Cook answered, "allow her to walk up with you and she will carry it for you."

"No need of that," Prince Konrad said. "I'll carry it myself." He reached over and Newle handed the tray to him. Then he left.

The moment the door closed Cook was down Newle's throat.

"You put bread on his tray!" she accused as she dealt a blow. "Don't think I didn't notice!"

The door opened again. "Oh—forgive me if I forgot—but my cook and scullery boy from Fairfalcon are here. You are dismissed. Newle is to be moved from the scullery. I'm sure we'll find some work for her upstairs. Good day!" and his head popped back upstairs.

Cook went white for a moment and then, without a word, hung up her apron and left. Newle stared at the fire.

She sank down onto a small stool by the fire, leaned against the stones of the fireplace, and the next thing anyone knew, she was asleep.

THE BEGINNING OF THE SIEGE

I remember it clearly—the following week had been seven days of chaos and fear. People from all around the kingdom kept pouring into the castle city, each and every one having had their homes ransacked by Fairfalcon soldiers. Slowly we watched as the soldiers outside the gate kept growing in numbers each day. Marja and I kept to ourselves in the back of the castle, watching as preparations were made for the siege.

It wasn't long before all the big, beautiful windows had been boarded up and the servants' and gentries' rooms had been moved closer to the core of the castle, far away, where no catapults could get at us.

At the beginning, we had space. My mother and I doubled up together with Marja, but as more gentry kept coming in, we sent them away. We could do little to help them, and in the case that our country fell, it would not do to have everyone taken out in one fell swoop.

After that week, it began. A farmer and his wife were coming out of the king's city when two arrows twanged and the farmer and his wife were dead. That was only the beginning. Soon after morning light, the thud of stones hitting the outer wall of the city could be heard.

It had begun.

"Marja!" I called out. People were lining the halls, haggard faces listening with detached disbelief as their homes were broken to pieces. Father was in his throne room putting the last finishing touches on his army.

"Marja!?" I hadn't seen her in hours. "Marja!!"

"Stop shouting," I heard her say as I whirled around. "I can hear you."

Marja was sitting on the floor, her hands covering her ears.

"Marja," I began, excitement glittering in my eyes. "Father took me up to the tower today."

"Oh Scarlet!" she cried. "They could have killed you!"

"No, father says the catapults can't get to the castle until they have been moved into the city. The city wall has not fallen yet, so up here in the castle we are safe. And soon my father will be leading his troops out to war," I explained.

"But still, try to stay safe." Slowly she stood up.

"Come on. Let's go watch the soldiers march out. Nearly everyone's going to be there."

"Only nearly?" she asked, something strange in her eye.

"Stefan will be there." I told her, smiling. "He's going out with my father. Don't worry, he'll be coming back." Then, changing to mischievous, "You do like him, don't you?"

"He's rather handsome," she answered, blushing to the roots of her hair.

I nodded. Stefan was one of the few tall men who showed the faint roots of elfish ancestry. With his laughing eyes he held every young woman under the age of seventeen under his spell. But those eyes lived for only one lady: Marja. Stefan had taken her under his protection after her parents died, and there wasn't a girl in the kingdom (besides me) who didn't envy her.

Slowly we made our way to the front gate. Long before we reached it, Marja's pace slowed. Whether or not the castle was in the range of the catapults, she still didn't trust the wall.

Carefully we slipped out into the courtyard. Father was mounting his horse, his armor clanking and flashing in the morning light. The other men were cinching up their horse's saddles, readjusting armor, saying last goodbyes, and mounting their horses.

"Marja, over there." I pointed and watched as she dashed over to the tall young man.

I turned away, I didn't need to watch them say goodbye. It was not for me.

Father, his already graying hair shining in the light, dashed out of the gate. As women cried, the men quickly mounted and followed him.

The last I saw of Father was his cloak fluttering out behind him and his armor glittering.

Marja fainted. The strain was too great for her.

"Chicken."

I turned around. Mart Haarbrink, heir to the title of Pegest Shallows, my cousin, stood watching as the last soldier stormed out.

"Chicken yourself." I answered angrily. "Why didn't you go with them? You're old enough, and you have reasons to."

I dashed over to Marja, carefully checking her head for blood. I knew she would revive in another minute. These faints had come often enough.

"Stupid little girl," Mart muttered under his breath, but not low enough for me not to catch it.

"Cowardly little boy." I retorted. "You haven't got the courage to fight for what's right. Marja and I would go if they would only let us."

"Well." Mart began, leaning against the cold stonewall with an air of superiority. "My father wouldn't let me. He says it's a fool's errand to lash out against an enemy so great."

Marja's eyes fluttered open or I would have yelled at Mart.

"Are you alright?" I asked.

"Sure." She grasped my hand and I helped her up. "What was that about?" she asked.

I glanced back to where Mart had been. He was gone and I wasn't surprised.

"Mart was just being himself," I answered.

She nodded.

Mart had become a big problem the past few days. Every year he and his father came to the annual celebrations at the castle, but I had always been able to avoid him. His family had been the first to flee to the castle for protection when the word got out that we were invaded. Cowards.

Mart was the kind of boy who could get on your nerves without even trying. From scaring the chickens in the hallways, to actually pouring out a jar of precious water, his jokes and pranks ranked from harmless to rude.

Marja and I followed him back into the castle. Slowly pacing the still halls that we had become accustomed to these last few days, we carefully strained our ears for sounds from the city. At first it was quiet. Our steps—one faltering, one strong—echoed back to our ears without our permission.

Then, from outside the castle, the lull before the storm ended and the storm itself broke.

Marja bust into tears and leaned against my shoulder. I listened between her breaking sobs, hoping for a cheer to rise up from the city, searching for a sign that we would win.

"Scarlet?" Marja whispered at last, "Let's go, I don't like it here."

I nodded, barely wishing to tear myself away from those mesmerizing sounds, but cringing at every eerie cry that made its way up to our ears.

"Come on!" she called, already half way down the hall. "Faster!" I reluctantly ran to catch up with her. We didn't say a word till we had reached the inner core of the castle.

The people there already knew. They were looking around as though they were lost. They had heard the tempest roaring outside the gate, they had heard the cries as people fell on the field of battle. No one would make eye contact with us as we meandered our way through the halls.

"I feel so sorry for them," Marja whispered in my ear.

I stumbled over a bump in the rug and she caught me before I fell.

"Thanks," I whispered back. "And yes, they look pitiful."

Mart's father, my uncle, rudely brushed past us going in the other direction.

"Chicken, like father like son." I muttered under my breath.

He didn't apologize. Not that I wanted him to. The less Mart and his family said, the better. I remembered there was a time when Marja would have been mad at me for not caring about the members in my own family, but as she spent more time with Mart, she had come to wonder why I put up with them so much.

"Careful where you're going!" Mother mindlessly brushed past us in pursuit of Uncle.

Marja and I watched as she turned the corner and stormed out of sight.

"Come on! There's sure to be an argument." I smiled. "Let's go watch her blow him up!"

Without waiting for a reply I dashed after mother, Marja reluctantly following me. We arrived just in time to see her catch up with Uncle.

"What are you thinking?!" she cried. "Our men need you out there."

"Sister," Uncle began, calmly sitting down on one of my mother's nice plush, ornate chairs. "You know I cannot go out to war because of my health. Why just the other day I nearly had a fainting spell. My wife can tell you it's a miracle that I lived to tell the tale. My apothecary says it was my heart." Mother looked down on the pitiful excuse of man that was my uncle.

"I already talked with Nana. She told me everything, from how the birthing of the cows went, to the dance she went to seven years ago. She never mentioned anything about your heart."

Mother's voice quavered, I could tell that she was very angry. Uncle just sat there, stunned and unsure of how to respond. But before he could open his mouth, Mother was off on another rampage.

"And what about that fully capable young boy you have? He only sits around here making mischief. Only a minute ago I had to pull him out of the cattle pens. He was trying to ride the cows! Give him a real horse to ride, give him something useful to do!"

"That boy," Uncle began, slowly this time, carefully weighing his options, "is all his mother and father have. You wouldn't tear him away from us, would you?"

"You have a country and countrymen. And that country belongs to them too. Would you tear that country away from them so your son can live? He is a coward. You can give him everything he wants, but deep down he is a boy, and maybe you have lost this sense, but every boy senses the need to fight for what he believes in and for what he holds dear."

"That boy only holds his family dear!" Uncle began, clearly losing it. "That is why we aren't sending him out. He would rather be with us."

"Then what, may I ask, is the boy to do when our country falls and he and his parents are taken to the execution block for being of royal lineage?"

As Uncle shook with rage, I flashed a smile at Marja. It felt good to be getting a little back at the people who annoyed us.

Marja only looked slightly amused. I know she didn't approve too much, but I didn't care.

"When my husband, the king, gets back, I'll be sure to have him look for some armor for the two of you. And of course, if you feel that you have overstayed your welcome, I'm sure it won't be much trouble to help you take your things out and move some other more deserving person into the apartments that you currently hold."

Mother turned to go but suddenly remembering something, turned back for another moment. "Oh, and Duchess Ella of the Barren Islands has come to us for refuge. She fought the invaders off of her islands for nearly a month before her castle was broken and she was forced to retreat. The king and I would like to thank her for her sacrifices, but putting her up in my room would hardly be comfortable for her. She's nearly sixty, and I already have the girls. Your family of three has five rooms. I'm sure you can spare one for an old war hero. I've already started moving her things in. Nana, your wife, can help me. I'm sure she can spare a moment from embroidering those extravagant clothes for your son." Mother stormed off the scene. I dashed to follow her, Marja coming in behind.

"Girls," she began without turning around. "You heard me, I need help moving the duchess in. Do you have a moment to spare?"

"Scarlet and I have all the time in the world," Marja said before I could intervene.

"I doubt that the talking to will change anything," Mother said, switching subjects. "My brother is too much of a coward. But at least I have another room. If I had my way, they would all be squeezed into the pigpen! One room with no furnishings! It would serve them right."

Marja shook her head as we lengthened our paces to keep up with Mother as the halls grew silent.

I knew Mother wasn't thinking about anything except Father, and I knew Marja wasn't thinking about anything except Stefan. All I could think about were those blasted relations of mine and that wasn't even a very pleasant thought.

It took a good bit of the rest of the day for us to set up the duchess's room. Little could be done to make it more comfortable. We stole a table from the hall, put a scrap of cloth on it and prayed that the duchess wouldn't mind. For a bed, we set some boards over a few crates. Again, we prayed that the duchess would find it suitable to her needs. Due to the many people we had to room and board, supplies were short. Already Marja and I had to share a bed in Mother's room.

CHAPTER THREE

Newle slept way past dinner. The midday meal was cooked, delivered and the dishes taken care of, dinner was sent out and the dishes taken in again. But she slept through it all. When she finally woke, there was a strange lady with a piping hot dinner waiting for her.

"What happened to Cook?" she asked sheepishly, still wiping sleep from her eyes.

"Don't you remember child? Prince Konrad sent her away," the woman answered.

"And who are you?" Newle asked.

"His cook!" she laughed. "And my son. He helps me."

Newle looked around the room and noticed that there was a small boy with her.

Newle nodded, "A scullery boy."

The woman laughed. "Dear little girl! More like my assistant, my helper."

Her voice and laugh was pretty, and the little boy looked happy.

"Now girl," the woman began. "First thing's first—dinner for you. Then I'll lend you one of my dresses, we're close enough in size. The prince wants to see you."

"What for?" Newle inquired, standing up to sit down in the offered chair. She began to dig into her dinner.

"Oh you poor, starved little lamb! He's probably going to set you up with some nicer position. Or you'll stay with me so that my little Himdir can go to school. You shouldn't worry about it," the woman assured her.

Newle wolfed down her dinner in record time and then went with the woman who lent her a dress.

"The brown under servant's garb is as unbecoming as a sack," she noted. "You can have my green dress. With your black hair and green eyes you should look like a princess."

Once again Newle nearly panicked. *Did she know?* But the woman just kept right on talking.

Newle stood and did nothing while the woman pulled out the dress, dressed her, and then brushed her hair and washed her face. It reminded Newle of when she was a princess and had everything done for her, but those times were in the past. She couldn't allow herself to live them again.

"There," the woman said when she was done. "Pretty as a picture." She walked around Newle and arranged two or three folds and a lock of hair. Newle tucked her necklace back under her shift so the woman wouldn't see it.

"A warm, sensible dress that you can still work in," the woman said, still observing the effect. "Now, upstairs, to the left and then the right. I'm sure you know the way."

"The way where?" Newle asked, trying to stall for time.

"The throne room, child," the woman chided her.

Newle knew the way, but something was holding her back. She didn't want to go up.

"Can I help you with anything?" she persisted.

"Mercy no! Now just run along."

"What's your name?" Newle asked, continuing to buy for time,

"Samantha, now go!" and the woman—Samantha—basically pushed Newle up the stairs.

Newle found herself stumbling up the stairs, her footsteps slow and heavy. She knew Samantha was watching her plodding ascent, but still she bided her time.

The king will recognize me, she thought. *The green dress only makes my green eyes more pronounced. Green eyes, black hair. Surely he will know I'm the princess!* but Newle continued walking. Konrad would be waiting for her, she knew.

Before she knew what had happened, she was outside the door to the throne room, had knocked, entered and given a curtsy to the prince. His father, the king, was nowhere to be seen.

"The bread you sent up with lunch was good," he praised.

"Thank you, I'm glad your majesty liked it," Newle answered, trying to act the part of a servant.

"I'm afraid I can't find any work for you in the castle." Prince Konrad explained reluctantly. "You can always go out to the village to find work."

"If it pleases your majesty," Newle began cooly. "But Samantha could perhaps use me in the kitchen."

"How?" he asked, looking at her almost suspiciously. "She brought the little boy to help her."

"She was explaining just a few moments ago that she would like a helper in the kitchen," Newle explained as quickly and in as few words as she could.

"And you still want to help in the kitchen?" he asked, looking at her curiously.

"No," Newle replied curtly. "But she would like to send her son to school. If you find another girl or boy to help her out I could teach him right here in the castle."

"You've been to school?" Prince Konrad asked, very surprised.

"Yes. I went before my family came to bad times and I had to help out by getting a position," she lied. "I can teach arithmetic up until nearly college. I know reading, writing, and everything else."

"You know," Prince Konrad began, taking his cue from her and replying with a stern standoffish look, "I somehow knew from the moment I saw you in the kitchen that you were probably educated. I knew there was a waste of talent."

"So may I?" she asked, continuing to sound high and mighty. This Prince had no business here, and she needed to take back any impression he had after last night.

"It's settled! I'll send you down to the village school tomorrow to get tested. My father will give you free room and board, and considerable spending money. I'm sure you'll want new clothes too."

"Thank you." Newle said, giving him the satisfaction of a sigh of relief, she needed to stay in the castle. She couldn't leave it, not even for Marja. This was the closest she could keep to her past. She wasn't going to give that up. "Is that all, your highness?"

Konrad nodded and gestured to the door. Newle left, a little confused that a high prince would stoop down to take care of his servants.

Behind the closed doors, Prince Konrad could only look at the door in a stupor. *They resent my every moment here. I never wanted to mess with a peaceful country. If only my father didn't have delusions of me and my brother. If only he liked my older brother instead of me. According to the law my father must give the land to my brother, if only my father were content to leave nothing for me. If only he hadn't conquered this land for me.*

Newle's own thoughts somewhat echoed his. How could she say yes to any of this? It was all so preposterous! Fairfalcon was bloodthirsty and ruthless! He was still her enemy. But how could she resist the opportunity to be in the knowhow of the enemy? If she could even call them that. But how could she debate against having a real bed? And the next morning she was to have a real breakfast too.

Before she was done with that breakfast, the prince had already called her.

She went to the throne room with the firm resolution to be cold and haughty again. She had decided that her secrecy was more important than anything else.

"I've arranged with the school teacher in town to have you stop by in the afternoon for examinations. I've also arranged for you to have some pocket money right away," he handed her a medium sized sack of coins, choosing to ignore her rude and haughty behavior. "This will pay for anything you need to get right away. Pencils and chalkboards, books and such. There should also be enough to pay for some fabric for a new dress, cloak, and hat if you need any of that," he looked intently at her for a moment but she didn't say anything. The look on her face was enough to tell him she was not going to even try to be pleasant. He wanted to reassure her that her country was safe, but the only thing that nagged at his mind was his orders from his father to go to Westfay to look for the princess.

Newle, not knowing what to say, bowed and turned to leave.

"Goodbye!" he called out after her, and she left.

All that morning she was buying supplies she would need for herself. She figured that after her examination she would have a better understanding of what she would need for teaching.

She went to the school in the afternoon, had her examination and passed with flying colors.

Then, on her way home, she bought a grammar book, a primer, and a small slate with chalk.

She had no fear that her pupil wouldn't learn. She thought he looked studious and would be keen to his lessons.

For the next week she taught the little boy how to read, write, and add simple sums together. She prospered under the good cooking of Samantha, and flourished under the new management and kindness.

She was making three new dresses during the school hours and helping out in the kitchen when she wasn't working on that.

As a princess she hadn't really worked on practical sewing, but she seemed to be learning.

She thought about her new position. The people loved their princess. They wanted her back. They would follow her to the end of the world. The moment their hero rose out of the ashes of the old Hedgecliff, they would follow her.

Even though she knew all this, she also knew she wasn't ready to be queen yet. She needed to wait a little longer.

Prince Konrad seemed elusive. She hadn't seen him since he had given her the money. It was almost as though he had gone on a trip again. Something seemed to draw her to him though, almost without realizing it. She started searching the halls for him even though she knew she shouldn't. How could she? This was the man whose father ordered her country to destruction. But still, something made her look for him in the halls. Was it his interest in the servants? Dare she say, his interest in herself?

So, when Prince Konrad came out of hiding and Newle started passing him in the halls, she decided to pursue his friendship, if only because she would gain valuable information from it (at least that's what she told herself). It would be hard to wait till she was ready to be queen if she had already made an enemy.

After passing him in the hall one day, Newle went down to the kitchen to begin giving lessons to Samantha's son, Himdir. Himdir proved to be a good pupil and had been zooming through his lessons, so Newle had decided to give him a treat.

That day the kitchen was aglow with knights and dragons as she told the stories that kept her country alive. She told of the first settlers that came from across the sea. She told how they had broken away from their former rulers and had started their own country. She told about the one and only dragon ever to be seen on this side of the sea, and how the first knight battled thirty days and thirty nights with the foul beast before they were both killed, falling over a treacherous cliff. When she looked up at the end of her story, she was startled to see not one, but two listeners. Konrad was leaning in from the door, unable to mask his amazement.

"And that's how we got the name Hedgecliff. Hedge was the name of the knight who battled the dragon while falling off a cliff," Newle wrapped up, turning away as if to leave.

But Konrad would have none of it. "You're not done yet," he began, sitting down on the ground.

"But Newle," Himdir interrupted before she could say anything. "Did he have any children?"

"Yes," she answered, settling back into her chair. Why was Konrad here? Had he just been passing by and overheard her? Or had he come down specifically to see what she was up to?

"So if I met someone with the last name Hedge, or Cliff, or Hedgecliff, they would be related?" the prince asked, breaking her thoughts.

"Oh no!" Newle replied. "That name is now sacred. No one can use it because we wouldn't want people taking the credit for their ancestors' deeds of heroism."

"So if I became a knight and I killed a dragon, no one could use my last name?" Himdir asked.

"Yes, but we don't have any dragons here these days, they only live in the east," Newle explained. "But you could do something else to gain that kind of favor." She looked fixedly at Konrad, hesitating before carefully continuing. "The village people are gossiping about making the princess's name sacred."

"What's her name and what did she do?" Himdir asked.

"Her name," Newle began a little nervously, "Is Princess Scarlet Elwen Silvergleam Oreldes. She led an attack on Fairfalcon, and the last stand against the king. She gave the people hope when they had none."

The prince was sitting in the corner and she didn't look at him when she said this.

"But," Newle brightened up, trying to bring the attention away from the princess. "Every name means something."

"Really?" Himdir leaned forward on his stool at her feet,

"Yes, yours means handsome young boy." Newle replied with a smile.

"And my mother's?" Himdir asked, his eyes riveted on her face.

"Samantha is a name as old as the hills," she explained, longingly.

"What a funny way to say that it's old!" Himdir exclaimed.

"It's a Hedgecliff saying. Anyway, *Sam* means inward beauty and *antha* means woman."

"What does your name mean?" the prince asked, coming closer and leaning in with interest.

"Nothing," Newle answered, looking away. She had already said too much.

"No, really. What does it mean?" he insisted. "It must mean something!"

"As a servant, my name must mean nothing because it cannot mean anything better than my employer. To be quite truthful, it's nearly as bad as slavery!" she blurted out at last.

The next moment she wished she hadn't, Prince Konrad looked angry and confused. "I'm sorry your highness, but it's true. Have you ever wondered why I never leave the castle? Have you ever thought about what it's like to work from morning to night and almost never get enough to eat? And just think about poor Himdir. He'd never been to school because he never had the time for it."

"If that's how you feel about all the kindness I have lavished upon you, I'll place it somewhere else," he said indignantly, standing up to leave.

"I'm sorry, but there's more than just Samantha, Himdir and me out in the world. You really truly haven't seen the worst," she angrily answered, also getting up to leave.

Himdir, oblivious to the tension blurted out: "What does Konrad's name mean?"

"His full name?" Newle asked with a sigh.

"Yes, Prince Konrad Thurindir Starseed Faervel," he answered, stumbling over the long words. Newle sat down again and Konrad didn't move, still wanting to leave, but how could he?

"Well ..." Newle began, was she giving herself away? But a little couldn't hurt. "Konrad is a ... it is a deep name going far back in time, it means bold ruler." Newle hesitated now. "Stop!" a voice in her mind screamed. But she couldn't. It felt so *good* to show the prince that she was more learned than he was, to have them actually *listen* to her. "*Thurindir* is handsomest young man. *Starseed* is already translated. It used to be Lichterson. *Lichter* meaning sky light, and *son* is just plain old son, or seed-of. It is quite usual to see a name already translated if you are royalty. *Faervel* is the oldest name because it is your last name and has been used by your fathers before you. You are the root of fear conqueror."

The room was quiet for a moment as the prince thought this out. Then he asked: "What does the princess's name mean?"

Newle started, this was the second time she had come up in this conversation. But she soon put her fear to the side, if she refused it would draw suspicion. "Princess Scarlet Elwen Silvergleam Oreldes. *Scarlet* means tough outward beauty just like Sam means inward beauty. *Elwen* is literally compassionate young girl. *Silvergleam* is already translated just like Starseed. It used to be *Shintnessey*. *Shint* meaning silver and *nessey* meaning gleam. *Oreldes* is the oldest of the names and means wise thought."

"How did you learn about the names?" Prince Konrad asked curiously. "I've never heard this taught in schools."

"I was an innkeeper's daughter," she lied. "My father had enough money to hire the best tutor around. It turned out that he was the last dwarf. He wasn't even a full dwarf, he was only half. He taught me the old languages and I lived in the most romantic dream of going to far off lands where they still only speak the language. I dreamed that I would then live with them, and learn everything they could teach me. Then I would become great among them and I would kill the dragons and rid the land of some great evil."

Newle knew it was wrong to lie like that, but part of it was true. She really had the half-dwarf as her teacher, and he taught her all about the languages that used to be. He had also told her about the dragon. He had even been the first person to tell her she was a princess. She had a friendship with him outside of learning.

"I wish you could teach it to me!" Himdir begged.

"I could if we had more time," Newle answered with a sigh. "But you must have time to help your mother in the kitchen. And I must help too." She looked sideways at the prince and he met her gaze before she gathered up her books. Himdir gave her a hug around the knees, and she left the room.

Newle felt terrible. She had remembered things she thought she had left behind. For a moment she had created a world of beauty, love, and adventure. She had shared it in the warm glow of the fire. In the moment she left the room, all of that had dispersed and crashed down around her ears. She felt as though she had lost it all over again that night.

Newle went to her new room and began sewing on one of her new dresses. Her room was bare and lonely.

A slave, she thought. *Is that really what I am? I know the prince says I'm almost a lady, but really? I work for someone else, my name means nothing, and I'm not ever allowed to leave the city. They would imprison me if I tried to leave through the gates and I would break my neck if I tried to climb over the high wall. I am a slave.*

Newle put down her sewing, pulled out her necklace, held it in her hand and tried to hold back her tears.

I'll never live up to my name, she thought. *I've been subdued to nothing.* The tears came in earnest now. *I'll never go and have adventure in the east. I'll never speak with another dwarf and I'll never see a dragon!*

Newle buried her head in her pillow and wept.

MARJA

Dinner that night was served in the throne room due to it being closer to the core of the castle than the banquet hall that was normally used on such occasions.

The tables from the banquet hall were moved to the throne room. The boarded up windows gave a gloomy air to the meal. Marja and I sat at the head table with Mother, Uncle, Nana, and Mart. There was little we could do about it—they were the only royal family who could sit up there and it would hardly do to only have mother, Marja and me.

Mother sat in the middle. To her right was her brother, and to his right was his wife. I sat at mother's left hand, to my left was Marja, and to her left was Mart. I kinda felt sorry for her, but I got to sit next to Mother, and that's what counted.

Dinner was small because rationing had already started. We only had a little water to drink, with so many people drinking out of only three or four wells that we felt safe going out to, the water had already fallen considerably.

Days passed, our army attacked and retreated back to the castle. Attack, retreat. Attack, retreat. Each day our forces dwindled.

Marja and I had little to do, and it didn't take long before we were stalking the nearly sixty-year-old Duchess Ella of the Barren Islands.

It didn't take her long to notice us and invite us into her sheltered cove.

"Dears!" she had said. "Come in and I'll tell you all about everything. And," she continued with a wink and a smile. "I'll keep that lazy boy away from you because he won't dare come to me."

Marja and I jumped at the opportunity to meet the old lady and escape Mart.

For being sixty, she was a fragile, darling little spitfire. Her health was decaying and her once-clear skin was parchment thin, and the brown and cream frock she wore washed it out and made her look more tired than I'm sure she was.

Though of royal lineage, when she invited us in, she was talking with my tutor who had been sadly neglected in the past few days and had not gone out to war with the others because he was too old and too short to be of use to us.

"Scarlet, dear," he began when he looked up after we had been ushered in. "I was just telling the duchess all about you." I nodded, not sure of what to say.

"Yes," Duchess Ella began, sitting down with a smile. "He was telling me about your language studies. It's fascinating that you can speak the eastern language. Can you speak it, Marja?"

Since Marja had moved in with us, my tutor and I had been trying to teach it to her, but I suppose she never fully had time for it.

"Only a little," she answered.

"But her accent is wonderful," I praised, wanting to make her feel better about it.

"Yes," my tutor affirmed. "These girls are wonderful, they make me proud of my name."

Marja and I looked at each other, and then the floor.

"It matters little," duchess Ella went on. "Though, if one day communications and trade are opened between the east and the west, you will be valuable members of our country."

"But sit down, dears," my tutor began. "We can talk of other things."

And indeed we did. Ella (for that's what we were to call her) told us all about how she had fended off the solders of Fairfalcon, even going so far as to lead our soldiers into battle herself.

"You must be a great leader among your own people!" I cried at the end of the story. "To follow someone into battle like that takes great courage."

"It took even greater courage to go into the battle yourself," Marja whispered. Battles and wounds and such had never been her favorite thing to talk about.

"It took great courage on both sides, girls," my tutor said with admiration. "No one can go into battle without courage." He paused to look at the floor for a moment. "But enough with that. Miss Ella is tired of our company. It is time for us to leave."

We said goodnight to her and departed. For those few moments in Ella's room, the siege had disappeared from our minds and had been gently lifted from our hearts. But the moment we stepped out of that room, we knew something was wrong.

"The horses are back," I whispered. We could hear them stamping in the courtyard.

"Come on!" Marja cried, her eyes lighting up. "Stefan will be there."

She dashed off before I could say anything. Following behind her, we swiftly made our way to see the forces.

Only fifty horsemen were in the courtyard when we arrived. The archers would stay night and day to fend off the attackers, and the horsemen took turns staying the night.

Stefan hadn't been among the ranks last night, and Marja had been waiting all day to see him for he would surely come today.

Father had again stayed out. He was nowhere in sight, so I accosted the first knight I could find.

"Your majesty," he began, taking off his helmet and kneeling. "Your father, the king, will not leave his men. You have no need to worry."

I bowed to the knight and thanked him.

"And what about the boy named Stefan?" I asked as I turned to leave.

"Your majesty," the knight was expectantly silent.

Tears sprang to my eyes as my head whipped around in search of Marja.

She was standing in the middle of the courtyard, her bewildered face searching each new knight who came in.

"Oh Marja!" I whispered under my breath. "Why?"

Slowly, as though in a trance, I made my way to her.

"Scarlet?" she began, looking in my eyes.

"Oh Marja," my voice cracked as I put my arms around her. "I asked the knight and he said ..." I didn't finish my sentence. The point had gotten across.

The two of us stood in the middle of the courtyard, barely noticing as the knights slowly left us to find their dinners. They had seen their comrades die on the field of battle, what did it matter if someone else had died?

Someone cleared his throat. I looked over my shoulder to see the soldier who had told me the news.

"Miss?" he asked. Marja looked up. "Stefan, I saw him get struck by two arrows, one on the helmet, and the other through the right side of his chest. He fell forward and down the outside of the wall. His body was cushioned by the bodies that had already accumulated. There will be no recovering him, his body is at Fairfalcon's mercy."

I glared at the soldier as Marja recoiled from my grasp.

"Miss, he went down in glory, there is no better fate," the soldier looked confused, was there nothing better than to die a glorious death? Yes, she wanted his life! She didn't care how he went, she wanted him alive!

Marja broke free and ran.

"You stupid soldier," I lashed out. "You should know better than that. Grief wants no company. She wasn't ready to hear those things!"

Quickly I dashed after Marja without a backward glance.

CHAPTER FOUR

The next day there was a new helper in the kitchen. Konrad didn't say anything, but the look he gave Newle when she passed him in the hall was enough. When she passed him for a second time, he called her over to talk.

"Teach Himdir all about the language," Prince Konrad told her, his own imagination sparked after the story yesterday.

"Do you really mean it?" Newle asked, her green eyes shining.

"Yes I do. I think this is a useful subject for him to learn. What if connections with the east are rekindled? He will be a pivotal person if he knows the language." He said it like he meant it, but there was something else in his eyes.

"Are you sure it won't be a bother?" she asked.

"Yes, I'm even going to set up a room for you to teach Himdir in."

"But I rather like teaching in the kitchen. The first snow was a few days ago and it's rather cozy in there. Don't you think?"

"Alright, I'll leave the teaching things to you," and he did.

Himdir had a favorite song that Newle sang to him every night as she grew to be like an older sister to the little boy. He would refuse to go to sleep until she sang it.

It was sad and beautiful at the same time. According to custom, it could be sung in two different tunes.

It runs like this in the other language:

Eloywen! Mina loyta ana ha naycht singen var nels.
Blewn var capit ana Lon ecalp an on Wel sels.
Lon varna haben ha dranken fa el nesil lan,
Zo Lon galth das He ville tace an jaynck fawn.
Furney a Capita yelns.

Newle had to make a new tune for the translation to their language. Himdir always fell asleep with tears in his eyes and Newle would leave his room with tears in her own.

Himdir said songs like that weren't written these days. You would hear about the soldier who had strength to go to war, but never about one who had to go to someone else for strength. And Newle firmly agreed with him. You hear about the soldier who could do everything, but never about the one who could only trust in another.

Newle grew more comfortable around the prince and even went so far as to exchange words with his father in the hall. She didn't forget who they were, but at times she nearly forgot who she was, where she had come from, and why she was there.

"Newle?" Konrad asked one morning.

"Yes," she answered, stacking her books and putting everything in order before picking them up.

"Well," Konrad began, taking her books for her and carrying them up the stairs. "I was wondering if you would like to go riding with me. If you know how, that is. We could take Himdir," he suggested, using the boy as a shield.

"We would love to I'm sure," Newle smiled. She hadn't been riding since the castle had been taken. She was itching to mount a horse again. "Let me put my books away and then grab my cloak before we go back down to get Himdir."

Newle dashed into her room, set the books down on her bed and grabbed her cloak from the nail on the wall.

Newle led the way back down to the kitchen and they caught up with Himdir. He put his cloak on, they went outside, and then around the back of the castle to the stables.

A nice dusting of snow covered everything and continued to fall steadily.

"Are we worried about the snow?" Newle asked as she saddled her horse.

"No, the stableman said that it would stop in the next few minutes," Konrad explained as he saddled a horse for himself and then one for Himdir.

"It seems to be lighter already," Himdir announced before Konrad gave him a boost onto his little horse.

"And just think," Newle said, as Konrad knelt down by her horse and gave her a hand up. "Soon it will be the winter festival, then sleigh rides, presents, and ice skating."

"Do you think I could do that?" Himdir asked, his eyes wide with anticipation. "Will you teach me how to skate?"

Newle laughed. "Of course! And I'll help you make any festival presents you need help with," she promised.

They started out at a slow pace so Himdir could keep up, but fast enough not to get chilled to the bone.

Their capes fluttered in the wind and the snow didn't have any time to stick before it was blown off of them.

They went away from the village. Soon the castle was lost behind them and they came to the wall that fenced everything in. They could go no further.

"We should turn around here, the snow is coming down faster," Newle suggested, a little worried. She could hardly see more than three yards in front of her.

"Sure," Konrad agreed. "But first, race you to that post!" He was off in less than a second, and Newle had to race to catch up to him. Konrad won easily. They cantered back to Himdir, and went slowly back to the castle.

Newle prepared a hot drink, and they all sat around the fire in the kitchen as Newle told stories about anything and everything.

"A long time ago," she began. "When there was no earth, everyone was a spirit. No one knows how they came to be, all we know is that they existed. There was one spirit who knew more than the rest and he thought himself into being. At this instant the rest were imprisoned, only to be set free after they had been used on this earth. He set up stars in their courses, and the planets to orbit them. Then he made elves, dwarfs, men, and beasts to populate these planets. He duplicated his knowledge and divided it among them, a bit to the elves, most to the dwarfs, and nothing to men.

"He began to get wild in his ways and he made a big mistake. He made magic, all sorts of magic! In the heavens, where he was, it took the shapes of flowers, animals, birds, smoke, and light. He put a stone in the middle of a mountain in charge of it. It was to distribute it to all the races.

"When the dwarfs found they had most of the magic, they began to mine a palace in one of the mountains near their encampment. The dwarfs did not mine the mountain with their hands, they used magic to do it. They did not guard the door to their palace, they wove spells that would bring anyone who entered it to the king and he would judge them. As a result of all this magic, the dwarfs had not been in half of the mountain. They did not know the dungeon in the heart of the mountain had the wonderful stone in it. The dwarfs began to rule the men very cruelly. As the men did not have magic, they lost crop after crop, beast after beast, and they had numerous diseases.

"Now the spirit from above looked down on all this and frowned at the cruelty of the dwarfs. He swore he would avenge the men. The spirit brought forth a man, Arainieous, whose name means "to destroy it." When he grew up, Arainieous swore he would destroy the magic or die.

"Arainieous went up to the mountain, his sword drawn and at the ready. Suddenly he was grabbed by magic and carted to the king. The king sentenced him to the middle dungeon. Arainieous was taken there and left. He saw the stone. It was glittering and beautiful, its nearly clear heart surrounded by ever-changing shades of blue. He reached out to touch it, drawn by its beauty. Suddenly the ground shook. The air trembled and the rock began to fall.

"Arainieous had set the magic loose from the stone. He escaped the mountain as he dodged falling rocks. No words can describe the damage to the palace of the dwarfs—it was in ruins, shambles, utter destruction! The unfortunate truth of the story is Arainieous only let loose the magic, he did not destroy it. Because he had sworn to destroy it and he hadn't, he died.

"The spirit from above started to gather magic into the heavens, but not until the end of the age will he have it all. Sometimes a spark of magic will meet a little child and that child will grow up to be a wizard. As the years go by, that will happen less often. One day though, all of it will be gathered. That will be the last day."

"Is Arainieous another name that no one can use?" Himdir asked when the story was done.

"Yes. You will never find a person named Arainieous," Newle answered. "My tutor told me this story of how our world was shaped. It's pretty, don't you think?"

"Very. But is it true?" Konrad asked. "I've never heard it before."

"I guess we'll never know," Newle replied.

They all said goodnight and in the morning woke up to find that it was snowing so much they couldn't go for another ride.

Newle, having grown more accustomed to the prince, invited him to join them for lessons. "No, I've been neglecting my duty as prince. I will be so bold as to suggest that I stay with my father today," he replied to her offer. "Perhaps in the afternoon we could go out if we leave Himdir behind," Konrad suggested, brightening at the prospect.

"Maybe," Newle replied. She really didn't want to go. Being alone with the prince was something she wasn't in a hurry to do.

Konrad, his pride hurt, turned to leave. "Alright, I have duties as a prince and I need to fulfill them."

"Now," Newle started turning to Himdir and grinning. "You've had enough lessons for the rest of the week. You just gobble them up! How would you like it if I showed you something really fun?"

"What is it, Newle? Is it as good as a story?" Himdir asked, jumping with excitement.

"Better!" Newle laughed. "Come with me."

She took him by the hand and led him quickly to the top of the highest tower in the castle. They didn't go out on the roof. They didn't need to for this surprise. Besides, it would be too cold.

"Perhaps some other time," was her reply when Himdir asked if they could go out. "Today we are going to slide down the rail, all the way down to the bottom of the tower!"

"Really?" he asked, his eyes widening.

"Come on! I'll show you how." She sat on the rail and grabbed it with her hand and slid down easily.

"Now you try!" she called back up. "I'll catch you at the bottom!"

"Coming!" he called back.

He sat down and grabbed the rail. He took a few shaky breaths and closed his eyes. He slid down just as easily as Newle.

"That's better than sled riding!" he exclaimed at the bottom after Newle had caught him.

"Then back up we go!" Newle cried.

They raced back up the steps and slid down again, and again, and again, and again, until they were breathless.

"Now do you know that else we can do?" Newle asked when they stopped for a rest.

"No, what else can we do?" he asked, sitting up eagerly, ready to play some more.

"Hide and seek!" she exclaimed excitedly. "Just think of all the rooms and the possibilities!"

"Alright then," Himdir said standing up and brushing himself off in his little way. "You start counting,"

Newle closed her eyes and counted to one hundred. It didn't take long and before she knew it, she opened her eyes. Not a soul was in sight.

While Newle was playing with Himdir, Konrad was helping his father.

"I'm glad to see you back, my son," the king said when Prince Konrad entered in the side door. "You've been spending a lot of time with the two servants," the king said with thoughtful contempt. "The small boy and the remarkable young girl."

"Yes, she's been teaching me all about Hedgecliff," he replied absently, trying to get his father to change the subject.

"Well I hope you haven't forgotten your position or manners," his father replied, watching to see his son's reaction.

"Forgotten them?" Konrad asked indignantly. "What do you mean?"

"Just that. In my opinion you are spending too much time with your inferiors. You must become much more than they can ever be. They are servants, you are prince," his father told him decidedly.

"But Newle's been telling me about this country!" Konrad exclaimed.

"And what do you need to learn about this country? You only need to rule it. Hmm? Tell me that."

"I need to know how the people think," Konrad explained crossing his arms. "Father, I am old enough to make my own decisions. Don't you think you should let me do that?"

"Yes," his father agreed. "Just as long as you are not making a fool of yourself at the same time."

"But I'm not making a fool of myself!" Konrad was exasperated. He couldn't make his father understand. "You should know better. Father, I'm learning new things."

"As you wish, my son," the king held his hands up in sign of resignation, exasperated at the pigheaded, low tastes of his son. "Just don't come running to me when you find you are wrong. You can run to the servants. I don't care."

Konrad would have liked to make a comeback, but at that moment a widow was announced. She was bearing a petition for the king.

"Your majesty," she murmured as she knelt on the floor. "My neighbor has been moving our boundary stones to expand their field." The tears began in her eyes. "Please have the stones moved back to their original positions. It's about six feet. With the removal of the land I will not be able to support my three sons. They might starve!" she pleaded.

The throne room was quiet for a moment.

"Konrad," the king said turning to his son with an almost wicked smile. "You're prince, tell her what you want. I will wash my hands of all you do." And he left the room to find an old history book of Hedgecliff—he had some reading to do.

Konrad turned back to the widow, the anger he felt toward his father clouding his judgment.

"My son," the widow began. "He must stay home because I cannot send him to school."

Konrad thought for a moment about Himdir and Newle, unable to dismiss his father's words toward them.

"Woman," he said after a moment of distracted thought. "I will send guards to have the boundaries restored. Rest assured that I have helped you,"

"Your highness! Bless your soul! Thank you! Thank you!" the widow bowed her head and left.

Before Konrad had any time to think about anything, another person was brought in.

"Your majesty, as the innkeeper I have been selected by my village to bring you news. There's a stretch of road that bandits are using to waylay passing tradesmen. We petition to have something done about it," the man pleaded. "We dare not go anywhere these days for fear of death. I have come here at the risk of my own life."

"I agree," Konrad replied absently. "I will send guards to escort you home. They will then patrol the road. I hope it will be enough."

The man looked a little startled and displeased for a moment. He accepted the escort reluctantly and then left. There was an almost hunted look in his eyes. Konrad didn't see it.

"This is going better than anyone, even my father, could hope," Konrad thought smugly, still trying to go through what he had said.

The next person, a young man, shuffled in. He was holding his cap in awe of his surroundings.

"What do you want?" Konrad asked, not paying attention and missing the fact that the man didn't bow or show the usual signs of respect.

"Someone has built a dam on their land, and now people can't irrigate their crops," he began. "It will be a huge blow to the entire country if our crops do not come in. There might even be a famine."

"I see," Prince Konrad began. "I suppose I can't just walk up to the man and tell him he has to take the dam down?" If only he could walk up to his father and tell him to take down the dams that alienated him from his own sons.

The man looked at him in surprise.

"Right. I guess I can't." Konrad sighed. "What would you do?" he asked, unable to think.

"Me?" the man asked surprised. Konrad nodded.

"I would explain it nicely to him and then tell him if he doesn't take it down then I'll take it down myself."

"Right," Konrad said. "I give you full permission to do that exact thing. If you have any trouble, you can tell him I will send guards."

The man bowed and left.

"Not bad," Prince Konrad thought. "I might have problems with that last man, but everything should be alright."

He stayed in the throne room till the entire hour of petitions had passed, still trying to process the information his father had told him. Then he left.

Konrad went all the way downstairs to try and ask Newle and Himdir to ride out with him, only to find that Newle had gone off to some other place to have lessons.

He stood there, realizing that in this huge castle, he would never find them.

She could be anywhere! She did say that she didn't want to ride today, and I have been neglecting my duties. Perhaps it would be wrong to try to go find her. Perhaps I should go do something my father would want me to do, Konrad reasoned with himself for a moment. *But I don't like making laws like he does. As a matter of fact I think it's wrong to make that many laws. I don't want to go horse riding by myself when I would prefer to take someone with me. Is there anything I can do?* He thought about it and hit upon an idea. He decided to hunt up his old sword fighting instructor and practice a little. But there was a snag, he hadn't even seen the weapons or the weapons' room in this castle yet. He'd been too busy with other things, so Konrad began the hunt immediately.

He really liked sword fighting, and it was strange he hadn't already found the weapons room, but something else seemed to have taken over his life recently. It was also strange that the first thing he thought was that it would be something useful to show off to Newle when he got around to it. It wasn't some sort of delicate art like she knew, but it was something he thought she would like.

Konrad had begun looking very systematically, and it didn't take him very long to find the weaponry—and Himdir.

"What are you doing here?" he asked when he saw the little boy curled up under a table.

"I'm hiding from Newle," Himdir explained simply.

"Why?" Konrad asked, curious as to why he was hiding. What had happened?

"We're playing hide and go seek,"

"Oh," Konrad said understandingly. "I see. Well come on out of your hiding place and help me pick a sword."

"A real sword?" Himdir asked, his eyes growing wide as he inched his way out from under the table.

"Yes. I'll even teach you how to sword fight. I'll give you a few lessons," Konrad offered.

"Really?"

"Really."

"Will you give some to Newle?" Himdir asked, looking over the swords.

"If she wants them," he promised.

Himdir gave a contented little nod and then began looking over the swords, not to pick one for Konrad, but for himself.

"You'll want a smaller one," Konrad suggested, guessing Himdir's intent. Smiling, he moving over to the half-sized swords.

Himdir resisted. "But I want a big one!" he complained.

"Here," Konrad told him. "Try to pick this up."

He pulled one down off the wall and handed it to Himdir. The moment it was in the little boy's hand, it crashed to the ground.

"Do you still want a big one?" Konrad asked, holding back a smile as he put the sword back up on the rack.

"I'll start with a small one today," Himdir told Konrad. "Tomorrow I'll need the bigger one though."

Konrad laughed as the door opened.

"Himdir!" exclaimed a happy voice. "I've been looking all over for you."

"Newle!" Himdir exclaimed with the excitement of a little boy, forgetting hide and seek for the moment. "Konrad's going to teach me how to sword fight!"

"Is he?" she asked, skeptically looking the prince.

"Yes he is. He even said he'll teach you if you want it."

Konrad looked away for a moment, he wasn't sure that Newle would approve. Instead, she glanced over the wall and chose a sword.

He saw her inspect it and balance it in her hand. It looked like she held it with surprising ease.

"They have a good store," Konrad commented.

Newle nodded. "Would you like a match?" she asked, looking at him.

"You know how to sword fight?" he asked, looking surprised.

"Yes, a little. Come on!" she jumped into position, saluting him with her sword.

"I don't approve of fighting a girl," he said, getting into position and saluting her anyways.

"Well then," she told him with a wild grin. "Think of it as teaching *a girl*, or defending yourself from *a girl*."

She thrust and he fended it off harmlessly. "Is that the best you can give?" she asked.

"I didn't want to hurt you," he told her as he thrust. Newle jumped out of the way and gave a swing at him.

He met it and the sound of clashing metal filled the room.

"Go it, Newle!" Himdir cheered.

Newle gave a push off and the two broke free.

"Give it back, Konrad!" Himdir cried, cheering for which ever side he thought was winning at the moment.

Konrad attacked and Newle defended herself with only a little effort.

"Come on Konrad, you can do better than that!" Himdir exclaimed.

Newle found a break in Konrad's attack. Quick as a viper she thrust full on at Konrad's arm, barely touching his skin and leaving the faintest little scratch.

"Go get her Konrad! Nice thrust Newle!"

Newle was beginning to get winded. With the sword blades only an inch from her face, she managed to slip out from under them.

Newle stumbled backward a few steps before Konrad recovered himself. He attacked again and Newle only just defended herself. Konrad was getting the better of the duel and Newle was almost done.

"Konrad! pull yourself together Newle! You nearly had him."

Newle gave a quick twist to her sword as she took a step forward. Several things happened in that split second. Konrad's sword flew out of his hand and a huge rip could be heard throughout the room as Newle tripped forward and fell harmlessly on top of her sword at Konrad's feet.

"Are you alright?" Himdir cried, running up to where she lay on the floor.

"I'm so sorry!" Konrad exclaimed, kneeling down and touching her shoulder.

"I'm alright." Newle told them, sitting up and laughing. "I'm the only person in Hedgecliff who would trip and lose a duel right when she was winning."

"You're probably the only girl in Hedgecliff that would fight a duel!" Himdir praised.

"Besides," Konrad began. "You didn't lose. You won! You disarmed me."

"But you knocked me to the ground," Newle explained. "You won!"

"Newle won," Himdir argued.

"Tell it to her!" Prince Konrad agreed, looking at her in confusion. What kind of girl was this? "She won fair and square."

"If you insist that I won, I must have," Newle gave in. "I won't argue with you both."

Konrad began giving a basic lesson to Himdir as Newle left the room to fix a rather large hole that had claimed a good bit of her hem. Before she left she heard Konrad ask Himdir what he had done that morning. She only just heard the response: "We slid down the railing."

DECISIONS MUST BE MADE

Marja and I drifted apart during the next month. I tried to help her, comfort her, share the burden, but she shut me out and wanted nothing to do with me. I was hurt, and honestly, who wouldn't be?

Day after day passed, Ella tried to comfort me, but she just ended up repeating the same words over and over again "All friends drift apart, whether sooner or later, all friends drift apart." It was hardly reassuring.

Mother had another tussle with Mart and his father. She convinced them to give up another room, but that was all.

Our stomachs were perpetually hungry, our thirst was never fully satisfied, our nerves were always on edge.

Mother came down with something early in the second month of the siege. She told me it was not too bad, that she was only a little under the weather, but after three days of her vomiting, I knew better.

"It's water poisoning," I whispered to Marja when I had the chance.

"Ask Ella," she muttered turning away.

I heaved a sigh. Marja had been like this for weeks.

"But it's water poisoning!" I whispered a little louder.

"No one else has come down with it," she angrily whispered back at me. "If the water were poisoned, we would all be sick."

I glared at her and stormed out of the hall. Maybe Ella was right—all friends drift apart sooner or later, all friends drift apart.

But surely that can't be the case with Marja and me? I reasoned with myself. *We're cousins!* I stormed past Mart's rooms. *Alright, so that doesn't mean anything. But we practically grew up with each other!* I stomped past my tutor. *Right, if you count a year as growing up with each other.*

In my rage I had made my way to the outer wall of the castle and into the courtyard. In another minute the horsemen would come storming in on their extravagant steeds.

I decided I didn't want to stay, but the moment before I could leave, I heard the clanking of armor and the sound of hoof beats against the cobblestone street. Quickly I wiped the tears off of my face and conjured a fake smile as I stood there, the only person who had come out to meet them.

The horses stormed in, sometimes two riders per horse. They had always come in like this, but today there seemed to be more riders doubling up. Were all of their horses killed?

I wondered if they had always looked this tired and beaten. My heart raced faster, was something wrong?

They poured in like water through a hole in a bucket, and at the last, there came a chariot.

Chariots were not altogether uncommon. Usually they came in dragging with one wheel. At this point, only one or two had come up to be fixed because, as of the last we heard, the battle raged on the wall, not the field, and so the chariots were not in use.

But this chariot that came in now wasn't creaking or jolting around. It ran smoothly over the cobblestones and stopped right in front of the door into the castle.

Curiously, I took a few steps over to catch a glimpse of who or what might be inside.

"Father!" I cried joyously. I hadn't seen him in weeks.

I saw his mouth move but no words came out.

"Father?!" I panicked and rushed to the chariot. He was being carried down on a litter, his left hand wrapped up and crossed over his chest in a clenched fist. His pale skin was dotted with beads of sweat and a bloodied handkerchief was wrapped around his head.

I dashed to his side and grasped his right hand as the litter bearers lifted him and began weaving their way into the castle.

Tears sprang to my eyes and I hardly noticed as the other horsemen dismounted, and began pushing prisoners toward the dungeon. "Father will deal with them later," I whispered to myself. "Or mother if father doesn't get up too quickly."

Swiftly wiping tears from my eyes, I conjured up a half smile for father.

"Scarlet?" he coughed weakly. "Scarlet?"

"Yes Father?" I answered, the tears already coming back to my eyes.

"Take this," his right hand unclenched and he looked up into my eyes.

"Your signet ring?" I asked, shocked he would suggest such a thing.

"Take it," he pressed it into my hand and carefully closed my fingers around the silver band with the scarlet crystal on it.

The litter bearers turned into a room.

"You need it!" I cried back at him as they closed the door behind him.

I don't know how long I stood outside Father's door. As a princess, they couldn't reprove me and make me move on. But as only a princess, they wouldn't let me into speak with father.

My heart climbed a mountain at every noise I heard from the other room.

As the noises became more frequent, I left my vigil for a kinder one.

"Mother?" I knocked on her door and waited for an answer. "Mother?" I knocked again.

"Come in," came a weak voice.

I slipped through the door, a mug of water in one hand, and the ring still clenched in the other.

"Daughter," I could hear a smile and reproof in her voice and it chilled me as I thought of how I would have to break the news to her. "Marja has been with me all morning but left to help the cooks get the food ready for the soldiers. Where have you been? Why weren't you with me?" she gently reproved me.

I handed her the water and sat down at the edge of her bed, the room was very dark.

"I was busy, Mother," my voice broke as I fought off the tears. I couldn't tell her.

"It's alright, Scarlet." I could still hear the reproof in her tone. And why shouldn't she? My friend would stay with her but I was her own daughter and couldn't even tell her my father was dying.

In the dark of the room, I slipped the ring over my finger.

It didn't fit; it was too big.

"What are you doing?" Mother asked me quietly.

"Nothing," I lied slipping off the bed and going to Mother's dresser.

I groped around in the dark until my hand hit a chain. I slipped the ring through it and after clasping it, dropped it over my neck and slipped it under my shift.

I'll bring it back before she notices it's gone. I'm sure I can get the ring back to Father before then.

I refilled mother's mug and slipped out of the room. She was lightly sleeping. Dinner was being served in the throne room. Even though I was hungry, I didn't want to face the people who had, no doubt, heard of everything.

Slowly I slipped through the hallways, creeping away from the people as quickly as I dared.

I looked back at the door to the throne room with loathing.

"Excuse me, miss," I bumped into someone.

"I'm sorry," I automatically answered, looking up at the young soldier.

He looked down at me in surprise. "Your Majesty," the soldier knelt on the ground and bowed his head. "Lord Telmar and Lord Cedric are awaiting you in the western tower."

"Why?" I asked, hoping against hope.

"Your father isn't going to get better, and the queen is still sick. The only ruler Hedgecliff has is you."

Hardly daring to breath, I followed him to the western tower.

We walked through the halls, turning at each corridor to make our way to the tower. There were people milling about the halls. I guess they had heard about their king.

I marched up the stairs to the tower with a sinking heart. Would the entire war rest on my shoulders?

"Your Majesty," the two lords bowed and kissed my hand as in the fashion of the day.

"My lords," I gave the slightest bob to show respect.

The soldier that had fetched me was dismissed.

"Princess Scarlet," Lord Cedric began. "As your father's closest advisors, we have been in his confidence since the siege began. We have also been in consultation with his doctor. I hate to be the bearer of terrible news such as this, but we have been told that he will not survive the night."

"May I see him?" I asked.

"No," Lord Telmar spoke before Cedric could answer. "Due to several different injuries, it is not wise for him to have visitors."

Tears welled up in my eyes. I would never see my father again.

"Your Majesty," Cedric began, giving Telmar an unforgiving look. "It is best for everyone. But we have important matters that must be discussed, here, at the top of the highest tower, at night, when no one can see us or hear us. "

I shivered and wrapped my cloak closer around me.

"You see," Telmar began, looking out across the black night, his slightly curling hair rustling in the breeze. "We are not winning this battle by much. One wrong move, and our generation will go down as the last resistance against the Fairfalcon empire."

The cloak wasn't doing much to keep me warm. Something besides the breeze sucked the heat away from me.

"You see, Princess," Cedric began, grasping the hilt of his sword with a fearsome glitter in his young green eyes. "We have a traitor among us who is feeding the enemy information. Each time we find a hole in their defenses, we exploit it only to find there are one hundred archers in place to fend us off. If I could only get my hands on him!"

His youthful enthusiasm seemed shadowed by dark tones too deep for his age.

"What do you suggest we do?" I asked.

"Ignore the traitor," Telmar said at last. "He will surface on his own."

Cedric shook his head, but couldn't come up with a way to catch the traitor so they dropped the subject.

"Either way," Telmar began. "As both the king and queen are unable to make decisions for the country, we must ask you for permission to make them ourselves. That's why we called you here tonight."

I nodded. I knew that they were asking for the ring, and I knew that it wasn't mine to give away. But I couldn't explain that to them, they wouldn't understand.

"I cannot," I answered at last. "If there is a spy, there is no reason why it can't be the two of you. I'm sorry, but you'll have to bring your ideas to me."

Telmar sighed but Cedric bowed and smiled.

"I know it will be a nuisance Telmar, but this way we can be sure that no one is getting the information."

"Your Majesty," Cedric began. "The only problem that I can come up with is that you will be wanted near the front action so the decisions can be made at a moment's notice."

"You should really reconsider giving it to one of us," Lord Telmar pushed. "We cannot be going back and forth to and from the castle every time we have to decide something."

I thought about it for a moment. "Is there really any reason why I cannot go myself?"

The two lords stood back in horror.

"Your Majesty!" Lord Telmar began. "The outrage! It's impossible!"

"Why not?" I asked glaring at him.

"You could be injured."

"So? My father was injured, hundreds of other soldiers have been injured. Why does it matter if I get hurt?" I lashed out at them angrily.

Cedric smiled. "If you don't mind, your highness, I don't see why not. We can outfit her in the armor I had when I was ten. Its light enough and will give her protection."

I smiled and looked to Lord Telmar to see what he would say.

"Your Majesty, this is not a good idea. Are you sure of this?" he asked, his face strangely withering.

"I'm certain."

Cedric smiled. "Good. Lord Telmar and I will give you a quick overview of what the situation looks like."

He led me over to the side of the tower and putting an arm around my shoulders, pointed out the positions of each army with a little help from Lord Telmar.

"So the wall around the city is nearly surrounded?" I asked. Truth be told, I didn't understand much of what Cedric said, but I was going to try my hardest.

"Yes," he began. "Except over there, by the trees to the south."

"And," I continued. "There are only two gates in and out of the city?" he nodded. "And the trees are offering too much cover so our archers cannot see them?" he nodded again. "So why can't we send them a delegate to ask them to fight on even ground?" I asked at last.

"Fairfalcon knows they already have the advantage and would never agree to that." Lord Telmar broke in.

"Alright," I continued, undeterred. "So what if we used that one spot where they don't have archers?"

"How?" Cedric asked, clearly puzzled and interested.

"We'll dig underneath the wall and send out a small attack party," I explained.

"I don't see how that would help us," Telmar began. "You clearly know nothing of war and shouldn't be allowed out at the front."

"Continue," Cedric urged. "I'm sure we can somehow use a small attack party."

"My idea is that we use them like outlaws. Small, quick attacks on the enemy's vital areas. Water trains, food imports, you name it. Attack quickly, decicivly and then fade back to do it again."

Cedric nodded, "Sure, if we can pull it off without letting the enemy know."

I smiled in the dark and headed toward the trapdoor that led back down to the inside of the castle.

Cedric lifted the heavy door to the trap and I took a few steps down.

I looked over my shoulder and the two lords bowed.

"I will see you two in the courtyard tomorrow morning at five sharp. Goodnight."

I slipped down the rest of the stairs and back into the lit halls of the castle. Spooky shadows danced across the walls as I made my way back to the room I shared with Mother and Marja.

The door slowly creaked open on ill-oiled hinges, but the two sleeping forms didn't move.

I crept around the mat that Marja slept on, and quietly lay down and covered myself with the one thin blanket and cloak I had.

CHAPTER FIVE

A week later, the people were allowed to bring their pleas to the king again. Konrad insisted that he join his father in the throne room again.

Once again the king left Konrad in charge of dealing with the people. This time things were different.

A farmer and his wife entered. "Your majesty," began the farmer. "Why would you take my land and give it to the widow next door? We have never done you any harm and we never moved the stones! We wouldn't dare! But you have taken away our space and now our sheep cannot graze. Please move the stones back."

"But the widow told me that you had moved them," Prince Konrad began as his heart sank to his boots.

"My husband wouldn't dare!" the woman exclaimed.

"And don't you dare accuse my wife of moving the stones. I can tell you she didn't do it," the farmer exclaimed, putting his arm around her as though to defend her from all harm.

He assured the two that the thought had never entered his mind. Konrad thought for a moment. "Perhaps we should bring the widow back."

"Yes!" the farmer exclaimed. "Bring the thieving woman in and make her pay for her crimes."

"I didn't mean it like that ..." Konrad began to explain.

"Pardon my saying so, but either way you meant it your majesty, we should bring her in," the farmer's wife kindly told him.

"I'll have her come in. You will come back this same time next week," he commanded them.

They left. Then a messenger came in with a message.

"The village of Coldfog has been abandoned. A man came in this morning with the king's guards. The rumor had started that the guards had come for war. Everyone left."

"Bring that man to me," Konrad ordered with a sigh. "I'm afraid that nothing really went right last week."

The man with the irrigation problems came back. "Your Majesty ..."

"Let me guess," Konrad interrupted sitting back on his throne. "The man won't take his dam down and is willing to fight to keep it."

"No!" the man exclaimed. "Where did your highness get that idea?"

"Never mind," Konrad sighed, "Why are you back?"

"The man agreed and we helped him break the dam. The water had built up and when we broke the dam, we flooded our fields. Our crops have only a little time to live!"

Konrad thought all these issues were even worse than war. "Dig canals for the water to flow through out of your fields." Then he thought about it a little more. "Make sure that it doesn't flow onto the road or into someone else's field. I want to be hearing the last of this right now."

"Yes, Your Majesty," the man bowed and left.

"Darn it! This ruling thing is harder than I expected. It feels like my kingdom is falling down around my ears."

"Truer words have never been said, my son," the said as he king entered the room. "Anyway, I've come to give you a piece of news. I found that old text I was looking for!"

"And how is this news?" Konrad asked, searching his memory for anything about the text.

"It tells all about the customs of the people of Hedgecliff," the king explained.

"But Newle already told me all about them. I'm confused as to why you need this," Konrad admitted.

"Ah! But your friend might have hidden things from you. She is just a servant. Nearly a slave!"

Konrad remembered the last time he heard that word. "She wouldn't lie, and she wouldn't hide the truth. Besides, what do you need with their customs?"

"I wanted to know if there was anyway we could identify the princess," the king explained as he rolled out a scroll on the table. Konrad bent over it for a better look.

"I've already told you I'm not interested in finding the princess," Konrad grumbled, turning to leave.

"And I've already told you we need to find her," the king insisted. "Anyway, the book says the king wears a ring. It's made out of a metal that looks like silver but is more precious. It has a stone on it that is scarlet. The stone can be flipped up and there is a seal on it. This ring is used to identify the ruler, and there was plenty of time for the king to give it to his daughter before he died. If I know anything about anything, she won't be parted from it if she wants to make a comeback to retake the kingdom. And I assure you she will!"

"I'm not interested," Konrad repeated. "In fact, finding the princess is the last thing I want to do. I still don't understand why you can't see it the way I do."

"It's because I don't need to see things the way you do. I already know what's right for you and the kingdom."

"Father, just stop messing with my personal business," Konrad commanded angrily. "You cannot control my life like this. I am a grown man."

"Yes I can if I'm doing it for your own good," his father pressed. "And I assure you I am!"

"But you're not. You're just trying to control my life!" Konrad crossed his arms and turned away.

"How is teaching you about politics controlling your life? I only said the one time that *if* we find the princess, I highly suggest you marry her," the king replied forcefully.

"And why would I want to do that?" Konrad asked outraged.

"Because the people love her, if we killed her they would revolt. Despite what it looks like, we are not strong enough to keep them from doing that."

"Then why can't we just exile her?" Konrad asked. "I still don't see why you have to arrange my marriage. Besides, mother asked you with her dying breath not to arrange a marriage for me."

Konrad's father ignored the question, he had already been over this with his son the morning Lord Grissel had suggested it. It hadn't ended well then, it wouldn't end well now.

"If you marry the princess, the people will love you," he explained again. "It will strengthen your position to the throne when I am gone. You remember what Lord Grissel said he overheard the woman in the street say."

"Yes I do. But I chose not to think of it," Konrad stood up. "This conversation is useless and I must be going. I have better things to do than talk to someone who just doesn't get it."

The king started into a fit of coughing as Konrad left. *Bother that old man. I almost wish he were dead,* Konrad thought as he stormed off. *Perhaps I should go and apologize*, he thought. *It really wasn't my fault, but he might not have meant it like that.*

Regretfully, Konrad slowly turned back to the throne room and pushed open the door. The king was still standing where he had left him, only just recovering from his coughing spell. But Konrad could only stand there, watching his frail father. Where had the time gone? Was it just a few months ago when he had gone riding out everyday?

He had never apologized to his father before, and even now it was hard for him to say the words. Konrad left the room with a heavy heart after promising his father that he would be back next week to finish up with the people.

Up until the moment that Konrad left the room, his father, the king, had watched him closely. The king was surprised. His son had never been so polite and considerate before.

What has gotten into that boy? he wondered as he hobbled into the other room. *I shouldn't wonder if it was the effects of that girl. I must admit that she is a wonder. Something is very off about her and I aim to find out what it is. I should invite her to dine with Konrad and me. Perhaps* ... but he never finished the thought. He was interrupted by another fit of coughing. *Bother this climate, you get a cough and keep it. I'll have to send to Fairfalcon to get my physician.* Then he went out for a ride with his armed guard.

When Newle and Himdir were done with their lessons, and as it was very cold out, Konrad couldn't take Himdir out for a ride.

"Perhaps we could go sliding down the railing again. Please?" Himdir begged Newle as he tugged on her skirt.

"I don't think so," she answered, coloring up a little and looking away. "It really isn't very ladylike."

"And what do you care about that?" Konrad teased smiling. "You never worried about that before."

"Whatever," Newle gave in. "Alright Himdir, let's do this." The moment she said that, Himdir jumped up and down. He dashed out of the room, ran down the hall and out to the stairs. Newle laughed as she followed him.

Konrad offered her his arm and she accepted it with a full heart. In this manner they strolled after Himdir. Down the hall and up the stairs.

"Race you to the top!" Himdir cried as he jumped up the first steps, followed closely behind by Konrad and then Newle.

Himdir won and was already on his way down when Newle finally made it to the top.

"A bit of a climb," she said sitting down on the top step and waiting her turn.

"Just a little. It's not bad when you are not running," Konrad commented, sitting down and sliding out of sight as Himdir ran back up the stairs.

Newle sat down on the railing and began sliding down.

Konrad was still at the bottom when she got there. Newle had again promised Himdir she would catch him at the bottom, so she waited.

"Newle," Konrad began, his face a perfectly illegible mask. "I need to talk to you about my father."

"Why?" she asked smiling. "What's wrong with him?"

"Lots. I don't even want to be prince anymore. Or at least I don't want to be his son."

"Oh, Konrad," she exclaimed, closing her eyes to remember what it was like. "Is being prince that bad?"

"Yes," Konrad said with contempt. "And I'm sure that being a princess wouldn't be any better."

Newle started for the first time in weeks. *Had he figured something out?* she asked herself. *Perhaps there is still time for me to run away before he tells anyone*, she thought.

"Father wants me to marry Princess Scarlet," Konrad sighed.

Newle gave a little nervous laugh to hide how her heart jumped to her mouth. "Why?"

"Because the people of Hedgecliff love her and if we killed her they would revolt and we don't have enough troops to fight them off."

"Why can't you just banish her then?" she slowly asked. *Perhaps*, she thought, *I can convince him to let me go if I promise not to tell his father.*

"Because if I marry her it will secure my place on the throne in the eyes of the people," he explained. "It's very well thought out by my father, except for the fact that I don't want to do it."

"Well," Newle picked her words carefully. "Perhaps you can wait till your father is dead. Then you could marry whomever you want. Or you could find the princess yourself and tell her to go away without telling your father."

"Well ..." he trailed off and seemed to be trying to decide something. "Perhaps I will wait till when my father is dead. After that, and after I have gotten rid of Lord Grissel ..." he hesitated. "Perhaps we should have a talk then."

Newle's imagination ran wild as her heart raced, but she remained calm and said, "About what?"

He took a step closer, "You know exactly what I want to talk to you about. In the meantime we won't say anything. Understood?"

"Yes, I see." Newle responded carefully. A single wrong move could ruin everything.

The air was tight with tension. Himdir slid down and Newle caught him. She spun him around before setting him down, then they ran up again, leaving Konrad downstairs by himself.

He doesn't want to marry the princess, and yet he just told her to wait a little while for him, Newle thought as she ran up the stairs with Himdir. *If I were to get married to him, I would have to tell him who I really am. What a mess I've gotten myself into.*

That moment she made a decision. When the weather got nice in the spring, she would leave. Marja and the castle didn't matter—this was for her life now. Through the gate or over the wall was still to be decided, but that didn't matter. She needed to get away. She didn't belong in the castle anymore and things were getting too dangerous. She did like Konrad, maybe even loved him, but that wouldn't stop her. Nothing could.

She watched as Himdir slid down the banister and then went down herself. The moment she could see the bottom, she saw that Konrad was standing ready.

It all happened in a second, and in a second it was all over. Her heart few as high as the sky when he caught her and it burst into a billion pieces when he twirled her around while looking deep into her green eyes. His brown eyes and tousled hair stared back at her.

"Again!" cried Himdir, when Konrad set Newle down.

Himdir dashed up the stairs. Konrad stood holding Newle's waist, her skirts still twirling as he looked down at her.

The moment Himdir's small legs disappeared up the stairs Newle broke away. Making some feeble excuse about having left her books by the fire and a fear they might catch a spark and burn, she ran down the hall and took the door down to the kitchen.

Konrad stood for a moment at the bottom of the stairs. The moment she left, he didn't want to be there any more. It was as though the light had gone out of the room. He lost himself in thought leaning against the wall. *She probably even knows how to help the people in the villages better than I do.*

Konrad silently caught Himdir at the bottom of the stairs and told him to go to Newle.

Newle ran all the way down the stairs and into the kitchen.

"Good afternoon." Samantha greeted her at the bottom.

"Good afternoon to you, too." she replied, a little breathless and absently.

Samantha's motherly eyes picked up that something was wrong, but she wisely said nothing. She realized that if Newle didn't want to say anything about it she wouldn't. If she did want to talk about it, she would. That was that.

"Could I send you out to the butcher?" she asked instead.

"Of course! Let me just run up and grab my cloak." Newle agreed, jumping at the opportunity to see Marja, especially after what had just happened. *Anything to get away from the castle, if even for a moment,* she thought.

Newle grabbed the books from beside the fire and ran up the stairs. She opened the door at the top of the stairs a crack to make sure that the hallway was clear before she went up to her room.

Why am I acting like this? she thought. *I really have nothing to worry about. It's not like he actually said anything.* But he had, and she knew it. She also knew if the offer were repeated, she might not be able to keep her heart from making a mistake.

She got to the safety of her room and set the books down, grabbed her cloak from the bedpost and was back downstairs before anyone could see her.

Newle got the list from Samantha and went out into the cold. She didn't bother to take a horse because she wanted to study the shop windows. You can't really do that from a horse.

If I'm running away, then I should take food, she planned as she began walking. *I'll have to buy that right before I leave so it won't perish. I should save up for it now. I'm going to need a disguise so I can sneak past the guards.* She thought a little more, *Perhaps if I go as I am then they will think I'm an important lady. They'll just let me through the gates without question. Then I'll have more money to spend on more important things. Like room and board on the way.*

She realized that if she were running away, Konrad would send people to run after her, and his father would be suspicious of her real identity, especially if she were caught. She couldn't spare to be seen.

She went into the butcher's shop through the front door.

"You, a front door guest now, Newle!" the butcher exclaimed when he saw her.

"Yes, I've taken up being a teacher in the palace. It's really nice," she absently told him, searching the room for Marja.

"Ah so you teach that arrogant little brat the prince, do ya?" he teased, taking a look at her list.

"Oh no!" she exclaimed, hating that Konrad and his name managed to follow her wherever she went. "I don't teach him." But her curiosity got the better of her, "Why, what has he done this time?"

"Nothing short of starting a war in Coldfog and moving some poor widow's stones out six feet and starting a little fight between the neighbors," the butcher explained with a laugh.

"Tell me," Newle asked. Her heart went out to the people of her country and she almost wished there was something she could do for them.

So as he was wrapping up her order, the butcher told her all about how the prince had moved the stones and about how he had nearly started the war.

"I thought the prince was better than that," she told him at the end. "I'm sure none of this was his fault, I admit that he really should have thought more about sending guards into a village right after a war."

"Aye, he should have. If only we had the princess back," the butcher wished out loud. "She would set things right."

She would, Newle thought, grinning. *And she is going to do something about this.*

Newle thanked the man, asked where Marja was, and left with her order. Slipping around back, she embraced Marja again, dying to tell her everything that had happened.

BEING ME

The next morning, right at 4:30, I woke up and slipped around Marja and Mother and back out into the hall again. There wasn't much for me to do but eat. I had skipped dinner last night due to not wanting to talk to people, and I had to be gone before breakfast would be served.

I slipped down to the kitchen and ate some bread that had been left out. I was sure no one would mind.

Fifteen minutes before five I was in the courtyard waiting, my black cloak drawn over my shoulders and pinned together in the middle with a silver leaf brooch. The chain with the ring on it was tucked underneath my tunic and shift.

I had taken the tunic from Father's room. It fell right below my knees and you could see six inches of my leg before my boots covered them from mid-thigh, down. Both tunic and leggings were differing shades of brown, as were my boots. My shift extended another three inches in every direction beyond the tunic. The sleeves, the hem, the neck.

My own sword was strapped to the belt at my waist, and I had a bow and quiver slung over my back.

I hoped I cut an intimidating figure. Though, truth be told, I probably looked like a skinny little boy trying too hard to look grown up. Perhaps when Cedric came back with his armor, that would help a little bit.

I hopped up and down in excitement. An adventure at last! I was restless after having been locked up in the castle for weeks. Mother and Father would get better. Nothing could stop that from happening. I was too excited. Anything could happen!

It grew a little bit brighter, the silver white gray of dawn spreading over the courtyard like wildfire.

Cedric brought three horses into the courtyard, the loud clip clopping of their hooves echoing in the light dawn.

"Here," he dropped a package at my feet and turned to tend to the horses.

I flipped the cover off with my foot. There was a spotless set of armor consisting of a chain coat, one wristlet of leather for my steady arm for shooting, two shin guards, and a light helmet.

I stood looking at them, unsure of what to do.

"Well," Cedric began, hardly glancing over at me. "You could take off your cloak, scabbard, and belt so you can slip that chain mail over your head."

I took his advice and in only a moment the glittering steel encased me in its heavy embrace.

"What's next?" I asked.

"Tie those shin guards on."

I picked them up and clumsily managed to tie the leather straps together, but the moment I let go of it, it slipped down over my foot and came up past my knee. I tried a few stumbling steps before I noticed Cedric smiling down at me.

"Stop it!" I laughed, failing in my attempts to take it off before I made a bigger fool of myself.

"You had it upside down," he informed me as I finally got it off. "But either way, it's obviously too big for you."

"So what's next?" I asked, leaning over and putting it back in the pile.

"The wrist guard." he said. "I see that you have a bow so you should know how to put it on."

I nodded and slipped it over my left wrist. Carefully I tightened the lacing till it was snug. I tied it in a quick knot and grabbed my bow to take a test draw.

The motion gave me extreme pleasure. You stretch out your left arm and pull straight back on the string with your right. Both arms felt great, although my draw time was a little slow.

I pulled at the lacing to stretch it just enough before I belted the chain mail and made sure my sword was easily accessible.

"Do you really know how to use that?" Cedric asked, stooping down to gather the shin guards.

"The sword?" I asked.

"Yes. Who taught you?" he looked at me curiously.

"Yes, I know how to use the sword and my tutor taught me."

Cedric nodded, obviously not too impressed.

"Let's test you," he slipped the rest of the armor right behind the door and faced me.

I sighed and drew my sword as he did the same.

"On guard!" our swords met in mid air in the neutral defense position of *arcada*.

He gave a slight nod as though impressed for choosing a stancethat would allow me to use my small size and make him do all the work. I smiled back innocently.

"Go!" he cried at last.

Quickly we both moved closer in, me to make it hard for him to move quickly, and him to make it hard for me to use my small size.

He lashed out at me in a lower side maneuver and I parried with a slash up and out.

"Good," he smiled as he backed out and sidestepped around me a little bit. I kept my guard, knowing he would not be satisfied with a simple defense move.

I was right. The next moment he was attacking furiously and I was literally kept on my toes, defending from all sorts of foreign moves I had never been taught before.

He was wearing me down with a strange, quick attack when I noticed a pattern. I took one little step to the right and lashed out at his leg with the flat of my sword. He was taken by surprise and took a step back when I began my attack.

Having been worn down by the quick defense that I had to make before, I chose a strong attack pattern and stuck with it. Needless to say, I needed to be another foot taller than my opponent and at least another hundred pounds heavier for it to have any effect.

"Bad choice," Cedric commented.

He defended with the same tactics and they began to work because he was a foot taller than me and weighed a good bit more.

Our swords met in mid air as I tried to break his concentration with another arcada move.

My sweaty arms and hands quivered under the weight as I vainly tried to stop him from winning.

In the next second my sword slipped out of my hands and my knees broke from underneath me. His sword slipped down my sword and closer to my face as I closed my eyes and tried to roll out from underneath it before it was too late.

His sword clashed against the cobblestones.

I opened my eyes slowly and uncurled myself from the tight ball I had become. I checked my face, arms, and legs. They were all there and I gave a sigh of relief.

"Are you alright?" Cedric didn't look too concerned as he offered me a hand up.

"I think so," I took the hand up as I noticed for the first time that Lord Telmar was staring down at us from his perch on the steps.

"Lord Telmar!" I called up at him and motioned for him to come down.

"Lock your knees next time," Cedric told me. "And don't stand your ground so much, you put yourself in a vulnerable position when you could have just run away. Other than that, you'll do. Basically, learn when you get yourself into a battle you can't win."

I nodded and sheathed my sword. Hopefully I would never have to unsheathe it again.

Lord Telmar mounted, and Cedric and I followed suit. We turn the heads of our horses toward the gate and then let them fly.

We galloped down the main cobblestone street and through the city.

The city was still inhabited by people who couldn't pull enough connections to find shelter in the castle. The few who were brave enough to be out bowed as we rode through. A few of the ladies called out blessings on our heads as we passed them and the men, too old to join in the battle, cheered and took off their hats as we came by. Children smiled and one was even bold enough to give Cedric a flower as he slowed his horse for them. No one seemed to take any notice of me. I guess they never thought I would come out of the castle dressed in armor and with a helmet pulled down over my eyes.

The city's streets were strewn with rubble from when the Fairfalcons had been pelting them with rocks. A few still stood in the streets and people walked around them carefully. The children hid behind their mother's skirts as we passed.

CHAPTER SIX

After breakfast a week later, Newle went down to the kitchen to give lessons to Himdir. When she arrived, only Samantha and her new helper were there.

"Samantha, where is Himdir?" she asked puzzled, looking around the room.

"That prince came down only a few moments ago, he offered to take Himdir up to the throne room to see how the country is run. Very polite of him," Samantha answered, looking closely at Newle for any sign.

"Then I'll just skip lessons for today," Newle said with a sigh. She had been looking forward to this. She had come up with a particularly good book to read. "Do you need any help in the kitchen?" she asked.

"Oh goodness no!" Samantha exclaimed. "I almost forgot. The prince said I was to tell you to come up and join him and Himdir."

Newle's heart sank even more. She didn't want to offend the prince, so she bade goodbye to Samantha and went up to the throne room.

She stood outside the doors for a few moments before entering. She could hear a heated debate was going on inside.

It must have something to do with what the butcher was talking about a week ago, she thought as she pushed the door open.

After the door closed behind her, Newle stood a moment on the carpet, surveying the room before she was noticed.

Prince Konrad was sitting on the throne, his arms on the hand rests, his back as straight as an arrow and his face grim with decision and puzzlement.

"Newle!" Himdir cried, running up to her and jumping into her arms as she bent down to catch him. "Konrad is trying to help these poor people figure out who moved the boundary stones. They might not have been moved at all!"

She walked up to him and gave a curtsy, still holding Himdir. "Perhaps you should take a step away from it to get a better perspective and they should go over their stories again."

Annoyance flowed visibly through his face, but he gestured for the widow and the farmer to start over again.

The two people explained their sides of the story and each begged him to help them. Then Konrad, thoughts whirling through his mind, asked an interesting question: "Widow, how old are your sons?" *Did it really matter if someone was brought to justice if both parties would be pleased?*

The woman answered, "My three sons are nine, twelve and fifteen, your Highness. My husband died right before our youngest was born."

"Perhaps it is time for them to be apprentices," Newle suggested. "They can be close to home and still live with you, but they will be learning how to be self sufficient before you die. It will be better for all of you and you can even keep one of the boys home to help you with the land. It's a perfect arrangement. This way you are getting more income, we can move the stones back so that farmer and his wife don't starve, and your children learn to fend for themselves."

"Exactly what I was thinking," Konrad jubilated.

The widow thought about it for a moment. "I see," she began at last. "The arrangement is better for all. But what if the farmer did move the stones? If he did I would like him to be brought to justice."

There it was, the one thing he couldn't be certain of—justice.

"I can swear that I didn't not move the stones. I will even give you two of my lambs in the spring to assure you of my good will," the farmer promised.

"Is that all?" Newle asked with a smile, turning back to Konrad.

"Yes, I will follow your advice," the widow thanked her.

"And I thank you for clearing this up," the farmer thanked her, making a bow and leaving the room.

The old widow turned as if to leave, but shot a few sentences over her shoulder before she was gone, "Bless you miss! Bless you sir! With the country in your hands I will never fear for justice."

The door closed behind her and another person was announced. It was the man who needed his road patrolled because of bandits. Konrad reluctantly explained to Newle what happened and she laughed.

"Did you really think you could send guards into a war-torn place and expect them to not think you wanted to kill them?" she giggled, setting Himdir down. "What if you send in a man to teach them how to defend themselves. No guards to do it for them. They will complain about you not really helping them, but it will. If you carefully broadcast it to the highwaymen, they will live in fear of being seen."

The prince was a little ruffled about Newle stepping in like that, but before he could reprimand her he had a great idea, "And if we raise the price on their heads, the bandits will hide and the people will hunt them out to get the money. The people will learn how to fight the highwaymen if only for the price!" he exclaimed.

"Exactly!" Newle praised, giving a smile of delight, a little jealous that he would get the praise for it and not her. But a moment later she stopped—had she given herself away? Was she exposing herself more each time she interjected into Konrad's affairs? Were they going to find her out?

Konrad, seemingly unsuspicious, beamed at her as his father, the king, entered the room.

"Ah, I was hoping to see you both," the king exclaimed, rejoicing at the opportunity to fulfill his plan to get to know Newle more. "Konrad I've decided to invite Newle to dine with us. Nothing formal, just dinner."

Konrad stared, puzzled at his father for a moment before turning to look at Newle.

Newle was startled. It was almost as though the thoughts she had just been thinking were now coming true.

The king walked up to Newle and extended his hand as she gave a slow curtsy. She took his arm. She took the arm of the man who had ordered her father's death, and calmly walked with him down the hall followed by Konrad.

This is wrong! her heart screamed as they walked into the dining room. *Your father is dead and you're walking, arm in arm, with the man who killed him!*

Newle's heart struggled within her.

"So, my son," the king glanced back. "How did the people's pleas work out this morning?"

"Well I was pretty stumped but I managed to figure things out. Did you know that Newle has some really great ideas?" he reluctantly admitted. "She explained a lot about how I need to approach her people because they are very different from the people in Fairfalcon."

Newle wanted to scream at him to stop talking, but the king had already picked up again.

"I hope my son didn't put you out too much," the king said, turning to Newle with a fixed look. This was just another detail to add to the list of strange things about her.

"Oh not at all, Your Majesty," she blushed and decided to ignore her heart for a moment. It was only for her own good. If she were to refuse to eat dinner with the king, he might get mad. Or worse, find out who she was. "Anything for my people."

They sat down at a round table so Newle was sitting next to both the king and the prince.

"Perhaps you will do us the honor of your presence more in the future," the king politely said, trying desperately to open the door for more opportunities to figure her out.

"I would never intrude like that, Your Majesty!" Newle cried. Anything to not do this again! "You have your own business to attend to."

"Anyway," he brushed it aside and cut to the heart of what he really wanted to say. "Tell me all about yourself." Newle's heart sank as she set down her fork. Was it safe? "Who are you?" he continued. "Where are you from? How did you come to the castle?"

Newle took a deep breath and began to tell him the fake history she had made for occasions like this.

"I'm an innkeeper's daughter. I lived in the village Edgeburn, which, as you might know, is an unsavory part of the kingdom near the border. My father was ruined in a raid and I was sent out to find my fortune. That's when I came here. I began asking for work and the cook took pity on me and she took me in. The rest you already know."

"So, that brings us to another question," the king began. "Were you here before Fairfalcon took over?"

"Yes," she answered carefully. *What is he getting at?* she wondered.

"Then perhaps you know what the princess looks like?" he prodded, setting down his fork and looking her in the eyes.

"I never saw her," she lied. Her heart was pounding. She knew she was on thin ice. "Please don't ask me to betray my kingdom. I won't, and if you continue to ask I will leave the table." Newle spoke with fire. She knew she had a right to refuse. She knew the king couldn't pin her down with anything just because she didn't want to betray her kingdom.

"Calm down, I didn't say anything of the sort," the king defended himself.

The second course came in and Konrad had the sense to change the subject.

"Father, I finally figured out how to fix that problem about the boundary stones." Konrad began, taking credit for Newle's work, if only to bring attention away from her.

"Really?" the king asked, turning from Newle to his son. Konrad had to explain what he did and why he did it, and before long the king nearly forgot about Newle being at the table.

"Wonderful, son," he cried when the story was over. "This reminds me of something I've been thinking about for a long time. I think it's time for your people to get to know you a little better. They need to become more accustomed to your face. I advise you to go out riding in the village more often. People need to realize you are the next ruler. You could even host a ball," he suggested.

"No ball, Father," Konrad told him. "If you insist that I go out more often, then I'll go out. But you can't make me host a ball. It's out of the question. Perhaps," Konrad began, looking at Newle sideways. "You will go out riding with me sometime?"

"I can't promise anything," she told him looking straight ahead.

"Well then it's settled, but we'll have the ball anyway," the king gave a little wave to an attendant. He nodded his head and bowed out of the room.

Konrad decided not to argue the point with Newle at the table so he focused on his food.

The dessert came in and was dished out. For the first time in what felt like forever, Newle tasted strawberries and cream again. It brought back sweet and sorrowful memories.

They ate dessert in silence. Before she left, the king invited her to supper after she had given lessons to Himdir.

Newle accepted only because she didn't want to anger him, then she went back to the kitchen where Himdir was waiting for a story.

She took out the arithmetic book and opened it up. "It's time for a real lesson," she told him, writing some problems on a slate.

"Why can't you just tell stories all day long?" Himdir asked.

"I'll spend so much time with you that I have to run and change before supper. The king asked me and I didn't refuse so I have to go."

"Will you wear the blue dress you've been working on?" Himdir asked. "I think it looks beautiful."

"Yes," she replied. *Thankfully it doesn't bring out the green in my eyes*, she thought. Then to Himdir: "The king told me it would be formal. He has invited some lords and dukes to dine with him."

After the lesson she extracted herself from the kitchen and went up to her own room to change.

She pulled out a blue dress with a scoop neck and draping sleeves lined with gold. There was a train that trailed out behind her and ended with a gold band of cloth around the edge of the skirt. She passed a gold belt around her waist and tied it in the front after the fashion of the day.

As a finishing touch, she untied her hair and let it fall over her shoulders.

Prince Konrad was waiting for her outside the door when she was done. He offered her his arm staring at her in admiration.

"You look amazing," he told her, pulling a little piece of hair away from her face as he looked down at her.

"Thank you," she replied, looking back up at him. Her heart sank and she looked away as she remembered she couldn't let herself do this.

How can I ever be happy? she thought. *I do love him, but I can't let myself do that. Every moment more I spend with him I should be spending twice that time getting ready to escape. That last snowfall blocked every passage in the mountain and I can't get out till spring. I don't know what I should do, but perhaps I should at least shun him a little more.*

They walked arm in arm into the banquet hall after the king as every man and woman stood up and bowed or curtsied accordingly.

Newle's eyes welled up with tears she could remember when she had walked into this exact same hall on her father's arm. Everyone had stood up and showed honor, just like they did now.

That night the room had a festive air to it and everyone greeted the king and princess with cheerful smiles. From the safety of her father's arm, she had surveyed the room.

"Father!" she cried, her childish excitement making her forget her manners for the moment. "Look at how happy they are to see you!"

"Daughter Scarlet, they are not here to see me," he explained to her with a smile in his kind eyes. "They have come to see you."

Newle's father led her to the front of the room where she stood for a moment before he took her and settled her in a chair.

"Father?" she asked, curiously. "Why are they here to see me? I haven't done anything."

"They are here to see you because they know one day you will do something for them. One day you will be queen." Newle smiled as she remembered those words.

Why did he have to die? she asked herself as Konrad led her to a seat and she sat down. *It would have made my whole life that much easier. And now I wouldn't be betraying my mother, father and country by consorting with the enemy.* Even that made her smile. *My father would have said that.*

The king stood up and began a speech but Newle wasn't paying any attention.

"My daughter," her father had said, now in her memory. "These people will travel with you to the ends of the earth. You can lead them, and they will follow you. You must lead them well or they will leave you for another, worthier ruler. Everyone has a burden. It is your job as ruler to make it worth their while. Remember this, and you will never go wrong," he had told her. "I'll never forget." Newle whispered.

The first course was brought in.

"Newle," Konrad began. "Father's taken a liking to you." Her heart stopped. "He's never asked a scullery maid to dinner before." Konrad gave her a grin.

Newle didn't know how to answer that without giving anything away, so she just tossed him a watery grin and fell to eating.

"Right," Konrad turned back to his food with a sigh and picked up his fork. "I guess you're as puzzled as I am."

Konrad dug into his food and Newle heaved a sigh of relief. *Thank goodness he stopped asking questions*, she thought as her eyes scanned the room. *Unfortunately I'm sure he's not the only one.*

Newle sharpened her ears and leaned closer in.

"Who is she?" she heard someone say over the murmur of the other tables.

"Princess or something," came a nonchalant reply.

"Come on, aren't you curious?"

"Nah, and it's none of your business. We stand by the old king. It doesn't matter who the new king's son has taken an interest in." Newle blushed.

"But the old king is dead! He's not coming back! Don't you think you should take some interest in what the new king is doing?"

"Sure, I take interest every time he reinforces a tax. I take interest every time his soldiers patrol the streets. I take interest every time ..."

"Shush!" the other voice warned. "That's treason!"

The two voices dropped below a whisper before Newle could find them in the crowd.

Keep taking interest, Newle urged in her heart. *You never know when I might need it.*

Konrad tapped her arm. "Something bothering you?" he asked with concern.

"Nothing," she lied, turning back to her food and picking up a fork. "Nothing."

Konrad leaned back. "Then perhaps you can tell me something."

Newle smiled, "Yes?"

"It's nothing really," he began. "I was just wondering."

"About what?"

"The origin of the language, is it from the North?"

Newle smiled. "East, where dragons, elves, and dwarfs live. I was told humans also live there, but they have dark hearts. They have the dwarfs under an iron fist." she smiled. "But that's only what I've been told." Two minstrels came out and bowed as the room hushed. "Later ..." she whispered to Konrad.

"Tonight," the minstrels began. "For your enlightenment and entertainment, I will be presenting one of the ballads of Fairfalcon. It will be presented after their traditions. I will tell this story in three parts as if I were the main character, moving forward each time a section is complete, according to the traditions. My friends, salutations." The king smiled as the minstrel began. "Tonight I will tell the story of the first winter."

The man told the story, but it was twisted. The story had been about love and a victory over Fairfalcon, but it had been rewritten. The story was dark and the end had been changed to please the king.

Newle stopped her ears and felt nauseous. It hurt her to the core to hear her kingdom talked of in that way.

"Next," the minstrel continued when the story was over. "I will tell the story of Hedgecliff." Then began the tale Newle had told only a month ago about the knight named Hedge who killed the dragon while falling down a cliff.

"I liked that story from the moment you told it," Konrad whispered in Newle's ear. The nauseated feeling passed and she felt strangely pleased.

The night progressed and soon the banquet was soon over.

"Father?" she had asked him long ago. "When I become queen, will you help me?"

"Of course," he laughed, a sad look in his eyes. "I'll always be there for you. To pick you up when you stumble and to guide you when all things seem dark."

"Dark, father? What do you mean?"

"Ah, my little philosopher. When you do not know the way and nothing is familiar I will be there. I will be familiar." Princess Scarlet had snuggled up to her father.

"I'll hold you to your promise," she had whispered. Newle repeated that line in her head, *I'll hold you to that promise.*

THE WALL

As we neared the wall the people disappeared and were replaced with silent houses abandoned for better places. Then, as we came even nearer to the wall, the houses were occupied by soldiers, knights and the like. We slowed down to a walk and after a moment, completely dismounted and tied the reins to a post.

"You will have a small tent over there. All of your father's things are still in there so it won't be too hard for you to pick things up. We'll get you to give us the signature to order out that little attack party," Telmar said as he led me to a tent. I sat down in a simple little chair before a low table and wrote out a quick permission for them, signed it and sealed it with the ring as proof of the fact that I was indeed in possession of it. He took the paper and nearly ran out of the tent, leaving me to settle in as best I could.

There wasn't much to the tent, it was just creamy white with a small cot and the table and the chair. There was a chest, bound with iron and rivets, padlocked. The key was on the low table, but I decided to leave that investigation for a later time.

There was an open chest with a compass, a map and a few tunics that I recognized as my father's. The sight brought tears to my eyes and before I knew what was happening, I had buried my head in the stiff folds of the fabric and I was crying.

I had dried my tears right before a soldier popped his head into my tent.

"Your Majesty?" I recognized him as the soldier who had told me about Stefan.

"Yes?" I answered trying to keep my red eyes out of sight.

"Lord Cedric offers to take you on a tour of the battlements."

"Sure. Tell him I will be out in a minute."

The soldier nodded and ducked out. I pulled my cloak back on and slipped out to find Cedric.

He was standing on the stairs to the wall talking to Lord Telmar. They were putting together a list of soldiers for the sneak attack.

Cedric excused himself and led me up the stairs to the wall.

We had archers every ten feet and I wanted to walk all the way around the wall, but I knew that it could take all day, so we just focused on taking a look at the part where we would launch the small attack party.

It seemed harmless enough and so I decided to follow through with it. Lord Cedric would lead the attacks on the water trains and such.

"We'll move another thirty archers here when we launch our attack. They will be in hiding so that if there are people out there, they won't be on edge. We'll need the archers in case there are people out there and we need to defend our party against a sneak attack."

Cedric nodded and jotted it down.

I continued, "Lord Telmar and I can hold things down while you are out. Remember, I am giving you complete control of the party. And you can be sure that they might not even come back. You understand that, don't you?"

He nodded, "What do you want us to do when we get out there?"

"Attacks on water trains, attacks from behind, and the like. We will be making an attack at the plain by the church. You can probably attack them from the side and distract them while we make a last stand."

He took that down as a note and then carefully rolled up the piece of paper, "I'll memorize this before I go and confide in one other person. Then our plans cannot fall into the enemy's hands, and if I am killed, the plan doesn't die with me."

I thanked him and gazed out at the trees.

He rested his elbows against the wall and leaned out to look down.

"Do you think there are soldiers out there?" I asked shivering.

"I honestly don't know," a strange note slipped into his voice. Could it have been fear? Did he have second thoughts about followings his ruler's orders? I pushed those thoughts out of my mind and focused on the trees in front of me.

This was no time to second-guess my subjects.

I turned from the wall and dropped the corners of my cloak. They dragged against the stones of the walk as I paced it.

What if Lord Telmar is right? I asked myself. *What if I am no good at this? What if I lead them into something worse than my father did?* I reassured myself by saying: *Cedric and Telmar wouldn't follow me if they knew I was wrong. But* ... I thought a little bit longer. *What if they are faking it? What if they are the traitors?* I reminded myself not to second-guess them and I turned back to the wall.

"It's pretty," Cedric said at last. "And altogether too quiet." I nodded.

The dark and still trees did seem foreboding.

Cedric looked away and I followed his gaze. If there were anything out there, the lookouts would inform us.

CHAPTER SEVEN

Days passed after the banquet and Newle only saw Prince Konrad from a distance.

She was fine with this because she could spend more time planning how to escape when spring would finally come, but every time she saw a glance of him in passing, her heart yearned to join him.

Newle decided with a sinking heart that she would have to leave before the mountain passes were clear. She didn't want to, but she really didn't have any choice.

Newle began riding a chestnut horse into town when she had to do errands for Himdir or Samantha, or when she wanted to see Marja. The horse was a loan from Konrad and she was pleased to have it. It meant that when she was to leave, no one would think it was odd for her to take a horse out.

Once, in the town, she heard one of the king's messengers heralding a ball in the castle. Her heart quickened with two things—joy and fear.

I'm sure Konrad will ask me, she thought. *And I know I can't refuse. I'd love to go, but the more I spend time with him, the more likely I am to be exposed!*

She didn't know which way to turn. No matter what she would do, the lies she was living would be closer to the surface. Newle could only hope Prince Konrad wouldn't ask her to come with him.

"You'll come with me to the ball? I know it's in the spring, but it's only a few months," he asked when he bumped into her in the hall the next day. Newle's heart jumped as high as the sky. "I told my father I didn't want to have the ball, but sometimes he needs to have his own way."

She answered before she could even think about it. "Of course," she told him. "If I can't go with you then I won't go at all." *That much is true*, she thought. *I won't go to the ball unless he begs me.*

"Then I'll see you at the ball," he told her as he left.

Newle sighed in relief. She knew that every moment she spent with Konrad, her secrets came closer to the surface and closer to being exposed.

Konrad was back in another second. "Will you also come riding with me?" he asked, his eyes begging her to agree.

Newle's heart jumped as high as the sky again. "Oh yes!" she cried. And then, because she didn't want him to know that she really did want to come with him that badly, "I just love riding and such. It's just wonderful." She blushed, knowing he could see right through her.

"Then how about I see you down by the stable in twenty minutes?" he asked, smiling down at her, fully seeing through her excuse.

"I'd love to," she replied as she walked away.

What have I done now? she thought. "*Consorting with the enemy,*" she heard her father reply. *The moment I can possibly get away, I'm going,* she walked a little farther only to be stopped in her tracks as an idea hit her. *I haven't even decided that I'm going to do when I get away! Do I plan a rebellion? Do I just spend the rest of my life in exile?* The anxious thoughts tugged at her heart and refused to go away. *What if I go and find a dragon? What if I go east and follow my dream?* Her heart quickened with excitement. Would it be possible for her to follow the dreams she had when she was a child? *What if I go and find elves and dwarfs? Can I make it that far?*

Newle began to take steps to the library in the castle. The last time she had been in here it was to gather books about Hedgecliff and its history for Himdir. She remembered seeing a small map that outlined all that was known about the east. It had captivated her imagination at the time, but now it captivated her spirit and her cause.

She tiptoed into the library and shut the door quietly behind her. She dashed over to the bookcase she had remembered putting the map on. She riffled through five books and three stacks of paper.

"Come on," she whispered, she knew she had to find it, now, or never. "It's got to be here somewhere,"

Panicking, she dashed to the other side of the library and leafed through three books. Panic swelled her throat.

She began tearing books off the self. A folded piece of paper floated to the floor and she snapped it up. "Thank you," she whispered, kissing it and then slipping it into her pocket.

She didn't have much time. She dashed out of the room and after putting on her cloak, she went out to keep her appointment with Konrad at the stables.

"Ready?" he asked as he led her horse out of the stable, it was already saddled.

"Almost," she replied, leaning against a post and catching her breath with deep gasps of cold air. After she had caught her breath and pulled her cloak closer around, he gave her a knee and a hand up before mounting himself.

"Where are we off to?" he asked, turning his horse.

"Well, your father did want the people in the village to see more of you," she suggested, knowing that if they stuck to the plan, it would be a safe route for both of them.

"Right. Village first, then we can head out into the country," Newle hoped that they wouldn't get that far, but she didn't say anything. They galloped off into town, only slowing to pass a cart or two.

"Fine day," he commented when they finally slowed to a walk in the town. Newle nodded. She didn't want to say anything.

"I'll admit it was rather nice of you to come," he added as he nodded to a few villagers who had bowed.

Newle nodded again. She was sure it wasn't wise to say anything. Snow began to fall as they picked up the pace through the village. Every bone in Newle told her to slow down, but she was fascinated with the cold breeze in her hair and the tears that streamed out of her eyes with the wind. She wouldn't trade it for anything in the world.

Newle, a little unsettled, took another look up at the castle over her shoulder. Relaxing, she settled herself further into her saddle. The village was small and it wasn't long before they had passed through it and were walking toward the wall that circumferenced it.

"Why is that wall here?" Konrad asked, breaking the silence as they turned to move alongside it.

"It's to keep people in and to keep people out," Newle vaguely answered, remembering the last time she had been there. Had the bodies been cleaned up already? Had the hole under the wall been filled in yet?

"I think it's a shame," he commented softly. "The wall should be torn down. Or at least made bigger to give the people more room to breath."

They walked in silence, passing one of only two gates in the wall. It pointed east.

Newle examined it as she passed, taking in every detail. One day soon she would have to pass through that gate, and she would never return.

There were three guards and they all bowed as she passed with Konrad.

"I wonder ..." he began.

"Wonder what?"

"If we could convince them to let us out a little farther. I am the prince," he joked.

Konrad cantered back to the gate, his streaming cloak and hair a startling contrast against the white snow. A magnificent picture that sent shivers down Newle's spine.

The guards knelt to the ground, shaking. The prince had never come to examine the wall before. Each guard had fleeting thoughts about questionable actions they had made, thinking that the king would never find out.

"Guards! Open the gate so I can continue my ride," he ordered in a solid tone.

The guards trembled. "We are not supposed to let anyone out," they replied in hushed tones.

"Well, we are not anyone. Make way!" he replied, gesturing Newle over. The guards hesitated for a moment but gave in and pushed the creaky gate open.

"Thank you," Konrad said as he jumped down and led his and Newle's horses through the gate.

It screeched shut behind them and they were left in a silent wood with the snow, quiet and soft, falling all around them. Birds silently took flight into the perpetual dusk of the forest.

Relaxing, Newle thought as her heart soared. Her heart felt like breaking, it was so beautiful, quiet, still and sad. *I'm outside the village and then it's only down to the sea when spring comes. But I can't expect to wait in this forest till spring without being found.*

The next moment she forgot all about it because out of nowhere came a huge snowball that startled her horse. It jumped in the air and for one terrifying moment, Newle felt for sure the horse was about to topple backwards. But just as soon as she had the time to think that, the horse bolted and Newle, slapped across the face by a branch, fell into a soft cushion of snow.

Konrad was laughing. "Look at you!" he cried. "Startled by a snowball."

Newle was about to send one in his direction when a change in his face made her stop.

Konrad was sitting with his back as straight as an arrow and his face was as cold and hard as steel. "That ring," his voice broke the silence like a knife.

His voice was commanding as Newle, with a sinking heart, looked down at her necklace. She knew what he had seen before she even looked.

"My father described it to me once," he told her, his voice far away and quiet. "He told me that it belonged to the ruler ..."

Newle panicked and stuffed the chain back under her dress, but it was too late.

"You lied to me," he accused, his brown eyes raging with fire. "You made me tell you everything about what my father was planning so you could betray me!"

"Prince Konrad," Newle began, looking up at him from the ground, tears welling up in her eyes. She hadn't planned for him to ever find out, and that cold look in his eyes hurt her to the core.

"Silence you ... you traitor!" he shouted, stunning Newle and freezing her words in her throat and her tears in her eyes. "You are Princess Scarlet Elwen Silvergleam Oreldes. Don't deny it!" Newle said nothing as she choked back tears.

His tone changed. "Why? If you had only told me the truth, things could have been different!"

"Do you think so?" her voice chilled him to the bone as she stood up. "Do you really think your father wouldn't have killed me? Have you thought of the risks I have taken and the consequences I have avoided by telling you that lie? Have you ever thought in your entire life?! You thought you could be king and you tried it! You failed! You're a spoiled brat! You never asked permission to barge into my life! You never think about others!"

She buried her eyes in her cloak, leaned against a tree and sobbed. Konrad stood stunned. His face clearly scared. He had never known her to be like this. *But*, he reasoned with himself. *I have never known her to be a princess.*

"You'll never know what it's like!" she cried.

Prince Konrad's anger got the best of him as he drew his sword. "I'll bring you to justice for shouting treason like that!" he cried, his hurt pride shining through in his actions.

"I know you would never force me to come with you," Newle answered, standing firm. "I have heard you with my own ears say you would never fight a girl. "

Konrad was taken aback. This forceful girl, no, *woman*, in front of him was more than he could handle.

Konrad struggled within himself, and putting his sword back in its scabbard, "I stay true to my word."

For a moment no one said anything. There was nothing to be said.

The silence of the wintry forest pushed at them from all sides. The snow continued to fall silently and the deepening gloom condensed as the temperature noticeably dropped.

The quiet was broken as Newle's horse walked back from where it had jumped and run off to when the snowball was thrown. Newle mounted again, defying Konrad's offer to help her up.

He's not as spoiled as I said he was, she thought, feeling only a tinge of remorse.

"I never needed it," she said aloud, her voice cutting through the gloom and dark to hit a soft spot in his heart. She knew she couldn't go back to the castle and Konrad couldn't force her to.

There was nothing for it.

"Konrad," Newle said at last,

"Prince Konrad to you, servant," he growled looking off into the trees.

His hurt eyes searching for solace.

"Then that's Princess Scarlet, thank you," she replied.

The silence grew for an uncomfortable moment.

"I cannot go back to the castle," she continued,

"I see, Princess," he muttered, forgoing eye contact.

"Then," she thought some more. "This is goodbye!" she whispered, turning the head of her horse to the east. "Perhaps one day we'll meet again."

"Wait!" Konrad cried, the color draining from his face as he finally turned to look at her.

It was too late. She was gone.

"No!" he shouted, starting to gallop after her.

He knew it was useless. "Don't leave Newle!"

He galloped to a stop and turned back to the village, riding in at full speed.

Only half formed sentences flew through his mind. *Emotional girl ... send out guards ... search the forest ... she lied ...*

He banged on the gate shouting, "Open! Make way for the prince!"

The soldiers, frightened by his voice, unfastened the gate quickly. Konrad could tell by the look on their faces that they wanted to know what had happened to his companion, but Konrad didn't have time for questions.

He turned his horse to face the castle and was off before the guards had a moment to say anything. His horse, sweating and pushed to the limits, slowed down a little just outside the town.

The villagers were dashing about in a furry. Konrad, impatient to get back to the castle, plowed right through them. It didn't matter.

Suddenly, a man in the crowd suddenly cried out, "Make way! Make way!"

Konrad unmounted and pushed against the flow of the crowd. It parted in front of him.

"Your majesty!" a messenger on horseback was standing in the clearing.

"Your father fell while you were gone," he was told.

"My father?" Konrad asked in a daze. Too much was happening at once.

"Yes, we've been looking all over for you! He fell right after you left. He asked to send for you. He says he's dying," the messenger told him bluntly, motioning for the prince to mount and follow him.

The people fell back a few paces. The rumor had been passed around, but to hear something from the king's messenger was different. Suddenly there was a feeling of fear in the air.

Konrad mounted mindlessly and galloped off to the castle. He wasn't about to lose two of his dearest friends on one day.

Konrad took the stairs leading to his father's room two at a time. When he got there, something told him he was too late.

"Your father is nearly gone," the attendant told him as he pushed his way through doctors and apothecaries trying to reach his father.

In a trance, he heard a weak voice asking, "Where is my son? Why does he not come?"

Everyone moved aside letting Konrad get his first glimpse of his father as he rushed to him.

"My son," the king sputtered. "The doctors say it is my heart. They tell me I will die. Before I go, I must name you as my heir. Servant, bring me my crown."

Konrad knelt, holding his father's hand and fighting back tears. He had never expected it to be like this.

The servant solemnly came back and handed the crown to the king.

"Son, with all the authority I have on this earth, or in heaven, I pronounce you king of Hedgecliff. Do you accept this responsibility?"

"Yes Father," Konrad's voice broke as the tears freely fell from his eyes. "I do."

Old King Orchalon, his hand shaking, placed the crown on his son's head.

Konrad felt its weight as the weight of the kingdom on his shoulders.

"Go my son, leave me," King Orchalon brushed his son away.

King Konrad dashed out of the room and to the spiral staircase. He leaned against the wall.

His mind was working, but nothing came out. At midnight, he was told it was over. Konrad didn't go to bed that night but sat up by the kitchen fire, thinking until morning.

Newle's horse galloped through the woods as the sun sank down the hill. Branches lashed out at her face and in the deepening gloom, noises startled her horse at every turn.

She only stopped when it became too dark for her to continue further without risking injury to herself and her horse, but even then, she only slowed to a walk.

I must put distance between me and my kingdom, she thought as she began to take inventory of what she had with her when she escaped.

The map, she smiled. *What a blessing! My money. Thankfully I never go anywhere without it. And I have my horse and the clothes that I have on.* It wasn't much, but Newle knew that she was starting out with more than others have started with.

She stopped in the middle of a clearing to take a look at the map. Her kingdom spanned only another thirty miles to the east before it came to unmarked territory and then a large expanse of water. Up to the northeast there were mountains with only one or two passes in them. She would never be able to make them in the winter.

Before, I was planning to cross the mountains and then go east, but now perhaps I can find this body of water in the exact east and find a small port village that will take me across. Then I won't have to cross the mountains or even go south toward Fairfalcon. It's more direct this way too. And even if I can't cross, I can at least stay the winter there.

Newle stared up at the moon and looked for the western star. "I know he's up there," she whispered as a cloud crossed over the moon. "Come out and guide me!"

The cloud moved and she saw it.

Behind me and to my right, she thought with satisfaction. *I've been going nearly the right direction this entire time. I just need to straighten myself out and walk east.*

Newle reoriented herself, slid off her horse to give it a little rest, and walked east.

Never stopping or ceasing, she walked or rode, giving her horse times of rest. *We'll be there within two days*, she thought when she stopped for a cold drink from a running stream. *I don't need to eat between now and then, although I still don't know if there will even be a village for me to find food in.* She began walking again. *And I shouldn't even need any sleep, although I might have to stop for my horse to rest. Then I can just take a little repose at the same time. But first things first—I must get out of Hedgecliff.*

The night progressed as Newle began to dwell on everything that had happen.

He'll send out guards the moment he gets home, she mused. *I can't stop till I get out of Hedgecliff.*

She passed a few small houses and a small village or two but they never knew she was there.

Why did I even do that? Why didn't we talk this through like civilized people? He had his own reasons to keep me in hiding because of what his father would do if he knew.

The villages would all wake up in the morning and everything would be just the same as always. Her presence meant nothing to them.

Just as the trees began to thin, Newle saw the sun coming up in the east.

In another hour, the trees were all gone and Newle was navigating by the sun, not the stars.

After another hour she saw the last village on her map. She pulled hard to the south to go around it so they would never see her and in another hour she saw the sea.

"How did this ever happen?!" she asked as she slowed for a last glance of Hedgecliff, of Konrad, of Marja, and of Newle. She was Scarlet again.

She turned to follow the edge of the sea north, her horse stumbling and dragging its head.

"Keep it up, old boy," she encouraged him. "I'm just as tired as you are. Just wait till we see around this peninsula, then we'll rest."

She unmounted and carefully led it around the rough spots. Newle wanted to go on forever—tireless, fearless, always hopeful, but she knew she couldn't. Her dreams could be just around the corner and that knowledge invigorated her.

She got around the peninsula, tied her horse to the tree, and slept next to him for warmth.

She woke later that day and continued on. Her stomach squeezed and she felt weak. Hunger ate at her legs and every time she got off her horse to give it a break, she was back up sooner each time. Her weak arms and mind had no time to think when a branch presented itself. Her arms and face were torn and scratched. White torn skin and scrapes where beads of blood formed covered her.

That night she could hardly sleep. Newle wondered if there was even a village, she wondered if she was going in the wrong direction, she wondered if she would die out there and if anyone would ever come looking for her.

The next day any energy she had left was gone. The rest of the day she could scarcely keep herself on her horse. The cold nipped at her nose and ears and she was nearly numb with it. But before the last light of the sun went down she saw it: a light.

It was a little town on the edge of the lake, and there was a ship in the water, her deliverance.

THE FIRST SKIRMISH

Later that day, a messenger came from the castle. He informed me Father has passed away and Mother was getting worse.

Everything seemed hopeless. What was I to do? I carefully put them both out of my mind so I could focus on other things. There would be time for tears later.

Suddenly I heard cries spring up from outside. I dashed to the door of my tent and raised the flap.

Arrows flew past and men fell from the wall with sickening thuds.

"Your Majesty!" I heard a desperate cry. Out of nowhere lord Telmar came rushing out at me.

"You're not safe here!" I felt for my bow and arrows, they were still strapped on my back where I had left them. My sword had also never left my side.

"Leave them behind! This is no place for you," his voice growled as he roughly grabbed my arm and dragged me toward the wall.

"What do you think you're doing!" I cried, struggling to get free of his vice-like grip.

"I'm taking you to the wall! It will shield you from arrows coming straight at you, and if you sit under the stairs it will even shield you from arrows coming from above."

He whirled me under the stairs and ran off before I could say anything.

The shouting grew louder like a thunderstorm does. It had started out fairly quiet, but quickly grew to a fevered pitch as more men landed with a thud at the base of the wall. I tried to look away, I tried to be brave, but nothing could keep that sinking feeling out of my heart and mind.

My hands pressed against the wall and my heart pounded faster. An injured man called out to me, but my ears were deaf to him. Slowly I became aware of him. He had an arrow struck through him, but it didn't look fatal. A pool of blood was beginning to form on his tunic and I looked away.

"Help!" He faintly called out. Arrows whizzed around him and one twanged right next to his ear.

I couldn't let my people die like that, they defended me from Fairfalcon. Wasn't there something I could do in return?

I dashed out and ripped my cloak off and into little strips. I wasn't thinking. I set one or two on him and put his hand on top of it. He gave me a faint smile before I moved on to the next person.

Out in the open, some were getting stuck twice by arrows that flew over the wall. Needless to say, there wasn't much I could to for most of them.

Arrows dashed past me and one even struck my armor helmet and glanced off to the side.

Men called out blessings on me as I passed from one to the other, but I didn't think (the job I was doing required me to not think), otherwise I would go running back under the stairs to stay till the battle puttered out on its own.

Before I knew what was happening, I had already gone back to my tent and grabbed my canteen and another blanket to tear up. The arrows flew thickly as I dashed back out and up the stairs. I gave up a silent prayer that the two lords wouldn't see me, and I set right to work.

It was furious. The fighting, the cries, I had never dreamed of anything like this. Sitting back at home in the castle had made me think that it was an adventure. Now I knew that it was a glorified grave.

"Defend!!!" I heard screamed out over the top of all the other noise. "A ladder! Defend!"

Twenty other people took up the cry as I grew closer to it.

Through the confusion I could see it all. A ladder had been put up against the wall and it was all they could do to keep them from pouring in. As it was, nearly ten enemy men had made it up and were engaged with my soldiers. I turned to run but it was too late. Someone was already blocking my path. My sword was drawn in an instant and already working to defend me.

They attacked with the same strange discipline that Cedric had used. It must be something unique to Fairfalcon and Cedric had picked it up in his free time. I thanked him silently because I already knew how to defend from it and could easily break their concentration.

One managed to rip his sword through my tunic, but it only left a little scratch. My hair fell out from under my helmet but I didn't have any time to push it back. They just kept right on attacking.

Soon smells wafted through the air. Blood and sweat mingled together in a vomit-inducing haze that hung about everything.

After we had managed to fend off the ladder and send it plummeting to its death on the ground, I was drafted into a group of archers. No one noticed me very much, and I never had time to go back and tend to the wounded like I had started out doing.

It was almost mind-numbing how easy it was to shoot an arrow and watch as another human fell to his death.

Soon the light began to fail and the arrows ceased to fly. I heard Telmar out in the distance calling men to the night watch. Everyone else could catch some rest.

I careened down the stairs and back onto solid ground. I felt like kissing it except for the blood and bodies.

"Your Majesty!" it was hardly Cedric's voice it was so rift through with shock. He grabbed me by my elbow and pulled me close into a hug as I struggled to get free. "You don't know how worried I have been!" I elbowed him with my free one and in a moment I was loose.

"Keep your hands off me!" I muttered at him angrily, tired and angry after everything that had happened that day.

"I beg your pardon," he looked surprised and angry.

I sidestepped several moaning bodies as Cedric followed me back to my tent. I handed the bandages I had made to him and I angrily told him to do something useful for once and for his own good to stay away from me.

I ducked back into my tent, Lord Telmar was awaiting me. "Your Majesty," he began as I sat down. "We worked on the digging all day thanks to the little distraction that we had. We will dig all night and it should be ready before tomorrow morning."

I thanked him. "We'll wait till tomorrow night then and we'll do it under the cover of darkness?"

"Yes, Cedric will lead them out tomorrow night," I heaved an audible sigh. "We have a list of people that are going out with him."

He handed it to me and I scanned it over. I didn't recognize any of the names so I handed it back and said, "Whatever you two think is best." He bowed and left.

My chainmail shirt was heavy so I lifted it up and over my head. It felt amazing to be able to breath again and not stoop to hold myself up.

I straightened up and stretched. I laid my bow and arrows on the table and sat down on the edge of my bed. I unstrapped my sword and hung it from the bedpost.

CHAPTER EIGHT

Konrad could hardly come to terms with everything that had happened in those last few hours. His friend, someone he loved dearly, had left because of him. But how could she have done anything else? She was in danger here. She couldn't stay.

And his father—gone forever. He was alone. Only his country remained to his name.

Konrad stirred from the fire only after three servants had called him. The servants had not wanted to wake him, but the people wanted a speech.

"Give them a speech yourself," he growled as he stirred the ashes. The servants left, worried, and Samantha came in with Himdir to make breakfast.

"Where's Newle?" the boy asked coming over to the king.

"She is gone," Konrad said firmly.

"Why didn't she tell me?" the boy asked. The hurt look in his face touching a soft spot in Konrad's heart.

"She didn't even tell me," Konrad whispered, looking into the fire, trying to sort things out in his mind.

"When is she coming back?" Himdir asked with childlike concern.

"I don't know," Konrad stood up, still not making eye contact. "It might be a while. Don't worry, Samantha. I'll organize things so that Himdir can continue his education."

"My King," came Samantha, clearly she had already been told about it, but still didn't know what to say.

"She hurt all of us, but she had no choice. There is a kingdom outside waiting for me to give them a kind word. They need me now that my father is gone."

His voice sounded hollow, but there was resolve behind it. He left the room and went up to give the speech.

"My countrymen," he began. "I apologize for making you wait. As you know my father is now dead. I have been heavily hit by this blow and I am not ready to take on this responsibility. But desperate times call for desperate measures and I will ascend to the throne. I will try to fill the place of my father, but I know in my heart that I can never fill the place of ... " a murmur of confusion ran through the crowd, who? Who could he never replace? "I will do the best I can, but is it enough? I have wrestled with myself, and have aged beyond my years. I wondered if I was ready for this, if I would be able to keep peace. There are many things a king must be able to do, and I have become aware during the past few months that there are some things I cannot do. I will do my best and you will support me, I know. I will never abandon you, in peace and plenty, or in war, famine, or hardship."

The crowd said nothing as the king, his shoulders dropping with the weight of his kingdom, went back into the castle.

I don't want to be king, he thought. *There is no one to lean on. The real question is: do I go after Newle or do I let her go? She wants to leave. She has left her people. Should I even try to bring her back? She is safe now that my father is gone. But no, I pushed her away, I told her she was no longer wanted. She is gone.*

His thoughts were interrupted by Lord Grissel entering,

"My king," Grissel began in his whiny voice as Konrad started, the first time hearing someone call him by his new title. "I come to offer you my help."

"And I refuse it," Konrad barked. "I didn't want your help when my father was alive, and I don't want it now. You are dismissed."

"But my lord ..." Grissel began, realizing his mistake in thrusting the new title on him too quickly.

"No, be gone!" Konrad cried, turning to him. "I don't want you!"

"Your Majesty, your father made it clear to me on several occasions that were he to die, I should be your helper. You would not want to go against your father's wishes."

"He is gone," Konrad began, "and I am king. You are dismissed."

Grissel looked angry, but left the room, a plan and a letter already forming in his mind. He would get his revenge.

Princess Scarlet, or Newle, pulled into the town just as the last light in the sky faded and the stars blinked into being.

She dropped off her horse and faintly led him to what looked like an inn.

Well, here's to hoping, she thought as she tied her horse outside and opened the door.

The smells that pushed at her nearly made her faint with hunger.

There was ham, and cheese, the overwhelming smell of gravy and turkey and over it all was the perfect smell of bread.

"What can I help you with, miss?" came a voice from behind her. It took her a moment to realize that the man had spoken in a mixture of her own language and the one the dwarf had taught her. It brought a smile to her face as she realized she was going in the right direction.

"Dinner. And stables for my horse. He is tired and will require coolingdown," she explained, trying to get the right mixture of the two languages.

"You're not from around here," the man commented as he wiped down the table and then pointed her to a seat. "It's not that I mind, we get foreigners every now and then."

"You're right," she replied. "I'm from Hedgecliff."

"Really?" the man asked in surprise as he leaned against the table he had been wiping. "Then how come you know what I'm saying? Most folks from Hedgecliff don't have the faintest idea."

"I've lived on the border all my life," she lied.

"And what name can I put on your reservation?" he asked, pulling out a note pad and pencil.

"Scarlet," she replied. *They'll have never heard of me down here.* she thought. *From here on out I'm going to by my real name. No more lying about it.*

"Pretty name, Miss Scarlet. I'll send the boy out for your horse right now."

The man gave a shrill whistle and a boy clattered down from upstairs. The man explained to the boy that he was to take care of the horse. Then he went into the kitchen, saying he would be right back.

Scarlet surveyed the room. It had the coziness of an inn and every curve of the place had the feeling of being hundreds of years old. It wasn't only because the place was dim, but every beam and board of the place looked heavy and massive. There was an old sea captain and his friend conversing loudly by the roaring fire, and there were another two or three men sitting at a table.

The sea captain reminded her that she needed to cross the lake or the sea or whatever it was and that she couldn't do it alone.

"Here you go miss," the innkeeper smiled as he brought out a piping hot plate with turkey and gravy on it. "When you're done, you can just go straight up the stairs and to the last door on the left. It's a pleasant room with a nice look to the eastern sunrise."

Scarlet thanked him and dug into her dinner with relish. It all tasted so good! The turkey was pleasantly moist and the gravy was not too salty (as it has a habit of being).

For the first few moments, Scarlet was just wolfing down her food without paying any attention to anything else, but soon the voices of the sea captain captured her thoughts.

He wasn't speaking her language at all! He wasn't even speaking the language of the innkeeper! He was speaking the eastern language with no additions!

"We're out a first mate since the last storm and we lost our cook too," he was saying.

"Why don't you just hunker down for the winter and stop being a fool?" his companion asked, sipping at his drink. "Your cargo can wait till spring like the rest of us."

"I've got my debts to pay, same as you. I could do without the first mate, but I really do need a cook. If I could only get to the other side of the sea, then I could find one. But there aren't many people around here who would want to take a one way trip in exchange for being a cook."

"A cook?" Scarlet asked, turning around. Her dinner could wait if there was a way to cross the sea.

"Yes, a cook. What's that to you?" the captain asked looking her over from head to foot.

"Nothing. It's just that I was once a cook and I need to get to the other side of the sea. I could cook for you on the way down, and then since you should be able to find another one, I'll be free to go my way and you go yours."

The sea captain turned to exchange looks with the other man, but the moment the captain had started talking to Scarlet, the man had gone back to his dinner.

"Clever thinker. But the main thing is: can you bake bread?" the captain asked.

"Can I bake bread? The prince himself ordered bread from me!" she cried, her excitement growing. *Oh, if only it would work!* she thought as she began pinning every hope on this one chance,

"All I have to do is take you to the other side of the sea and you'll cook for us?" he questioned, not quite sure if it was a trick.

"Yes, and when we get there, I leave you and you go find another cook," she explained.

"It's a deal. By the way, why can you speak our language? No one here knows it."

Scarlet replied, "I've always had an ear for languages, and as I live on the edge of Hedgecliff, I know a lot of them." She obviously couldn't tell them about the dwarf.

"Are you staying here tonight?" the captain asked.

"Yes," she replied.

"Then I'll see you down here in the morning and then I'll take you down to the Raider. By the way, the names Wycliffe Gloom. Yours?"

"Scarlet Albrektson. Nice to meet you, Wycliffe Gloom. I also have a horse I'm rather fond of. Would it be possible to take him along?" she asked hesitantly.

"Take a horse!? Are you out of your mind?" the captain roared.

"Then I guess I'll have to sell him in the morning." she said with a sigh. "Perhaps the innkeeper will want it. He is rather nice,"

"Who? The innkeeper or the horse? The innkeeper charges too much, and I'll bet the horse looks like a mule!" Captain Wycliffe Gloom laughed at his own joke as Scarlet rolled her eyes and finished up her dinner.

"Well goodnight," she said as she went outside to check on her horse before bed.

"Yeah! Bright and early tomorrow," he laughed. "Just think of it," he said, turning to his friend. "Bringing a horse on a trip like that?" he laughed.

She glowered, but went with it. She knew she was lucky to have any transportation at all.

He seems a little ill-mannered and crude, but I'm sure I won't have too much trouble with him, Scarlet thought as she went to bed that night.

She could have slept till the cows came home the next morning, but thanks to having a window to the east, she woke up with the sunrise instead.

So hungry, she thought as she stood in front of a mirror, arranging her hair and dress before she went down stairs. *I'll need to stop around and buy a few things before I head out. A map for one. But perhaps that can wait till I get across the sea. They won't have a map of across the sea over here. Then I'll need a knapsack for putting all my things in. Rope, some fabric for another dress—I'm sure it will be freezing out in the sea—and good, sturdy boots. I need to keep enough of my money for a horse and food when I get across, which means I can't buy anything too expensive.* just the fact that she was planning for a long trip that she might never come back from was enough to make her feel excited and anxious to be off. *This is it!* she thought. *This is the day I realize my dreams!*

She took the stairs two at a time down to the common room of the inn, and sat down for breakfast.

"Morning miss," the innkeeper greeted her when she sat down. "Eggs and bacon?"

"Yes please, and would you be interested in buying a horse?" she asked, looking up at him.

"A horse?" he asked, surprised.

"Yes. He's in fine condition," she urged.

"You mean the one you came galloping in on last night?" he asked.

"Yes. That horse," she reiterated.

"Fine, I'll take it. What do you want for him?" he smiled. It really wasn't like him to jump into a business deal like that, but he was worried about her when he heard she was going with the sea captain who was practically known as a pirate in these parts.

"Payment for my stay and twenty Chrono Tluapee, I've heard that's what they use across the sea."

"Twenty? A horse like that needs thirty!" he insisted, trying hard to make sure her path was well funded.

"Really?" Scarlet asked in relief, another ten Chrono Tluapee would be helpful in a tight spot.

"Yes and I'm willing to pay it." He decided to come clean, "I heard you talking to the sea captain last night, I wondered if there was some way I could help you." Then his tone changed to concern, "I hope you haven't decided to go with them?"

"I have," she grudgingly admitted. "I need to get across the sea and I need to do it without too much money. What other choice do I have?"

"You could at least wait until spring. The seas won't be as rough then," he suggested.

"I can't wait until spring. I have to go now."

"Well then I can only pray that your trip goes well," he set down a mug of sludge-like coffee at her spot.

"Thank you," Scarlet replied. "If anything, I really appreciate your buying my horse."

"Not a problem."

"Could you exchange the rest of my money for Chrono Tluapee?" she asked as she took a sip of her coffee.

"Sure thing," he smiled at her and then went behind his counter to get his money.

"You can never trust the banks these days," he explained as Scarlet pulled out her purse and they exchanged the money.

"There is your thirty for the horse, and another thirty from your purse. You have sixty Chrono Tluapee. What about the rest of it?"

"It's for supplies and the return home, if I ever come back," she explained, avoiding eye contact.

"Well miss, if you ever come home again, look me up," he said softly. "I always could use another hand behind the counter."

The thought reminded her of Marja. She would be worried when Scarlet stopped coming in to buy things. It was too late in Scarlet's mind. She had already committed. The past, her past, was gone. Only the east was left for her.

"Thank you. It's nice to know that I haven't burnt all my bridges behind me," a tear trickled down her nose and the innkeeper noticed it before she had time to wipe it away,

"Is it really that bad, miss?" he asked.

"I'm afraid that it is," she replied. "But you shouldn't know about that.

Thank you kindly for the stay and for buying my horse. If I could leave a message with you for captain Wycliffe Gloom as I have to go out and buy some things before I go, that would be nice,"

"Certainly, I'll just tell them that you skipped out for a moment to grab some things," he thought for a moment. "What are you going out for? I might be able to send you to some pretty cheap places to buy your things. They will be high quality, but still affordable."

Scarlet explained what she was going after and the innkeeper made a list of places that she could go to get what she needed.

"Thank you sir," she told him as she left.

The snow was heaped up high all around and Scarlet pulled her cloak closer around herself as she plowed through it all.

Her first stop was to get fabric. It didn't take long to choose a sturdy woolen brown. She figured that across the sea she might need to blend in with trees. It helped that her cloak was green. She would pack up the red dress that she had on and probably would never wear it again. It would be impractical where she was going.

The next stop was to get a knapsack. It needed to be big enough to hold everything and in the end she paid a lot for it.

I just hope that my shoes won't cost that much because I don't have that much money left if I'm to buy food and the map on the other side of the sea. Perhaps I should invest in a good knife and a bow. Then I can kill my own food.

Scarlet managed to find the boots and they cost only a little less than the knapsack. They were sturdy and she knew they would last a long time if she could keep them in good condition.

Not that I'll have time for that, she concluded as she counted up the last of her money to buy a dagger.

When she was done, she stepped out with all the things she had bought in her knapsack.

There should be enough room for food in there, she thought as she pulled her cloak around her more tightly.

The snow had stopped, but Scarlet had everything she needed. She still had some more money to exchange for Chrono Tluapee, but she never had time to do it.

The moment she walked in the door of the inn she was swept right out again.

"Come on cook!" Captain Wycliffe Gloom called. "You'll make us late!"

Scarlet was escorted to the harbor and led up to the Raider. That name gave her the creeps, but she tried to convince herself it might not be that bad. They walked up the gangplank and Scarlet was shown to the kitchen.

"The galley, miss." the crew member who was taking her on the tour explained.

"It might be a little tight," she thought out loud, "but it will be nice and warm."

"You'll sleep right here," he explained.

"But there's only enough room to cook in!" Scarlet cried in unbelief.

"Well there isn't enough room anywhere else, and someone always has to be in here to make sure the ship doesn't catch on fire," he explained.

Scarlet thought about it for a moment. *If you turn this down to wait till spring, you'll never survive out in the wild*, she told herself. "There isn't anything else for me to do," she agreed at last.

"Good," the sailor sighed. "Now I'll show you the store rooms."

He led her out on the deck and down a hatch to a small compartment with sacks and boxes of food.

"These sacks contain flour and the boxes have potatoes. The captain has his special coffee in this tub and the rest of his stores are here. His stuff is better quality than the rest of the crew gets. Normally, the cook puts a lot of food in this pot and then just adds to it as it gets low. Then he cooks something special for just the captain and his first mate. This trip we don't have a first mate so you only have to cook it for the captain." They left the small room and went back up to the deck. "Oh, and the captain likes to have fresh bread with lunch."

Scarlet smiled, she wasn't sure she was ready for this, but she was at least going to try.

"Thank you for the tour sir," she said politely. "When am I expected to serve the first meal?"

The sailor explained when the meals were to be ready and how she was expected to have hot water for tea waiting for the crew at all times. She was also told about how they had to ration everything out and that when she made soup, she could only give one ladle per person.

At the end of his explanation, she felt that being a sailor must be worse than being in prison, or being a princess.

But I can do my best to make it a little better, she thought as she went back down to the galley to settle her things and to wait the month-long journey. By that time, Scarlet realized, it would be spring.*work*

The time passed slowly for about two weeks without ship or land in sight. Scarlet spent time below deck cooking and above deck listening to the waves against the ship. They called her and seemed to be saying: "Come with us! We will show you the world!"

After those two weeks a storm could be seen brewing on the port side of the ship. Every sailor went about with gaunt faces, as they knew a storm at sea in the winter would mean sure death.

A day later it hit. The boat rocked as the waves' voices changed from the pleasant call Scarlet had become accustomed to, to the wild howl that made her want to follow their way even more. Many times during the night she was awakened as she was tossed from her bed and she heard those voices calling her to them.

All through the next day the storm raged, and during the one moment that the navigator came in for a mug of something hot, he told her there would likely be a change for the worst before midnight and that all hands would be called on deck. She must go up with them.

"What will I do?" she asked, ready to finally have something like an adventure. Sitting alone in the galley while the waves knocked against the sides of the ship was one thing, going out into the open deck while the wind howled away was another.

"Whatever they need," he told her as he went back up.

She didn't fall asleep that night, but was sitting ready for the summons as she listened to the wind howl and the ship rock and the waves wild scream.

Finally the voice of Captain Wycliffe Gloom called above the howl of the storm: "All hands on deck!!"

Scarlet stood up, and holding on to anything, she made her way up to on deck.

Rain pelted her and the spindrift from the sea tasted salty on her lips and helped the rain make light work of soaking her. For a moment she stood at the hatch, waiting for orders.

"You!" a crewman called, unable to recognize her through the confusion. "Help me pull on this line!"

She dashed as quickly as she could to the man and put her whole weight on the line and felt it slowly pull away from her.

The man shouted for more help and in another minute, five men were pulling the line through a block to a cleat and there they tied it off. It was then that she was noticed.

"Get back in the galley!" one of the men cried. "You'll be washed overboard!"

"But they need my help!" Scarlet cried over the noise.

"They don't! You'll only be in the way!"

Scarlet dashed over to another man who was trying to tie of another rope and she helped him. "What do you mean I'm in the way?" she shouted, but the man was gone. She never saw him the rest of the night. Later she found out line had been washed overboard.

All that night she helped and when day finally came the storm was all over and for the first time in days they could all see the sun, and land.

"Land ho!" the man at the mast head called.

Immediately there was a rush of crewmates to the side. Everyone wanted to see the land. Scarlet didn't have the strength. She was worn out by the storm.

TRAITOR

The next thing I knew, I had woken up. There had been a noise or something. It was still dark outside and for a fall night, my tent was hot and humid.

I turned over on my side and glanced about the room. The entrance to the tent was flapping in a slight breeze, I must have forgotten to tie it when I went to bed. I kicked my blanket off and tried to be as still as possible. I knew from experience that I would doze off in a few minutes.

The moon shone in just a little bit, illuminating the sides of the tent like a silver moth.

The tent flap stopped moving in mid flutter. I stiffened. A hand appeared and then a head, and then a body with legs and arms.

It glanced around the room. It seemed pleased with itself and took a step forward. Voices came faintly from outside and the figure made a dash to get out of the entrance. The voices passed by and the figure became bold again. It stealthily crept up to me and drew a dagger. Suddenly I realized my danger. The figure stabbed and I deflected it with one arm while drawing my sword with the other.

Blood streamed down my arm and my wrist. It dripped on to the bed sheet and made little pools and rivulets. But I was still alive. I grasped my sword in my bloodied hand and rose to my knees. The man stood back, his arm against a dagger aimed to throw it at me. I caught my breath. I didn't have a shield, I had never had one. And what could a sword do against dagger aimed straight at my heart?

I raised my sword and hoped the dagger wouldn't break right through my sword when they intersected, if they intersected. Suddenly, before I knew what was happening, the figure's hand was gone. I heard an unearthly scream and I quivered, watching as two figures clashed together, one trying to strangle the other.

Footsteps pounded outside, a candle was lit and I looked upon a terrible sight. Lord Telmar was holding Lord Cedric as tightly as he could. Cedric was bleeding from a stump where his hand had been. On the ground was the dagger, his hand was nowhere to be seen. Men came tumbling in head over heels. Swords drawn and arrows nocked. Someone managed to pull the two lords apart and hold them.

I stood up, my arm still dripping in blood, my hand still clenched around the hilt of my sword.

Someone in the back called out, "What happened?"

Cedric held his head higher. "Your Majesty," he began.

"Silence!" I shouted over the confusion. "I don't want to hear from you, traitor! You were going to kill me!"

The soldiers holding Cedric tightened their grip as he struggled to get free.

Someone holding Telmar asked, "And what about Lord Telmar here? An accomplice?"

"I think Lord Telmar can speak for himself," I replied.

I sheathed my sword and sat down to nurse my arm.

"Your majesty, may I be permitted to speak?" Lord Telmar asked.

"Begin."

"I was watching your tent from under the stairs. I noticed a figure sneak in and I followed him. I saw him lash out at you, Your Majesty, and when he raised his arm to throw the dagger at you, I cut his hand off and tackled him. I heard him scream and the next thing I knew we were being pulled off of each other and held in place." He gave as much of a bow as he could with twenty pairs of hands on him.

I gestured to have him released. He had saved my life, and while I had doubted him earlier, I could doubt him no more.

Cedric glared at him. His once handsome face twisted and darkened with anger.

"If Your Majesty pleases," Lord Telmar began, kneeling in front of me and kissing my hand. "I will question the traitor and find out what his plans were. I also offer to go on the secret attack in his stead."

I gave him permission and soon I was seated at the low table with Lord Telmar's left hand on my right shoulder and Cedric on his knees in a half circle of guards. My arm had been taken care of only a little bit, but the blood had stopped running. To my left another soldier knelt, pen and paper on the table before him. He was to write out every word that was spoken and then configure the prisoner's sentence at the end. I would sign it and it would be executed. Telmar brought the meeting to order and the scribe began to take notes.

"Your Majesty," Telmar turned to me. "May I have permission to question the prisoner?"

I gave consent and he took a few steps closer to Cedric.

"There will be no need of that," Cedric growled. "I'm willing to confess everything." Telmar stayed put.

"I have been in Fairfalcon's counsel for years, but only just now has the opportunity arisen for me to actually help them. Yes, I told them everything. If there was to be an attack the next day, I would go out the night before to the wall and I would wave a torch around. It was a simple and harmless action that no one would question." I shuddered and tried to keep the tears from coming.

"After the king had been mortally wounded, I hoped the signet ring would be given to us and we would have complete control over the entire army and it would be easy to make a convincing last stand before surrendering to Fairfalcon. When I found out her majesty the queen was ill, I knew it would be very easy to finish this once and for all. But I hadn't reckoned on dealing with her daughter, the princess. Needless to say, when I found out she wouldn't relinquish the ring, I was furious. I knew I couldn't let it show and so I made it sound like a good idea. Much to my great delight though, Lord Telmar himself pushed that she give it to us and for a moment I thought perhaps the princess thought he was the traitor.

"After that, I knew her majesty had to be down near the front of the action. I knew I could probably scare her into going back to the castle, but another plan was forming in my head. I knew she trusted me, and so I offered to lead the secret attack. I knew that once out there, I could easily lead them into an ambush and be the only survivor. It would have foiled all of your plans and I would have been a hero in Fairfalcon. This afternoon I noticed her majesty didn't seem at all like she wanted to leave, even with piles of bodies all around her and so I ditched my plan and tried to get close to her." I squirmed.

"I thought I could perhaps become close to her and manipulate her into doing what I wanted. It didn't work and I had to come up with a new strategy. That's why I came here tonight. I would kill her, make it look like someone else did it, they would find her body in the morning, and Lord Telmar and I would have full possession of the ring."

The tent was quiet. You could hear the grass unbending as people shifted from one foot to the other.

Telmar cleared his throat, "We will now pronounce the sentence on his head. Princess?"

I glanced up, frighted. Was I supposed to do something?

Lord Telmar took it in in a glance. "Because this is a trial for a traitor, you are to open it to the floor for suggestions as to the most fitting death for him."

Unsure of how to say it, I stood up, one hand firmly set on the table, the other crossing over and holding the others elbow. I began, "The floor is now open for suggestions as to the most fitting death for this traitor."

I sat down again, quickly. No one seemed shocked so I suppose I didn't say anything wrong.

Someone in the back raised his hand and Lord Telmar called on him.

"If Your Majesty pleases, have the traitor drawn and quartered." Several men chimed in agreement.

Telmar called on another, "Hang him from the wall and drop his dead body in among his own foul people!"

"And whip him before hand!" another shouted out. People began to rally around the two suggestions. To draw and quarter, or to whip, hang, and drop his body on the other side.

"Silence! Silence!" Lord Telmar called at long last. "We will hold a vote." The room stilled. "All in favor of draw and quarter, raise your hand."

Almost half of the room responded as the quiet scribe counted the heads twice to make sure.

"All in favor of whipping, hanging, and dropping?"

Everyone that had not voted before raised hands and was counted twice.

The secretary turned to me and handed me the results. I looked up at Lord Telmar and he nodded.

I stood up, shaky, knowing I was about to pronounce death on a fellow human being.

Dealing death from the wall had been easier than this. It was almost disconnected. You could see a man fall to his death but never know it was your arrow. You could shoot an arrow and never know if it killed someone. Even sword fighting was better than this. In sword fighting you knew that if you didn't defend yourself, you would die. You weren't killing to kill, you were killing to live. And in both, you could never know if you hadn't just hurt the man. He could be wounded and still push on.

And so now, as I stood to declare certain death on this man, my heart quavered. He had hurt me, he had hurt my country, but could I do this? Could I send this man to his death?

Yes, my heart whispered as I looked down at the paper. *I can do this.*

The paper read:

Draw and quarter: 15
Whip and hang and drop: 19

I took a deep breath, "By the power that has been given to me, in heaven and on this earth, I declare the convicted traitor, murderer, and manipulator, Lord Cedric, shall on this date be severely whipped, hung from the city wall so that all may see, and then dropped to the bodies and dogs below to suffer that same fate that all other traitors face when they die, namely, to eternally wander the face of this earth as a spirit until all the magic on this earth has been gathered into the heavens. So be it."

I signed that paper and gave it to Lord Telmar. Telmar looked it over and gave his signature of approval. He in turn handed it to the captain of the guards and he signaled his men to surround the traitor and lead him out to be whipped.

"Your Majesty," Lord Telmar began as the men poured out of my tent. "I know it hurt you to sign that. Should I have the men do it while you are at the castle getting your arm properly looked at?"

I glanced down at my arm for the first time since the trial had begun and noticed it had started to bleed a little.

"Alright, thank you." He bowed out of my tent and I went to go back to my bed but it was covered in blood. I glanced to the ground. The dagger was gone and I hoped the hand had gone with it.

I decided it might be best to arrive at the castle in armor. That way I could slip past anyone I might know without getting questioned about it. Back on went the chain mail, back on went my sword and bow and quiver. I slipped a red cloak over my shoulders and sat down at the table again.

I was so tired. I didn't want to be awakened in the middle of the night to have a trial. I didn't want to be caught up in the middle of a war. I wanted Marja back. I wanted to laugh with her and protect her from the simple petty things that scared her. How did I go from that to keeping an entire country from fears, fears that are more real than anything I had ever faced?

CHAPTER NINE

It took them a full day to reach it, and when they finally set out the gangplank, Scarlet had her bag packed and was ready to go.

She went up to the captain's quarters to thank him for the favor.

"Thank you Captain Gloom for letting me come, but now it's time we go our separate ways,"

"Separate ways? No. I've decided I like your cooking and I offer you a permanent residence aboard the Raider," he looked at her intently, waiting for her reaction.

Scarlet didn't know what to do so she walked out on deck. "Sir, this was never part of our agreement. I was to cook for you on the trip down and then you were going to get another cook."

"I don't care. You are never going to leave this ship!" he cried.

"Captain," she began. Was everything going to fall apart again?

"I'll pay you handsomely."

Crew members began to gather around. Scarlet didn't know what to say.

"I never said I would let you go after we landed," Wycliffe Gloom lied.

"But I never wanted to become the Raiders' cook," Scarlet protested. She felt she was losing.

"You can duel it out!" a crewmember joked in the back of the crowd.

"Yes! A duel!" came another voice as each member began to pick up the chant, "Duel! Duel! Duel! Duel! Duel!"

"I'll lend you a sword," the captain began with an evil smile. "And if you win then you can go free and I'll even let you take the sword. If I win you come back as our cook. Got it?"

Scarlet didn't even know what to say but she nodded. There was no way she could ever beat this sea captain at a duel.

A crewmember brought out a broadsword and scabbard and gave it to Scarlet. She hefted its weight for a moment, remembering the last time she had a sword fight.

"On guard!" a crewman who had put himself in charge as judge shouted above the chanting.

"Duel! Duel! Duel! Duel! Duel!"

"Fight!" he cried as the rest of the crew grew closer around them and cheered.

They circled around for a few seconds before Captain Wycliffe Gloom attacked Scarlet.

The crowd roared with cheers as Scarlet was caught off guard and nearly slipped on the wet deck.

They attacked and parried for a few moments before Scarlet got a lead. She attacked better than she had when she was fighting with Konrad or Cedric and was beginning to gain ground. The clash of metal on metal came and then the scrape as she pushed him off.

"Go it, Scarlet!" someone cried.

They broke apart for a moment but were back together and fighting in less than a second.

Scarlet waited patiently for an opening. When it came, she gave the same little twist to her sword as she stepped forward. In a moment, Captain Wycliffe Gloom was standing in front of her, with his sword on the ground five feet to his left.

No one said anything as Scarlet grabbed the scabbard from the ground and girt it around her waist. She sheathed the sword and picked up her knapsack from where she had dropped it on the deck.

The crowd parted for her and in less than a moment she was on land again and headed into the village.

The village was truly a work of art. The small cottages by the sea made Scarlet wish for a moment that she could settle down and live there. She was brought back to reality when she heard the people. Everyone in the marketplace was speaking the language the dwarf had taught her. She felt she had arrived.

She set down her knapsack, pulled out the dagger and tied it in place next to her new sword. The air was barely spring-like and in her woolen dress she was just right so she took off her cloak, folded it up neatly and set it in the bottom of her bag next to the silk red dress she had worn when she ran away.

There, she thought. *That's all behind me and the world's ahead.* She pulled out her heavy purse and went into a shop that looked as though it might sell weapons.

"Good morning," she greeted the shopkeeper. "How much is the bow?"

The man replied and Scarlet decided it would be worth it. She bought a quiver and ten arrows and then moved on to the next shop.

During the course of the day, she bought a map, provisions and traded her woolen brown dress for a cotton one that would be more practical. Then she bought her horse.

He was beautiful. He had a star on his forehead and was called Demonic Tide. Scarlet knew from the beginning she would only call him Tide.

As the light faded from the sky, she went around the village looking for the inn. People stared to see the young lady with the sword and dagger at her side. The knapsack was slung on her back, side by side with her quiver and the bow. She was riding bareback because she didn't have any money for a saddle, but her back was straight as an arrow and her royalty showed through as the fading light touched her face.

"She is a half elf," people would whisper behind her back.

"She was sold as a slave to the west and has come back to rejoin her people," the rumor spread.

The people didn't know her name and behind her back they called her *Kymilavarion*, meaning beautiful, revengeful, western wanderer. It was a rather long name, but the people wouldn't have settled for less. She was essentially a person of honor.

She dismounted outside the inn and the boy took her horse to the stables without a word. She entered and the room hushed as the innkeeper led her to a table alone in the corner and left to go bring out his finest wine and food.

A guest like her needs something special, he reasoned as he got out his finest roast that he had been saving for his own dinner and he sent his little girls out to pick some fresh herbs to top it with. He pulled out his best looking loaf of bread, put it on a plate and cut a few slices from it.

There, he thought as he artistically drizzled gravy on the roast and arranged a few sprigs of herbs. *Done.*

He brought the two plates out to the table and set them down. He didn't dare say anything but just bowed before going back into the kitchen.

"That's the elf," one man whispered to his companion at the bar table as the innkeeper came back out with the glass of wine. "They say she's a hundred years old."

"I heard she can speak any language she comes across," came another.

"She worked her way to this side of the sea by working for the pirate Wycliffe Gloom."

"She was rejected by her lover," came another. "She ran away because he didn't love her."

The gossip floated around the room as Scarlet sat in the dark corner eating.

"Her father arranged for her to get married to a prince and she rebelled," whispered a fellow who came to close to the truth.

Scarlet silently ate, ignoring the talk going on around her.

"She's fought dragons."

"She's come back from the dead."

"She's written the volumes of *Clynisy and Rulers with Traditions.*"

The preposterous views circulated the room as Scarlet brought out her map and began to pore over it.

"She's going on a journey of great length."

People continued to speculate and present their opinions as fact.

The room quieted when Scarlet looked up. Everyone turned their heads away from her and began to mind their own business.

Bother them, she thought. She folded up her map, finished the rest of her dinner in a hurry and then went upstairs to study her map by herself.

King Konrad's father had been buried after the usual mourning period for high-ranking royalty.

He had watched as his father's casket was lowered into the grave, his young head bowed under the weight of the king's crown.

I'll never abandon them, he thought to himself. *I will never leave them.*

A boy from the crowd broke free from his mother and ran toward the grave, crying. Oh how Konrad wished that he were young enough to break down into the tears he now held back and kneel by his father's grave.

We never agreed on anything, but I did love him, he thought to himself. "And that's what matters."

The last shovelful of dirt thudded against the wood of the casket.

Why? he asked himself again. *Why?*

The diggers filled the grave and all of the visitors left as the young king continued to stand, his head bowed at the top of his father's grave.

The snow began to fall in the quiet and cover the newly filled-in grave.

How much more appropriate would rain be? he thought kneeling down. "Father? I need your help. I can't lead these people by myself, and I never wanted to."

He didn't want to bear this pain himself, he couldn't. But the only two people he could share it with were gone. He was alone. How could he continue to live for himself when he had nothing left to live for?

But he did have something to live for. The people needed him. They had already gone through so much, why should he make it any worse? From that moment forward, Konrad was different, empty. Pouring himself out for his country, but unable to feel anything.

Scarlet bent over the map in the privacy of her room, but before she could study it to any detail there was a knock on the door.

She opened it and there was an old man in a long black cloak and with a long gray beard. He bowed.

"Who are you?" she asked, closing the door another half inch.

"Crovprix is what they call me," the man answered, pronouncing the x in his name with extra emphasis. "I know you're not really an elf."

"That shouldn't be too hard to figure out. What do you want?" she asked, closing the door a little more, why was he taking so much interest in her presence?

"Nothing. I know you are going on a journey because you want to see dwarfs and elves and dragons. Am I not right?"

Scarlet said nothing. Caution warned her against continuing this conversation, but her instinct for adventure kept her from closing the door all the way.

"Ah, you are wondering how I know these things, right? Well, I am, simply put, a wizard."

"What does a wizard want with me?" Scarlet asked.

"I have lived in this village long enough and I want to go back to my home. You want to go in the same direction. I will be your guide."

"Come in," Scarlet invited him, her instinct for adventure prevailing.

"And my friend?" he asked, gesturing to a short, dark shape besides him.

"He can come too, if he means no harm," Scarlet agreed.

The two shapes of the wizard and his short friend shuffled into the room.

"My friend will also come with us," Crovprix explained. "He is a dwarf."

"I had a teacher who was a dwarf," Scarlet told them.

"I know," Crovprix smiled,

"My name is Grurhoum Greatbrow," the dwarf explained pulling the hood of his cloak off of his head.

The dwarf stood only a little higher than her waist and even so he gave her a bow so that his beard touched the ground.

"I know that you come from royalty on the west of the sea," Crovprix explained, "Grurhoum was impressed."

"Is there anything you don't know?" Scarlet asked feeling a little uncomfortable.

"I can never know what human minds are thinking. Besides, I have been in this town for years waiting for you."

"Waiting for me?"

"Yes, I knew you would come one day and I knew you would want to go east. I decided I could wait another thirty years before I leave. Besides, these people needed me to get rid of the 'witch' population," he smiled in remembrance. "What's thirty years in the life of a wizard?"

Scarlet didn't say anything. She was still wondering if she could trust them.

"I also knew Grurhoum would need my help and I could only do it here."

"I am a dwarf from the wonderful mountains of the east. I was sold as a slave and Crovprix saved me. I am now going back to the east with him," Grurhoum Greatbrow told her patiently.

"And I also needed to get rid of this," Crovprix pulled a small package out of his cloak and handed it to Scarlet.

"What is it?" she asked, running her hand over the wrapping.

"As the second highest in my order, I was given a book. I know my days are running short and I must pass this on. Who better than royalty from the west? The western people need to know about these things too. You'll share the book with your county, and they will know about their brothers to the east."

"What if I don't want to do this? What if I don't have a country anymore?" she argued, tossing the book on the table and turning away.

"I can only tell what is, never what ifs," Crovprix explained.

Scarlet reached back and opened the book anyway.

"It's a book with stories about my country!" she cried, surprised. There were also stories she had never heard before.

"Your country?" Crovprix asked with a knowing grin. "I thought you said you didn't have one anymore. Anyway, it's a magic book, every time something of importance happens, it gets added to the book. It will always be complete,"

Scarlet blushed at the stab about her country. She hadn't meant to blurt it out like that. She wasn't even sure where it had come from.

"When are you planning on leaving?" she asked, trying to hide her embarrassment.

"Tomorrow. It will take some time for me to gather thirty years of magic, but it can be done," Crovprix sighed.

"After lunch then," Grurhoum settled it.

The two gave great bows and then left the room.

A dwarf and a wizard, she thought. *And they both know the way to elves and dragons!*

She was cautious, but there was something interesting about their story.

She lay down to go to sleep, but she opened up the book first and read the first few pages.

On one page there was a picture of a dragon and on the one after that was a picture of Arainieous inside the mountain of the dwarfs as it fell down.

So it is true! she thought as she finally closed it and put her head down. *It's all true, dwarfs and wizards.*

Scarlet, from her little room in on the other side of the sea, could only see a sliver of the moon but it seemed to be calling her back to Hedgecliff.

It's not too late to go back, she thought, staring out the window in concentration. *I can still tell Crovprix and Grurhoum I can't come and I need to go.* She tossed and turned. *I can never go back*, she reminded herself. *Not until the king is dead. Nothing can bring me home.* She hardened her heart toward the moon and found a comfortable spot to lie on. *Nothing can bring me back.*

MARJA AND MOTHER

I mounted my horse later that morning. The captain and his guards had already prepped the noose and brought the traitor out.

Lord Telmar had decided to go up to the castle with me. I could have gone up by myself and he knew that it would be better if he stayed behind in case of attack, but he didn't trust anyone anymore and had decided to come up himself.

I appreciated the gesture, but didn't have the heart to tell him to stay behind.

As our horses passed by Cedric kneeling on the ground, his shirt already off in preparation for his death, he called out to us.

"Be silent, cur!" Telmar bellowed. "I have had enough of you and your ways. I advise you to think about where you are going, rather than bother yourself about a place with people you will never see again."

My hair blew out behind me in the stiff breeze that had come over night.

"Her majesty has better things to do than to waste time on the likes of you," Telmar signaled to the other riders to advance and we pushed our way back into the king's city.

How could it be that I was not bothered by how graphic the death was yesterday, but my heart is quelled by the thought of one dying today? How could killing just one be so much harder than killing hundreds?

I pushed it out of my mind and spurred my horse on faster. I had better things that needed my attention than that traitor.

The others matched their pace to me and it wasn't long before we had reached the castle. Had it really been only a few days since I had last basked in the warm glow of firelight in the hallways?

But I had important things to get done. First, my arm had to get taken care of. It was a nasty cut. I'm quite sure that the knife hadn't been cleaned in years. My tutor, who was also a doctor, cleaned it out.

With my arm nicely bandaged up, I took leave of the men. They would be heading down to the kitchen to bring back food for the other soldiers. I quickly dashed through the halls searching for Marja. I couldn't find her anywhere. I spent fifteen minutes searching before my feet led me to my own room. Marja was outside the door, tears streaming down her face.

"Marja? What happened?" I cried, hugging her close, oblivious to her struggling.

"Get away from me, Scarlet! Your mother has been worried sick over you!! You don't deserve anything right now."

I carefully let her go and she indignantly brushed off and held herself with a prideful air.

"You would run away from your own mother and leave her to be taken care of by others? I'm not even her daughter and I care for her more than you do!" she accused.

"Marja, I'm sorry."

"No you're not!"

I glared at her and pushed her off to the side. I opened the door quickly and in a moment I was at the side of my mother's bed.

"Mother?" I called.

"Scarlet? Is that you?"

I smiled with hope. "Yes it's me. I'm back, see?"

"No," She whispered at last. "My eyes are too dim. There is no light in this room." She coughed. "You can't be my daughter." Her voice sounded weak and distant. "My daughter is dead. There was no way she could survive." Her voice was strained. "And my husband, my king! Why doesn't he come to me? I have sent messengers. I have begged and pleaded. What have I done to make him angry?!"

Tears streamed down her face and I caught up her moist and feverish hand.

"Mum! I'm here! Father is down at the wall. He is fighting the enemy," My voice caught and for a moment I couldn't say anything. "It will be alright, Mum!" I burst into tears. "You have to get better!" She recoiled her hand and feebly pushed me away.

"Send in my niece, at least she has not abandoned me. I do not know you! I do not know you ..."

I dashed from the room. Marja passed me on her way back in.

I didn't get very far before I collapsed in a heap on the floor and cried my eyes out. Marja found me there an hour later.

"Scarlet," she began, sinking to the floor and putting an arm around my shaking shoulders. "I'm sorry, there isn't anything we can do for her. I'm only here to ease her pain in her last days." She paused and took a shaky breath. "I shouldn't have said those things. I'm sorry. I know you're out there saving the country and all."

I wiped my tears away on the corner of my sleeve.

"Marja?" I began with resolve. "Can you promise me one thing?"

"Sure."

"The minute the wall is overtaken, I want you out of this castle."

"Why?" she looked surprised.

"Because I don't want to lose you too! Everyone in this castle will be killed for being royalty! You need to be in the city, away from the others. There you can lie low until we take everything back."

Marja hesitantly promised. I knew she didn't want to leave Mum. But I also knew she would do it for me.

"Alright Scarlet, but what about your mother?"

"I don't know," I leaned heavily on the wall. "She can't be moved from the palace till she is better. Don't worry about it. When the time comes, save yourself."

Marja was quiet.

"I understand," She whispered.

Footsteps and horses could be heard echoing down the hall. I stretched out my legs and helped Marja up.

"Miss Marja," I began, giving a mock bow and holding out my arm for her. "Would you please be so kind as to allow me to escort you down to the courtyard?"

"I thought you would never ask me," she smiled and accepted my support. Her slender and smooth hand just barely touching the rough metal chains and course tunic. I winced when I realized how pale that hand looked, her knuckles dark and striking compared to the rest of it.

I matched my pace to hers and smiled down on her.

Oh Marja! I thought. *Whatever would I do without you?*

We pulled out into the courtyard and she stopped.

"Good bye, Scarlet." she smiled.

"Say it again," I asked her. "Tell me again what you are going to do once the city is taken."

"Scarlet," She began, gently cuffing me in the arm. "I'm going to head out into the city to find a nice family to take care of me till this blows over." I could hear her voice quiver. "But what are you going to do?"

My heart sank. "I'll probably be captured and found out," I reluctantly replied.

"Bring this with you," Marja handed me a small bundle. "When the time comes, find yourself a private place and then open it."

I took the small bundle that was wrapped in fabric and I kissed her hand, still pretending to be the gentleman.

"Thank you m'lady, take care of yourself."

"I will!"

I bowed and she curtsied and I took a few steps toward my horse.

"Scarlet!" I heard her cry.

I dashed back and hugged, tears streaming down both of our faces.

"You'll be safe." I whispered, reassuring her.

"I know. Promise me you'll come back?"

"I can't Marja! The minute the city is taken, there won't be a stone unturned looking for me."

"Promise me!"

I sighed. "Marja, I promise to do my best to try to get away."

Marja recoiled, her face turning away from me in disgust.

"Marja, I'm going out there to save others, to save this city," I explained. "I cannot think of myself, this is for them, for you! I promise you when my work fails and there is nothing more I can do for you and my country, I will think about myself because only then will it matter. I promise that much, Marja. I cannot give you anything else."

"Your Majesty?" Lord Telmar had already mounted his horse and was waiting for me.

"Stay strong, Marja!" I finally said. "If at all possible, I will come back."

I dashed out to my horse and mounted in one quick movement. Carefully I tucked the small package underneath a little hollow in my saddle.

Telmar's horse dashed out and I followed, not having time to give Marja a second glance.

The few trees that lined the way back to the wall had all lost their leaves. The sky was dark and the easy breeze that had kept us comfortable in the morning now chilled us to the bone.

I slowed my horse a bit and pulled my cloak further around my shoulders.

We progressed through the city at a rather slow rate. The people who had been out the first time I had made this trip were nowhere to be seen. I pictured them cowering in their little houses, overcome with fear for their lives. I shook the thought out of my head and tried again.

I could see them coming out of their houses when we finally sounded the victory call. They would walk, crawl, hobble, and ride out to the city wall in hopes of seeing or touching the hero of Hedgecliff.

Smiling again, I singlehandedly pulled my cloak closer around my shoulders and spurred my horse on.

I took a deep breath of air and nearly threw up.

"What?" Lord Telmar rode to a halt, his nose sniffing the air in disgust.

"It's the bodies, Lord Telmar. When we were up at the castle our noses readjusted. It won't bother us once we get used to it again," one of the soldiers spoke up.

The stench was terrible. Blood mixed with sweat, mixed with the horrendous smell of decay assaulting our noses without our permission.

Truly I didn’t think it was that bad this morning.

We slowly pressed on. I took shallow breaths to try to keep the smell out. But needless to say, it didn't work.

CHAPTER TEN

Scarlet woke up the next morning, hardly feeling rested.

She had all morning to do nothing before Crovprix and Grurhoum would come to pick her up. She waited in the inn after she packed everything up. The village people nearly flowed in and out to see her.

They still called her *Kymilavarion.* Nothing could convince them otherwise. The people were simple and didn't know any better.

Scarlet waited all morning and was beginning to get worried when Crovprix the wizard and Grurhoum Greatbrow the dwarf didn't show up right at lunch.

Scarlet ordered a meal and was beginning to eat when the door was opened and Crovprix and Grurhoum walked in with knapsacks, cloaks and staves.

"It really is a bother to have to clean up thirty years of magic in less than one night, but I can assure you it will be worth it," Crovprix sighed, sat down across from Scarlet, waved the innkeeper over and continued. "I'm quite sure that Grurhoum didn't sleep all night, he was so happy to realize he was finally going home."

Grurhoum nodded and spoke, "I can't wait to show you everything in the east. I will personally take both of you to my mountain and show you all of the treasures we have made. I will even find armor for you, Crovprix, and I will find a chainmail shirt for you made out of things harder than steel. It will be light enough for you to wear everyday. You never know when you will want armor."

"I have come up with a route," Crovprix explained pulling out a map when Grurhoum paused. "We will travel to Grurhoum's mountain by passing over these two rivers to the north. They are impossible to cross unless you cross them to the north. Then we will go due east till we reach a road that is not on the map. It didn't have any name back in my day and it doesn't have one now, as far as I know. This road will take us up to the dwarf city Vamkuldir. There we will part our ways. Grurhoum will stay there with his free kin. I must move east until I die."

"And what about me? This rode only takes me to the dwarfs. What about dragons and elves?" Scarlet asked, feeling a little let down.

"It would be my suggestion not to take on the east too quickly," Crovprix cautioned. "Even though you know the language, you are unaccustomed to the ways of the people. But perhaps from there you could head south to Lililenor of the high elves. They should know where you can find a dragon," he gave a knowing look at Grurhoum, but Scarlet didn't notice.

"You mean to say that you have never seen one?" Scarlet asked in surprise.

"Never. It is not my job on this earth to fight dragons, find them or look at them. I have come for a different purpose," he answered her.

"Then what do you do?" she asked.

"That is for me to know," he said wisely. "Some things people don't need to know."

"That's a wizard for you," Grurhoum commented as he devoured a large fried egg in one bite. "Any day they could tell you stories of what they have done. Any day they could tell you stories of dragons and treasure. Any day they could tell you of magic. Any day I could tell those stories,"

"Enough Grurhoum. Any day you could tell enough stories to last a lifetime," Crovprix silenced him. "After you have visited the dwarfs, you can get a map from them and then journey to Lililenor and the high elves. After that, only fate can drive you to the dragons,"

"What are we waiting for?" Grurhoum cried. "Let's be off!"

"Patience," soothed Crovprix, "My lunch has not yet come and I cannot leave without it."

The table grew silent as the innkeeper brought in Crovprix's lunch.

He ate it in silence. When he was done, everyone mutely left the inn, mounted their horses and were off galloping through the front gate of the village and out into the wide open plane.

"To the dwarfs' kingdom of the east!" Grurhoum bellowed, free at last.

"To the east and the end!" Crovprix cried, a faint memory crossing his mind and giving him both fear and hope at the same time.

"To adventure!" Scarlet laughed, a cold glint in her eye.

I'm off! she wondered. *After fifteen years I'm following* my *dream and nothing's holding me back. And all it took was a little push out of the door from Konrad,* she shuddered and instantly tried to think of something else. *And when I have seen dragons, and elves, and have a coat of armor from the dwarfs, my life will be complete. Then I can settle down and write it all out in a nice, long book.*

The thought contented her for a moment, and when it was gone, only the flat, open plain lay empty before her.

As they started out after lunch, they were only going to ride for half a day so they could push the horses a little bit. They planned on stopping when they got to the first river and then waiting to cross them till the light of day.

"Many a time I have imagined myself making this journey," Crovprix started, "I thought that perhaps the world might end before I would make it."

"Ay, the world's end," Grurhoum affirmed.

"I never believed it would," Scarlet stated, "I have heard when all the magic is gathered it will end, but to tell the truth I still don't believe in magic."

"Don't believe in magic?" Crovprix cried giving Scarlet a terrible glare. "I'm nearly made of the stuff! When the rain comes down so hard that you cannot light a fire you will learn the truth of magic!"

"I'm sorry," Scarlet eagerly tried to fix what she had said. "I didn't mean it like that."

But the old wizard would not be consoled that easily.

"Don't believe in magic. Pah!" he muttered to himself. "Just you wait till we need it, then you'll more than believe it!"

"Perhaps you haven't heard about what will happen at the end of time?" Grurhoum suggested, trying to take Crovprix's mind off of magic.

"I haven't ever heard about that," Scarlet eagerly grabbed onto the distraction.

"Then let me explain," Grurhoum began. "The last day will be when all the magic has been gathered or used. My great great great great great grandfather was just a child when the magic was released. The humans were mad at us for making them our slaves through magic, so when it was gone, they turned the tables on us. It has been like that ever since and that is why I must go free my people. They have been in slavery for too long and it is time for change! We were meant to be a free people! Our own country of free men, each helping the other to create great works of art through metal and determination."

"But that doesn't tell me how the world will end," Scarlet pursued. "I do feel sorry for your friends and family, but this doesn't tell me how the world will end."

"A great calamity. That's all we know. It will wipe out everything. After that, no one knows."

"But I thought we knew more about it."

"We don't."

"We should."

"I do not dispute that."

They rode in silence for a little while longer,

"I remember those times," Crovprix commented. "After the magic was released. I was the second wizard to be made from the magic. For a while they all thought I was the first, but then the oldest of our order resurfaced and I have been second in command ever since."

"Is there a council? Or an order?" Scarlet asked.

"Not really," Crovprix explained. "We wizards only come together every now and then for big and important events. Very few of us have died actually. Only five died in the War of Gulrun."

"The War of Gulrun?"

"Yes, it happened right after the magic escaped from the mountain. It was then that the humans revolted from the dwarfish rule and enslaved them."

"So everything really circulates back to the dwarfs?" Scarlet asked.

"I should say not!" Grurhoum interjected. "At least not everything bad. We made the armor when the humans went up against the dragons when the humans woke them. The infernal curiosity! They had to go meddling in other respectable beings' business."

"But this whole story goes right back to the dwarfs though. And if you think about it right, it wasn't their fault they got all the magic. It was all that silly stone's." Scarlet reminded them.

"They still could have been better stewards of what they had been given," Crovprix suggested. "They could have helped the humans and not enslaved them."

"How could we when as a smaller, and even backwards race, they would have returned gift for plague?" Grurhoum defended his lineage.

"I don't think it really matters today," Scarlet told him. "It only matters that we don't do it again and that it is a part of our history. There is nothing you can change about that. But the truth of the matter is: what can you change now so your children will never have to feel that same shame?"

Grurhoum laughed. "You have hit the nail on the head and have hit it well! Truce. Just because of this conversation, I will personally make you a full suit of chain mail."

"Thank you," she spoke from the bottom of her heart. "I will hold you to that promise."

The rest of the day no one spoke, even after they had halted and struck camp, no one spoke. The silence was bearable and seemed nice after the long conversations of the afternoon.

"The constellations here are different than back at home," Scarlet commented when dinner was nearly over.

"Look there!" Grurhoum cried as he glanced up and began pointing. "It's the great warrior of the dwarfs."

"And the peacemaker to the elves," Crovprix suggested as he lit his pipe from the fire. "Have you ever noticed that in the dwarfish mythology, when someone does a great deed they are lifted up to the sky in the form of constellations? But the elves have the heroes from the stars come down to help them."

"That's because they are weak," Grurhoum huffed. "The dwarfs don't need supernatural help like that."

"What are all the constellations and their stories?" Scarlet asked. Here was time to learn about the great east!

"Well to the dwarfs, the great warrior was once a dwarf who led the biggest freedom revolt ever. Someday my brother will take his place among the stars as being the redeemer of all of my people."

"And to the elves?"

"He came down from the sky to teach the elves how to make peace throughout the land," Crovprix explained his finger tracing the sky. "The elves will never succeed in creating peace and they know this. But they still believe he is of great importance."

"And what about that one right there?"

"That is the dwarfish tree. We dwarfs don't like trees, but way back when we held the humans as slaves, there was a tree that lived in the heart of dwarfish land. Every dwarf would have meetings under it. It was chopped down when we were enslaved."

"The elves say it is the lamp." Crovprix began dreamily, preferring the Elven ways to the dwarfs'. "It has yet to come down from the sky to help them. They say it will come down at the end of this age."

"Perhaps," Scarlet began quietly. "Perhaps it will tell us how the world will end. Don't you think it's sad?"

No one said anything and in less than an hour, everyone was busy dreaming their own dreams.

"Everybody wake up!" Grurhoum shouted.

"It's not even light out yet," Scarlet complained, but sleep had already vanished.

"It will be light by the time that we get to the river. If we hurry, we can make it to my mountain by nightfall tomorrow. Then I can begin work on your armor."

"And then I can continue ever east to practice my magic elsewhere," Crovprix said, still dreaming.

"Well then! Move out everybody! We'll make breakfast when we get to the river. I'm sure some of you will want to wash up a bit before."

They packed up the little they had brought out, and then, after untying the horses, they mounted.

"Some people could never imagine me, mounting a horse without help,"

Scarlet thought with satisfaction. “I can do what I want and nothing can stop me.”

They headed due north listening as the silent plain slowly turned into forest. The silence was only broken by the sound of the horses and breaking twigs.

“This forest is too gloomy.” Scarlet said at last.

“It has reason to be,” was all that was said. Scarlet felt bad about having broken the silence and she did not pursue an answer.

Just as the sun rose above the tops of the trees, Scarlet heard the sound of running water.

“That’s it!” she cried, dismounting and running forward. She wasn't disappointed.

They unpacked food, cooked a meager breakfast by the side of the river, packed it up again and then crossed the river.

“One down, one more to go!” Crovprix's spirit lifted as he said these words. “I never thought I would ever see this side of the river again,” he took a deep breath, bringing back memories he thought he had left behind.

“Ahh ... can't you just smell the mountains?” Grurhoum jubilated. Scarlet sniffed the air and felt that nothing was different. Even the trees looked the same on this side of the river.

Someday, she thought as her heart began to soar. *I'll be so well-traveled that I will be able to smell the mountains and feel the difference in the air. I'll know every mythology and know the names to all the stars. There is nothing else for me to do with my life now that I am no longer princess.* She felt so free as she thought those words.

They passed over the other river less than an hour afterwards, and before lunch, Crovprix was getting worried about finding the path he knew about.

“I know we should have come across it by now,” he worried. “I know we have been going a little too north and we should go south and east now that we’ve passed the rivers, but I'm not doing that until we find the path.”

By the midday meal, he was nearly out of his wits. “We should have found it by now! I should have never taken all of you with me if I can't tell the way,” Crovprix exclaimed.

“Why can't we just use the stars to find our way to my kin?” Grurhoum asked, he was unruffled by the wizard’s anxiety. “It would be less stressful, don't you think?”

“Stressful? Finding our way through the night with only the stars as our guide?! Are you out of your mind? It’s plain stupidity,” Crovprix shouted.

When they had gone another hour without finding a trace of the road, even Crovprix had to give in.

“We'll take a rest and finish our journey to the mountain by night,” he said with a sigh. “I don't know if we'll make it there anytime soon, but I'm sure we won't die till the food is gone.”

They stopped and Grurhoum got out his bedroll, "I might as well try to get a few winks in before we have to start out again." Crovprix followed suit.

Scarlet sat down on a stump, not knowing what to do.

I could climb a tree, she thought. *I've never done it and it might be interesting.* She stood up and quietly walked out of the makeshift campsite.

This shouldn't be too hard, she thought as she picked a tree and took her sword and dagger off her belt. *I'll just have to tuck my skirt up a little*, she tucked it under her belt and grabbed a branch. *Now just a little swing. Humph, gotcha!* she stabilized herself on the first branch. *Not too hard. Foot goes there, hands grab branches and ...* she reached up, smiling. *Making progress.*

She slowly progressed up the tree, stopping only now and then for a little rest.

"It's not too hard," she whispered. "Just like climbing stairs. Ow!" she exclaimed as her foot slipped and her hands tightened around a sharp twig.

She situated her foot back on the branch and pulled a little twig out of her hand.

"Darn," she muttered as she let go of it and watched it flutter down the tree, "I've got to be more careful."

She slowly made her way to the top of the tree, and then looked around.

Not much to go by in a forest, she thought. *No way to see where a path might be.*

She looked around a little. "That's the end of the forest right there. We're not too far from it. Past it there's what looks like another river. It goes winding all the way to the ..." she caught her breath. "Mountains! And it's not a river, it's a path! We are so close we could get there by tomorrow if we don't stop today." she realized.

She began climbing down the tree, being careful to remember what direction the path was in. *So close and we could have passed right by it. Now we won't have to travel by night!*

Her foot slipped, "No!" she cried as she fell down the tree. Her cry and the following thud woke Crovprix and Grurhoum and they rushed to her side.

"Are you alright?" Crovprix asked, kneeling down.

"What were you doing up in that tree?" Grurhoum asked. As a dwarf, he did not understanding the human fascination of trees.

"I'm alright Crovprix. I was bored but that doesn't matter now," she told them as she got up, concealing a twisted ankle and untucking her skirt. "I saw the path. It's only a little ways forward. The moment we come out of the wood we should be able to see it. And Grurhoum, I saw the mountain! It was beautiful!"

"I know, it glistens like a jewel and shines like a star."

"Glistens like a jewel? Shines like a star?" Crovprix seemed amused. "Either way, she's seen it and we know where the path is. Let's be off! But first, let me do something about that ankle."

Scarlet, aware that she had not concealed it very well, sat down and waited for Crovprix to bring out a poultice and wrap it up or something, but that didn't happen. Instead, he began whispering half words and phrases. After a moment, he turned and walked away as though he were done, Grurhoum following him. Scarlet, very confused, stood up and followed them. It took her a moment before she realized she wasn't limping and it didn't hurt anymore. Scarlet, still stunned, walked back to camp and slowly mounted her horse. The dwarf and the wizard packed up their packs and then mounted.

"Lead on to the dwarf's kingdom of the east!" Grurhoum bellowed.

"To the east and the end!" Crovprix cried.

"To adventure!" Scarlet murmured. Was it really magic? Did magic really exist?

Scarlet led the way. For nearly an hour the forest was still surrounding them, quiet and dark.

"Wait! Look ahead," Crovprix cried.

"It's the plain!" Scarlet cried, for the moment forgetting her bewilderment at her healed ankle. "Just a little further and we should be able to see the path."

"Exactly what I was thinking," Crovprix smiled.

They pushed their already tired horses. In another moment they were out of the gloomy forest and in the open air.

"Now if Scarlet is right, we should see the path in another few minutes," Grurhoum commented taking the lead.

Scarlet was worried. *What if it was just a river?* she thought. *But there are no rivers on the map.* she reasoned. *But then again the path is not on the map.*

"Is that it?" Grurhoum, snug in his saddle, pointed at what looked like a faint shadow.

"Just as I remembered," Crovprix smiled as he adjusted his course. "See? I told you we wouldn't have to navigate by the stars."

Grurhoum and Scarlet shared a smile. They knew Crovprix had given in when it was suggested they navigate by the stars. They knew he had given up. They also knew it was because of Scarlet that they found the path. They knew.

That night they slept under the stars again. Scarlet heard about other constellations, filing away the information for her future use.

The next day they reached the mountain. Around it, there was a town with seven or eight streets passing through it and leading to the front gate of the mountain.

They circulated around the outside, looking in for a moment, Crovprix and Grurhoum each remembering the mountain at a different point in its history. Crovprix could remember all the way back to the peak of the dwarven empire, but Grurhoum could only remember the shambles it had been in when he had been stolen so many years ago.

It was then that Crovprix said goodbye. Nothing in that kingdom waited for him, but across the sea, faint as a memory, he knew who was waiting for him.

"I knew that this day would be coming sooner rather than later, and now it's come," he turned to Grurhoum. "Goodbye Grurhoum. Save your people and bring peace. I wish I could have done more for you when I had that chance, perhaps one day you will be up in the stars."

He turned to Scarlet, just as he had to another princess only thirty years before, "Goodbye Scarlet! Find your adventure, but don't forget your countrymen. They will need you one day. Good bye!"

Scarlet and Grurhoum, still stunned, watched as Crovprix turned his horse to the east with the golden sunset on his back.

"I hope he finds what he's looking for," Scarlet wished, waving at him. "Perhaps we will meet again."

"Goodbye old friend," Grurhoum let go of a single tear. "I spent all those days in the presence of people who enslaved my family, then you came along. You were my only friend and I will miss you."

A shadow crossed Crovprix's face as he waved.

Grurhoum and Scarlet began to walk through the town.

"It really is more like a city," Grurhoum commented when he had regained his composure. "Last time I saw it, it was much smaller. When I tell them you are a real princess, they will all worship you and your grace, even though they are a free people."

Scarlet felt uncomfortable at the praise.

"They have never seen royalty from across the sea and they probably never will again," he continued, "I will make sure my brother lets you live in the mountain for the duration of your stay. I will also begin work on your armor tonight. I will never rest until it is done, and why should I? Metal working gives me strength I have not had in years. It will be light and strong. I might even be able to have it cover your entire dress. Now that would be a project worthy of the dwarfs of old. How they would have loved to treat the princess of the west to a suit of armor."

They reached the mountain, a boy took the horses and they asked for an audience with the king.

"Who shall I say is calling?" the servant asked, eyeing the visitors suspiciously.

"Lord Grurhoum Greatbrow and Princess ..." Grurhoum broke off for a second trying to remember her full name, "... Scarlet Elwen Silvergleam Oreldes from the west. We have traveled from far-off lands and are exhausted. I have finally come home."

The servant nodded and went into the throne room. In another moment he was back.

"His majesty, King Herhem Greatbrow of the eastern mountains welcomes you."

He pushed open the door to the throne room and Grurhoum and Scarlet walked inside.

"Grurhoum Greatbrow? Son of Grurhour Greatbrow? Son of Grurgon Greatbrow? My brother? Is it you who have finally come back?" came a grinding voice from the throne.

Scarlet and Grurhoum knelt.

"Yes, it is me," Grurhoum whispered, tears in his eyes. "I thought I would never see you again."

"You escaped from the humans?" the king asked, descending his throne and offering his brother his hand. "The day you were stolen I fasted for three weeks. The whole city will be in rejoicing."

Grurhoum and King Herhem embraced for a moment.

"And even now you bring a human into my presence?" the king asked, turning and looking at Scarlet who had been watching everything.

"She is a princess from the far western lands," Grurhoum explained.

"A slave you have come by?" the king asked curiously.

"No, she is as free as you and I are," Grurhoum explained. "Her people had nothing to do with the slavery of dwarfs. She is our guest."

"Then that changes things," the king laughed and sat down on his throne to take a good look at her. "You may rise. Like he said, if you have not wronged our people, you are our guest."

Scarlet stood up and made a curtsy to the king, "Your Majesty."

"She speaks our language?" the king asked in surprise.

"Yes sir," she grinned. "My teacher had been a slave dwarf from the east and he could only escape to the west. He was a free man and would have done Your Majesty honor."

"I can see that," the king stared at her in surprise. "You even know how to address me. You may stay."

"Your Majesty," Scarlet bowed again.

"And for you, Grurhoum?"

"I have a promise to keep to the princess before I can join your army."

"And what is this promise?" the king asked curiously.

"I need to make chainmail for the princess."

"A princess in armor?" the king laughed. "Do they fight a lot in the west?"

"No your majesty. I promised it to her because she is in the east to find adventure. She will need it."

"But perhaps," Scarlet began, her heart sinking to her shoes. "Perhaps I should stay and help you win the war against the humans?"

"No," the king told her as she sighed in relief. "You follow *your* dream, only then can you follow someone else's. Never sacrifice your dream for another."

"Thank you, sir."

"Now, Grurhoum, you have armor to make!" Grurhoum and Scarlet bowed and left the room.

"Come with me," a servant told them. "Lord Grurhoum, brother to the king, will have a room in the heart of the mountain and we'll curtain off a section of the great hall for the princess. She'll be more comfortable with the space and the height."

"Thank you for your consideration," she thanked them looking a little dazed.

"Not quite what you were expecting, Scarlet?" Grurhoum asked.

"I didn't know quite what to expect. But everything is so different,"

"Good?"

"Perfect."

They reached Grurhoum's room and parted ways.

"I'll send dinner in soon. I see I don't have to send for your things. You have them already," the servant commented.

They left and soon Scarlet and the servant were in a hall.

"The roof is a little higher in here," he told her. "You should be quite comfortable."

"Thank you," she told him again as she walked to a makeshift bed roll that had been set up,

"I'm sorry but we don't really have anything your size. It would please the king to have you received in more splendor, but I'm afraid this is all we have," he apologized.

"It will be perfectly fine," she assured him.

"Then I'll send another servant up with some food and then you can sleep. Tomorrow the king will send a guide to take you around town and at night you will be invited to the king's feast," the servant bowed and left the room.

Scarlet, deep inside the dwarfs' mountain, couldn't see the stars or the moon for the first night in many weeks.

THE SECRET ATTACK

Our ride grew short as we closed in on the camp and the wall. Lord Telmar and I dismounted and climbed the steps to look out on the enemy.

"Are we ready for tonight?" I asked.

"Yes, the tunnel is dug and the soldiers are resting."

I pushed past two archers who were standing guard over the wall.

"You know your orders?"

"Yes, Your Majesty."

"Good."

I glanced out over the field of soldiers, tents, rubble and bodies. What had I ever done to deserve this?

As I turned back to face Lord Telmar, my eye caught on something.

"It's him isn't it?" I whispered.

"Yes," he answered.

I shivered, but not from the cold.

Out to the left there was a body hanging from the wall, it's blood still pouring out of wounds on its back and staining the shreds of clothes that it still wore. Its face was a blank slate, a bag pulled over its head so no one would recognize him from below. I knew that if the soldiers had their will, his head would be uncovered so that all could see and so the birds could pluck out his eyes.

"Thank heaven I wasn't here for that," I thought. "I could never have watched as the men did that to someone, anyone, even if he did deserve it."

I left the wall, that eerie image still dangling in my mind the way that its feet dangled in the wind.

Lantern light filled my tent as I waited to watch the small attack party leave. We all knew our hopes rested on them.

Telmar opened the flap to my tent and I walked out with him, the stars in the sky shimmering in the familiar patterns I had known since childhood. We silently walked to the tunnel that had been dug. Through the cold night I could hear whinnies from the unsettled horses and cries from the encampment just outside the wall.

Our footsteps echoed in my ear as we swiftly moved closer into the one place we could now get through the wall.

"Your Majesty," Lord Telmar bowed over my hand when we finally reached the place.

"I have complete trust in you and your judgment. Good luck," I answered.

He nodded to his men and one by one dropped into a dark hole in the ground. Lord Telmar brought up the rear. I watched as his shiny helmet disappeared from sight and I heaved a sigh.

Quickly I mounted the steps to the wall. In another minute I knew that Lord Telmar would shine a light up at us so we would know he was alright.

I saw the light bobbing and flashing before it disappeared into the forest. I nodded in his direction and gave up a little prayer for his safety.

In another two hours, the sun would come up and the rest of us would need to be in position. Today would make it or break it for us.

I walked back to my tent quickly. I left a small group of soldiers and a messenger with a horse in case the men came back, or worse, something happened to them, or even more worse, the enemy tried to gain a foothold there.

It was a risky move, not re-closing the tunnel, but I wanted to be sure my men had an escape route if the need came about.

In the meantime, I went back to my post, right where we would attack in a few hours.

Waiting was so hard. It felt like forever before the sun came up and we could just barely see the tents and the men moving around down below. It felt like forever before I could be certain that Telmar was in his place and ready, waiting for us to make our move.

I hesitated to call the shot. I worried it was the wrong thing to do. Would my people hate me if it was my fault we fell? And what if we did fall? Marja's words came back to me. Would I be able to get away in time to save myself? And when I called out to have the arrow shot, would I be able to keep my men under control? Would they obey me or would they run? Was it possible that this was the wrong decision?

Doubts flashed through my mind as fast as birds dive-bombing coveted chickenfeed. And just as fickle.

I'm sure I waited till past the last moment, but I finally gave the cue.

Arrows flew from our wall and we waited for the response. It came in less than a minute.

Arrows flew up at us as we continued the assault. I had instructed Telmar to wait until they had regained their guard and foothold. This would ensure that we were confusing them more than if it all came down at once.

Men fell from the wall and were replaced by more men. I continued to shoot arrows, but this time I had a bigger role to play in the attack.

"Keep it up boys! Good job, soldier," I encouraged them as I passed, all the while making sure they were attacking as much as they could. "It's just a scratch, something to tell your grandkids about," I smiled at the wounded.

People who had been assigned to posts quickly abandoned them in exchange for helping out in places that needed it more. In some cases, several feet of wall would be left as an open opportunity for ladders to be set up.

"Stay at your posts!" I called out to them. "I need more men here!"

It was an empty spot that I called them to, but a ladder had been set up. Men pushed around me and the first one up the ladder stepped out on the wall.

I attacked with my sword and quickly killed him. The other men were busy shooting them as they came up the ladder, so I felt it was secure enough to move on and find another spot to fortify.

The battle's focus moved from place to place as I was kept on my toes trying to defend the wall.

Suddenly, an arrow came out of nowhere and struck me in the leg. Pain coursed through my calf and up my leg and I stumbled close to the edge of the wall. Quickly I sat down and held my tears back until it was bearable.

"I have to keep going!" I whispered to myself. The shaft sticking out of my leg and quivering with every movement. I made a stupid decision and tugged at it. It stuck fast as my face turned red and tears shamelessly streamed down my face.

I pushed myself and pulled as hard as I could, as quickly as I could, and in a moment blood was streaming out of the open wound and coursing down my leg.

I ripped the bottom of my tunic and wrapped it around my leg and tied it as tightly as I could.

I didn't even stop to wipe the tears away. I stood up as quickly as I could and limped my way back to the action.

It really looked hopeless. Telmar hadn't attacked and I had no idea how we would hold the wall till last light. I really was the last person they should have asked for this job. Every soldier here has been in several battles before, but this was only my second. How was I supposed to lead these more experienced men?

I looked out across the field below, I was only a little wary of arrows.

The enemy's archers were shooting out from under little turtle shells of shields that the soldiers were hiding under. It was nearly impossible to get at them under that armor. I could see the knights lounging around. This part of the battle wasn't for them—they would come into play later.

If only Telmar would attack right now! He could catch them off their guard and we would have the advantage.

Slowly I turned from the wall to respond to a cry for the left, a ladder had been set up and they needed help fending it off.

Suddenly I stopped in my tracks, a different cry had called out from below. I dashed back to the wall and cheered. I could see a small group cutting its way through the Fairfalcon armies like butter. Arrows flew less quickly and I called out to the men to continue firing. We would use the break to our advantage and would distract them from Telmar.

I smiled as I went to help the soldiers who were fending off the ladder and drew my sword.

The sun fell behind the mountains and the arrows from below failed even more. We were winning!

I attacked another enemy and one of his own side's arrows felled him before the second blow.

The ladder was quickly pushed off and the other men dispelled.

Having already used all of my arrows, I watched the men below clashing and fending. Lord Telmar had the advantage of surprise, but they didn't have the numbers to last very long.

My heart quailed as they were forced back. I reminded myself that we hadn't expected it to help much, and everyone on that team knew they would probably die, but it still hurt to watch them fail.

Daylight failed me and the only clues we had were the sounds of the swords clashing below us and the cries of men dying.

Quickly everyone dashed to the wall and watched with unseeing eyes as we heard the massacre played out beneath us.

Tears flowed and I didn't even try to stop them. In the dark, no one would notice and besides, I could hear sniffles from the men and I knew they wouldn't snub me. I wasn't the only one.

Slowly, the sounds below turned to silence.The men couldn't tear themselves away from the wall, but I slipped out behind them and down the stairs. Anyone left would come to the tunnel and I was sure they would be followed.

I wanted to get some sleep before it happened. Then, we would fight in close quarters by the light of torches.

I didn't even take off my armor. I knew I would just have to throw it quickly back on and it would take too long.

One thing I did do was take off the one wrapping on my leg. I hurt like nothing else, but I wanted to make sure it would be clean and properly taken care of.

After that, I limped back to my bed and exhausted, collapsed on the clean sheets. I was out before my eyes even closed.

CHAPTER ELEVEN

Scarlet woke the next morning, nice and warm.

I could live in a dwarfish mountain for the rest of my life, she thought. *Except for the beds.*

Her back was sore, but what else could you expect after sleeping on a rock slab inside a mountain?

Breakfast had already been set out, and she devoured it before arranging her hair and smoothing out the wrinkles in her dress.

I suppose the silk, scarlet dress should wait for the banquet tonight, she thought with a sigh. It would have been nice to have changed.

A servant announced his presence. "I will be your guide," he explained with a bow. "We can leave whenever you are ready,"

He seemed to nearly stare up at her.

"You haven't seen anyone from the west, have you?" she asked, curiosity getting the better of her.

"Never. Much less a princess."

"Well, I'll tell you, it's not too much different."

"Really?" he asked in surprise.

"Yes."

"Being a princess, or being in the west?" he asked.

"Being in the west," Scarlet clarified.

"Right," the dwarf pulled himself together again. "Now are you ready?"

They turned out of the castle and began walking through the streets.

"This city has been here for years," he began. "It was built in the years of Arainieous, and was laid siege upon when the humans revolted. The city lay desolate for years, but we free dwarfs have begun to build it back up." Her guide hesitated, "And about your friend ..."

"What about him?" Scarlet asked, a little worried.

"He was up all night in the forge making armor. Why?"

"He promised me some when we were on our way here. He said it was a debt of honor."

"Well," her guide thought about it a minute. "You must be a real valuable person. He was making it out of the most precious and hard metal there is, Ijeslum,"

"Ijeslum?" she asked curiously, the word had never come up in her vocabulary lessons with her tutor, the dwarf.

"It gleams a pale gold and is stronger than steel. But there's another thing. He said he would have it finished before the banquet tonight. Ijeslum cannot be manipulated that quickly," he told her, sounding puzzled.

"I'm sure he'll be safe," she assured him. "Now, tell me, what is this building?"

Scarlet was looking up at a huge structure. It had stuck her as strange because it was built for a taller person, certainty not a dwarf.

"That is the oldest building in the city besides the mountain. It too is from the time of Arainieous."

Scarlet knew what he meant by that, and to save either one from embarrassment, dropped the question.

"The mountain was mined three years before Arainieous," he continued. "It was left to molder while we were all held slaves. That is why there is still Ijeslum in there today. Perhaps tomorrow I can give you a tour of the mountain and show you the beam of the tree in the sky in it."

They walked through the entire city.

Scarlet felt strange to be treated like royalty again. When a dwarf saw them, he would always bow with his beard touching the ground.

"How is the king planning on freeing his people?" she finally asked. "And from whom? Are there human villages around?"

"Villages? No. Entire kingdoms of them? Yes," he spat the words out of his mouth like they had a foul taste. "We lay raids on them from time to time and free our people one by one. I know you are not related, but those humans are troublesome creatures. Don't feel insulted."

"No insult taken," she assured him. "I can understand what you mean."

"Really?" he asked, his face looking hopeful. "You really are a princess. A princess not only in deed, but in word and action."

Scarlet looked away and felt guilty. "I left my country in the charge of enemies," she explained. "I'm sorry about it though."

The dwarf was startled. "Does being sorry really take away any of the hardships for them?" he asked, shocked. "You abandoned them?"

Scarlet nodded, aware she had just lost his admiration.

They turned to go back to the mountain. Tension split the air between them, but the dwarf began talking again, almost to himself.

"I know the hardships of living under a foreign ruler and not knowing when my king will come back for me. I know the agony of realizing that this pain will be mine for the rest of my life. I know ..."

They reached the castle and Scarlet found her way to her curtained-off section of the hall after quietly thanking the dwarf for the tour. She quickly changed from her brown dress to the red silk one from the day in the woods, but she tried not to think about that.

She buckled her sword and dagger around her waist in the custom of the western banquets and she pulled out the necklace with the ring on it.

"Everyone already knows that I am a princess. There's no need to hide it," she reasoned.

She found her way to the banquet hall and stopped short as she was greeted by King Herhem, brother of Lord Grurhoum.

"Princess, it is so nice to see you. Grurhoum has been telling me all about you and your quest. I'm having a map made for you right now."

Scarlet bowed, suddenly feeling unworthy of the title princess. If her guide was right, was she a true princess?

"What? No crown?" he asked, suddenly noticing his royal guest had no marking of royalty besides the ring on the chain.

"Your Majesty, I had not time to steal my crown before I left from home. It was not a priority."

"It's alright," the king told her. "But why do you come armed to a banquet of peace?"

"In my country, it is tradition to wear one's arms to the banquet. It can be used to defend the king if something wrong happens, and it can be used to fight friendly duels," she explained.

"You duel?" he asked, curious.

"Yes, Your Majesty. I wasn't planning on any fighting."

"Doesn't matter. You honor us by following your own traditions and giving us a simple taste of your country. And we dwarfs do fight friendly duels at banquets, perhaps you will win one?"

"Perhaps," she bowed.

"What's the name of your sword?" he asked.

"Stormcaller," she replied, the name itself bringing back memories.

"How did you get it?" he asked. Scarlet explained about getting the ship over to the east.

"Though a little dark, it's a fitting name for it," the king replied. "As the waves called you to us during the storm."

"Thank you," Scarlet told him.

"But it suits you." The king offered her his arm and they turned to enter the hall.

It happened just like the time she had entered the hall on her father's arm, Konrad's arm too. Every dwarf rose and bowed as she was led to the seat of honor.

The memories overpowered her for a moment before King Herhem brought her back to reality.

"Perhaps you will tell us a story later on?" the king asked when they had been seated. "One that we would never have heard?"

"Oh yes," Scarlet cried, filing away the memories for another time. "I would even sing a ballad, but I would have to translate it and it would never work out translated."

The king gave a creaky laugh, "Right."

The banquet began in earnest as everyone began to fill their plates and eat. Scarlet was overpowered by the number and variety of dishes to pick from. Each very different from the ones she was used to.

"*Mina hala*!" someone finally called out. "My friends! *Mina loyta*! My children! It is time for stories!"

That seemed to be the cue for everyone to push back their chairs and give a satisfying sigh.

"Tonight! For your entertainment, Princess Scarlet will tell us a story from the west," the king announced.

The room instantly grew quiet in expectation, no one wanted to miss the new story (not that the traditional ones were boring or old).

Scarlet, not knowing the traditions of the people, decided to follow her own.

"My friends, salutations," she began, still sitting down in the fashion of her people. "I will tell you the story of the rock constellation to the west."

Scarlet stood up and walked to the back of the room. "I will tell this story in three parts as if I were the main character, moving forward each time a section is complete. It is according to the traditions of my people. Forgive me if I insult you in any way by this story." The king smiled.

"It began on a clear summer night with all the stars and constellations in their proper places. It was the Festival of the First Moon of summer.

"Section one, I, Laqip, the priest of the moon was sitting on a rock, waiting for the summer prophecy to come to me. I waited for hours, but I knew the prophecy could not be rushed. It would come to me when it wanted to. But I waited for days, fasting and refusing to drink according to the requirements of the ritual. I had been priest for three years now and I knew it was time for me to resign and that the prophecy would most likely point to the next priest."

Scarlet moved to the middle of the room, "Section two, but then suddenly the rock I was sitting on spoke. It spoke about the fine day and why it had always liked the Festival of the Moon. I asked it why and it told me that every priest of the moon had sat on this rock, waiting for the prophecy. 'It was rather nice to hear all about the outside world every now and then,' it explained. *Perhaps one day I will give the prophecy myself*, it thought wistfully. Finally the prophesy came to me and I left the rock so I could tell the country."

Scarlet moved forward to the front of the room, "Section three, strangely enough I stayed the priest for years afterwards. Even through the war and the restoration afterward I was priest. The country was in a mess and the sanctuary to the moon was desecrated. No one remembered the Festival of the Moon that year except me. I went to the rock and sat down to wait. There was no need for me to forcefully fast that year—everyone was fasting whether they wanted to or not. The rock spoke with me again that year but this time it said: 'Go, make me the cornerstone of the sanctuary. When that is done everything will run smoothly.' 'But what about the prophecy?' I asked. 'That is the prophecy,' the rock told me. 'I have given the prophecy that I have always wanted to give, and now you will move me to the middle of the civilization.'

"And that is the end of my story. I moved the rock to the cornerstone of the sanctuary and I rebuilt it by myself. The country prospered and the rock got to be in the middle of the community, as it had wanted. When it wasted away, it was moved up to the sky to live forever in the memories of my people."

The room went silent as Scarlet bowed and went back to her chair.

Have I done something wrong? she thought. *Should I have asked what the dwarfs customs were before I presented it like that?*

The room was silent.

The king stood up, turned to Scarlet and gave her a bow, "You have pleased the people. It is our tradition to make noise for a story we dislike, and have a moment of silence to reflect on the words good story tellers have shared."

Murmurs began to run around the room like wildfire. "It was only a little story," she told them.

Two more stories were told and each of them were met with medium noise. Then the king summoned Grurhoum from out of the crowd, shifting the focus of the evening.

"Grurhoum Greatbrow, will you be my champion in the duels?" the king asked, loud enough for everyone in the room to hear.

"Yes Your Majesty, gladly."

Scarlet was curious, but wisely kept silent. She was sure to find out at some point.

Grurhoum stood at the front of the room while the king explained what was going on.

"I have appointed Grurhoum as my champion of duels," he announced. "Anyone who wishes to fight him may try. Anyone who beats him will be my new champion, and anyone who wants to fight my new champion may. This will continue until there is no one else in the room who would like to try. Then I will award my final champion and the banquet will be over."

Two people lined up to fight Grurhoum.

"Begin!" the king cried.

Grurhoum fought well, invigorated at finally being home again, and soon both opponents were limping back to their seats.

Scarlet was beginning to like the plucky dwarf even more.

"No one else?" the king asked in surprise. "Perhaps Princess Scarlet would like to try?"

"If your majesty wishes," she replied standing up with excitement. "But I don't think it entirely fair."

"Have my attendants tie one hand behind your back, while you will still have your height, you will be severely unbalanced." Scarlet consented. In another minute she was facing Grurhoum.

The battle lasted only a few minutes, but Grurhoum knew from the beginning he was outmatched. Though he could make quick and agile moves, Scarlet seemed to know too many ways to attack and defend.

"All hail Princess Scarlet! The king's champion!" the people cried when it was over.

"You fought well," Scarlet told Grurhoum giving him a hand back up. "I just didn't have enough of a handicap."

"Say nothing of it," Grurhoum told her. "Now it is time for me to give you something." Grurhoum went to his seat and brought back a small bundle. "Open it," he told her.

Scarlet untied the thick twine around it and then unfolded a pale golden chain mail shirt.

"It's beautiful!" she cried, holding it up to herself and admiring the fact that it went all the way down to her knees. "It's light and just thin enough to wear!"

"It's made out of Ijeslum, the hardest, lightest and most valuable metal in the mountain," Grurhoum told her with pride. "I made it myself,"

Scarlet thanked him again slipped it on over her head. The rustle gave her a feeling of authority and power at the same time.

The crowd murmured. They could more than appreciate the work of art that had been given to her.

"Perfect, if I do say so myself," Grurhoum told her. "A stunning work of art."

She thanked him and the king again before Herhem called the banquet to a close.

"Goodbye Grurhoum," she said as she caught him outside the banquet hall when it was all over. "The king will give me the map I need in the morning and then I'm off."

"So soon?" he asked sadly.

"I'm afraid so. I need to go follow my dream," she smiled at those words. "I'll never get anywhere if I just stay put."

"Right," he gave her his hand and she shook it. "I wish you could have stayed longer and seen more of our country, but one cannot always have what one wants. It was nice to know you."

"It was nice you know you, too," she replied. It bothered her that he was speaking as if she were already gone. "Perhaps someday I will come back to help you."

"Perhaps."

The next morning she set out early with her horse and headed south and east to visit some human villages in the Bucan Dynasty, bypassing the kingdom of Davia. She was selfishly hoping she could get a night's rest in a real full sized bed.

And something warm to drink, she thought. *It's not cold out but it would lift my spirits immensely.*

She traveled through small human villages all day, but rode in silence and never said a word. She had changed out of her red dress and into the brown, but she still wore the chain mail. She had tucked the ring back under her dress. These were humans—if they saw the ring, bad things could happen. Her sword and dagger were still girt around her waist and her bow and arrows were strapped to her back. Her knapsack was strapped to her horse so her back wouldn't be as encumbered.

The villages and cottages that she passed seemed to be desolated. *From the dwarfs no doubt*, she thought sadly. *I do believe in their cause, but doing it like this should be wrong. These people are too poor to own slaves. Why bother with them?*

As she progressed through the miles, the villages became alive. By the time night was gathering, she had found an inn to stay the night at. "The Doams Star," she read, wondering if there was some mythology behind the name.

She gave her horse to the stable boy and entered. "A room for one," she announced.

"Coming right up," a young woman told her as she juggled to keep three plates upright. "And dinner?"

"Yes please," she answered sitting down at a table.

The night passed like any other night. The next day she rode south and west and spent the night under the stars. This time there were no comforting stories about the elves and dwarfs.

The countryside was flat and green. It was almost summer at this point. Forests every now and then would sprout off to her left or right, but it wasn't until the next day that it became one long forest.

It's a wandering life, she thought to herself. *Just me, the trees, and the wind.*

The day after that she passed a cottage. It was burnt to the ground. It gave Scarlet the chills. Did she really want to take on a beast that could do that to someone's home?

She brushed those thoughts aside and focused on the mission at hand. It was night, and if she rode till midnight, she could get to the elves, or she could just wait until morning and get there at lunch.

When she found herself nearly nodding off, she stopped for the night.

I wonder, she thought. *The moon is nearly full now but it no longer beckons me. It no longer pleads for me to come back, to overthrow Konrad's father.*

She fell asleep remembering the stories Crovprix and Grurhoum had told her. About how the dwarfs go up to be the stars, and how the stars come down to meet the elves.

Just think what Himdir would say to those stories, she thought as she fell asleep.

WRAPPING THINGS UP

Just as I had expected, I was woken up soon after.

"Your Majesty, Lord Telmar is back!"

Quickly I jumped up and headed out of my tent.

"Telmar! You're alive!"

"Yes. But many others aren't. And even more have been taken prisoner."

My stomach squeezed.

"We'll move our forces to the tunnel and we'll block it."

"Exactly my thoughts, we can't be too sure they won't betray us."

"I hate to leave our people out there," I quietly said. "But, more lives will be saved if we collapse it now. I feel sorry for any men who won't get back in time."

"Don't worry too much about it. Ten other men have made it back, it's not just me."

I nodded and gave him permission to collapse the tunnel.

"What's that sound?" Lord Telmar stopped, his hand in the air for silence.

I listened and heard stomping.

"They're coming!" my heart jumped and I started to run to the tunnel.

"To arms!" Telmar called out. "Defend the tunnel!!"

Men woke up and dashed out of dwellings, grasping swords in steady hands.

Telmar ran after me and mounted a horse. I untethered it for him and he dashed off before anyone could say anything. I also mounted my horse and followed him, though at a much slower pace.

Men continued to follow me as I lead them to the tunnel.

We were too late. They were already pouring through and fighting with our men.

What had I done? What was I thinking? Why didn't I close up the tunnel when I had the chance? Would they ever forgive me for making that mistake? I pushed the thoughts out of my mind and joined in the action, hoping to rectify my mistake.

The men pushed out of the tunnel and were instantly engaged by someone. Before long, almost everyone was fighting with someone else. The people streamed over the city and I sent a messenger up to the castle. Now would be the time for Marja to leave.

We fought long and hard. Several times I felt for sure it would be my last.

"Retreat!" I heard called out somewhere.

"Fight!" I screamed. "Don't be a coward!" No one heard me. They pushed away from the tunnel and ran. I mounted my horse and pressed on, but in a moment I knew it was useless. I turned the head of my horse back toward the houses and I let fly. I needed a disguise, and quick. My horse stopped outside one of the houses and I dismounted and went inside. It was empty like I expected. In the distance I heard pounding on the door to the castle.

"Oh Marja, I hope you got out on time!" I prayed. Suddenly I remembered the package she had wanted me to have. It was still on my horse. He hadn't been unsaddled since this morning.

I took the package down and unwrapped it to find a simple dress, and soft belt, and a shift.

"Marja!" I cried. "Thank you! Thank you! Thank you!" I dashed back into the house and quickly changed. I knew a lady would never wear my knee high boots, so I took them and chopped them off at the ankle, folded them down to make a soft cuff and put them back on. I checked to make sure my necklace was tucked out of sight, pulled my cloak further around and went back out to change my horse over.

The first thing I needed to do was get rid of the obviously expensive saddle. Off it came and the bridle with it. I found an old blanket in the house and carefully draped it over his sweaty frame.

I hesitated as to what to do next. If I went further into town, I would no doubt be killed, and if I took my sword with me I would be captured. But, on the other hand, if I stayed here, alone, I would probably be found with my old clothes and weapons in the house and that would be the end of me.

Quickly I decided the best option would be to go out and further up into the city.

I stood on a stump and mounted the horse again. I headed him off in the direction of the castle and prayed I wouldn't be found out.

The horse's steps echoed on the pavement and sent shivers down my back. When I got as near to the castle as I dared, I let my horse go.

No going back now, I thought to myself as I slipped into a corner.

In the distance I could hear the enemy's soldiers marching, and by the sound of it, bursting doors open.

I needed to find a house with people in it and wait till they were found. At that point I would just be one of them to the soldiers and there would be no reason to question me.

Heavy thuds began to sound up by the castle.

"A battering ram," my heart fell to my shoes and tears came to my eyes. "My home!" I whispered. "Gone! No!!"

My knees gave way underneath me and my eyes burst into tears. My shaking back leaned against the doorframe. What was I supposed to do?

Slowly my tears dried, and my heart felt empty and heavy. I stood up and without even stopping to adjust the hem of my skirt, I purposefully stomped my way up to the castle.

I dodged in and out of streets, sometimes blending in with a crowd who had gathered in fear, sometimes slipping past guards and ultimately ending up at the one bridge to the castle.

I didn't even stop to chide myself for not leaving soldiers behind to protect it. I didn't even smile when I watched as a soldier dumped boiling water on the soldiers' heads because a moment later, he was pierced by many arrows.

I hid on the outskirts of the city, watching as the enemy plowed up the hill that led up to the castle. They had already made their own bridge to cross the moat and the thudding of the battering ram battered at the door like emotions battered at the door to my heart, but I too wouldn't let them through. After an eternity that wasn't long enough, the door caved in. Soldiers poured through, some staying outside the castle to keep people from entering and exiting.

Screams and shouts could be heard coming from the castle. I shuddered, thinking of them coming across my mother and then killing her. Perhaps since she was ill they would wait a little. Perhaps they would try to get her to tell them about me. And then Mart and his father and mother, Nana? Only now did I wish they would be spared. If only because they would be my only kin left.

Dark came and I stayed at my post. I couldn't take my eyes off of the castle, the den of thieves. The thieves that stole all I had ever known. First it had been Stefan, the brave loyal soul. Then my own father. How I missed him, even now. Then Marja. Oh Marja! The sister I never had, the friend I had left, the broken-hearted lover, but not truly broken. Nothing could ever break Marja. She was as beautiful as steel, and just as cold and hard. Though her health had been fragile, they could never break her. She was an old soul. Nothing could argue with that. I loved her more than I dared tell. I loved her like a sister, I loved her like a friend, I protected her like a child but I was as loyal as an old dog.

The night passed slowly as I watched those imposing walls, filled with hatred for the people within, knowing that many deaths were happening and there was nothing I could do to stop it. As the light dawned again, a small group of soldiers entered the castle. No doubt they had prisoners from the city to take to the dungeon.

I stood up, realizing what I had to do. I must turn myself in in exchange for their freedom. Something nagged at me, whispering that they couldn't be trusted to carry it out, but my heart was empty and there was nothing for it.

My steps faltered up to the garrison of guards, in an instant I was engulfed by weapons.

"Who are you?" one asked.

I cleared my throat. A noise back in the city made all of us turn our heads and for a moment I caught a figure moving in the shadows.

She was shorter than me and I could see by her dress that she was of low birth. The soldiers, not wanting to lose me, prodded me along in their investigation. Just outside the city we caught up with the little phantom.

"Who are you?" the soldier asked the newcomer.

The girl kept her eyes on the ground and said nothing.

"Answer me you cur!"

"Sir," she began, I knew her voice in an instant. "I'm only a servant at the butcher's. I was on my way back to him."

"I know this girl," I piped up. "She is telling the truth."

The soldiers let the other girl go. As she turned to run I smiled at her.

Marja, I thought. *I should have known. You promised. I didn't have to go in there and bargain for you.*

The soldiers turned back to me and suddenly, I didn't have a plan.

"Who are you?"

"A servant," I pulled the same trick.

"What kind? Where?" the head guard seemed suspicious, and I honestly didn't blame him.

"A scullery maid in the castle," I quickly answered. "I was in town when the soldiers came through." I suddenly burst into tears, knowing that I would really need to convince them. "What happened? Where is the cook? What are you going to do with me?" I tried to sound terrified. But I didn't fear anything that they could do to me.

"The poor girl," a sympathetic soul answered. "We'll let you up to the castle. It's been completely taken over so we shouldn't have anything to worry about resistance from a poor little girl."

I inwardly cringed at those words, but I had passed. They accepted me as who I said I was.

They let me through and I went into the castle. There wasn't much for me to do. I wandered those familiar halls, knowing they wouldn't be mine ever again. Knowing they were witnesses to the horrors that had happened last night. But mostly rejoicing that Marja had gotten out alive.

It didn't take long for someone to find me and send me down to work in the kitchen.

At first, as the days passed by, my battle wounds healed slowly with the wounds I had received to the heart. I didn't want to stay at the castle. But I realized there wasn't anything else for me to do. If I left, people would wonder. If I left, I would never have the chance to be this close to the heart of my kingdom ever again.

Even though I was only a servant, nearly a slave, nothing could have taken me away from my country. I did think about running away, but really, I never actually thought I would be able to follow through with it.

And so when I found my disguise revealed, I went in search of something to replace what I had lost. Something that could take the place of family, friends and country. But nothing I found could ever truly replace what I had known.

CHAPTER TWELVE

While Scarlet gallivanted through the eastern world (ignoring her responsibilities), Konrad was having his own troubles.

"A messenger has arrived," one of the servants told him, peeking into Konrad's study. "He seems distraught. I think you should see him immediately." Konrad was leaning over a pile of papers, frowning. "Can't you see I don't have time?"

"But really, sir." he urged.

"But really," Konrad began, looking up from the papers. "Someone stole a cow and the whole village is upset, nothing could be worse."

"But sir," he paused.

"I don't have time," Konrad's voice rose.

"The messenger said that he nearly died to bring you this message," the servant finally said.

Konrad sighed and pushed the papers away from him, "How long is this going to take?"

"The moment he delivers his message, it will be done."

"Bring the fellow in," he sighed.

The servant left and was replaced with a worn out messenger.

"Oh, King!" the messenger rushed forward and knelt with his face to the floor. "Forgive me for being the bearer of such news."

"Such news as what?" Konrad asked, his curiosity finally aroused.

"Your brother, the king of Fairfalcon, has attacked. He claims Hedgecliff is his."

"He did what?" Konrad was stunned.

"Attacked. He is claiming that Hedgecliff belongs to him," the messenger repeated.

"Belongs to him?" he asked, still stunned.

"Yes, he attacked your most southern villages. Three in all."

"Three?"

"Yes. He promised he wouldn't stop there, even now his army is advancing slowly north."

"Leave," Konrad ordered, conflicting thoughts and emotions battling for his attention.

"Your Majesty?"

"Leave, I tell you! Unless you know how to stop a war in its tracks, leave!"

The messenger bowed and left the room.

Now what? Konrad thought. *If the princess were here she would know what to do. At this point she may never come back. But when she does, I must still have her country to give back to her, if she wants it or not.*

He paced the room, the piles of paper concerning the cow, forgotten. *What are my armies like? Do I even have the forces for this? Why?* He sat down in a chair with his head in his arms and didn't move until Darien, the captain of his army, knocked on the door.

"Your majesty, the messenger told me what happened," he bowed, aware of the implications.

"So what?" Konrad grumbled.

"I did some checking up on your forces."

"And?" Konrad looked up at him.

"They are ready and willing to travel with you into battle. They are willing to follow you."

Konrad stood up and paced the floor, "Really? Do they actually know what that means? Do they really want that?"

"King, they are waiting."

Konrad stopped pacing. "How long will it take to get to my brother's forces?"

"If you are riding in full armor ... two days."

"Get everything ready. I'll want my armor and my horse. If we leave before sunset today we should arrive morning after tomorrow. Run!" Konrad sprang into action with his words.

"But your majesty, perhaps it is still possible to regain peace?"

"Peace? With my brother? Impossible. He wants this land and he wants his war. Now hurry! We have only a little time!" Konrad dashed out of the room to get armor and his sword.

Konrad and his army left before the evening meal, and by the time it was dark, they were gone.

Konrad and Captain Darien spent the night planning strategies and attacks. They considered the lay of the land, even the number of soldiers they figured each side had.

They talked for hours, each hour more fruitless than the last.

"There's no way I can see Hedgecliff winning," Captain Darien exclaimed at last as he rubbed his sore head. "Even if we have overestimated the numbers of Fairfalcon, we can never win."

"But Captain Darien, my brother cannot have this country. There must be something we can do about it?" Konrad begged as his last hope fled from him

"Perhaps," Darien wavered. "I hesitate to suggest this."

"Well?" asked Konrad disgustedly as he threw down his map.

"I knew the princess well, your Majesty," he told him, avoiding eye contact. "I taught her how to fight and use a sword."

"Well?"

"She would have a plan to get us out of this fix," Captain Darien turned. "Do you know where she is?" he continued. "Did your father kill her?"

"My father did not kill her," Konrad began to lose patience. "And I do not know where she is."

"You're right," Darien admitted. "I thought that as king, you might know where she is. If only we had Lord Grissel with us." Darien looked at Konrad, but there was no reaction. "Anyway, what will your plan be?"

"I will fight," Konrad said, as he stood up with resolve.

"We will lose. Your brother has the only high ground in miles. Our soldiers cannot fight uphill. We will be pelted by rocks from above and your brother's army can advance without much difficulty. They'll also be able to see us advancing for miles around."

"I promised myself I would keep this country safe, and that is what I intend to do."

"Perhaps your brother is worthier?" Darien suggested.

"Never. He will kill anyone who gets in his way. He cannot be trusted with anything," Konrad was shocked and angry at the implication.

"Then you will fight?" Darien asked.

"Yes," Konrad answered, fierce determination etched across his face.

"We will lose."

"Perhaps. But that is for me to worry about. Your job is to follow orders. Is that all?"

Captain Darien nodded and left.

"Oh, Father," Konrad muttered. "Why did you have to break us apart like this? Why did you have to tear us asunder? I didn't need a country, and why this one? None of this would be happening if it weren't for him. This country would be safe, he might even still be alive!" Something nagged in the corner of his mind. Newle would still be here if his father hadn't taken over this country.

Elves are tall mysterious beings, each living twice as long as a dwarf. They are happy and jovial, but always seem to treat humans as if they were nothing more than a picture in the background. They welcomed Scarlet with only a little hint of surprise. They even led her to their king. He completely lost it when she asked where she could find a dragon.

"Are you out of your mind?" the king roared. "The dragons have plagued our people for centuries. And now, when we have sacrificed our blood to battle them back, you would like to wake them again?"

"Your Majesty," Scarlet told him with a bow as she realized there would be at least another roadblock before she reached her dream. "All I want to do is see one. Nothing more, but certainly nothing less."

"Seeing is equal with death," he replied. "I cannot let you go. It is out of the question. If you insist on going to see them I will personally lock you up."

"Your Majesty, if I just told them I came from the west they wouldn't even think of you," Scarlet insisted, her dream falling apart around her ears. "I came to the east for adventure, I came to see the dwarfs. I came to see the elves. But most importantly, I came to see the dragons and have my dream fulfilled."

"Well I cannot let you see them," the king insisted. "I won't even have you stay in the castle with a vision like that. Be gone!"

Scarlet turned red with anger. She wasn't about to let it go so easily, but she knew better than to cross blades with a king. So she left.

Scarlet looked around after she left the throne room, no one was there.

"The insolence," she whispered. "I know he's king, but he's not my king! He can't order me around like that!"

"Lady Scarlet?" someone carefully accosted her.

Scarlet huffed, ignoring the greeting. "I am a princess. He could just wash his hands of me. Royalty should treat other royalty like royalty."

"Lady Scarlet?" the greeting came again.

"Yes?" Scarlet turned angrily to see the speaker.

It was a tall elf. Her golden hair and sparkling eyes fetchingly contrasted with her gray gown.

"To begin with, I'm Elincia."

Scarlet didn't feel like introducing herself, besides, the elf already knew her name.

"I heard what the king said and I agree with him," she began.

"Well if you agree with him, then go away," Scarlet verbally pushed her off to the side.

"I also heard that you are not allowed to stay in the castle," Elincia tried again.

"Good news travels fast," Scarlet muttered, taking long strides to get out of the castle as Elincia tried to keep up.

"I was only going to propose that you could stay with me," Elincia suggested. "My family would be honored to have the princess from the west stay with us."

"Well ..." Scarlet hesitated, why was Elincia trying to be friendly? "I suppose I could stay a little while. Until I convince the king to let me see the dragons."

Elincia smiled, "You'll never convince him to let you see them. But come, follow me."

Scarlet was led through the castle and out into the street where Elincia stopped to wait for a carriage.

"So, I heard you are only fifteen?" Elincia asked. She didn't even try to mask her curiosity.

"Sixteen, since the incident with captain Wycliffe Gloom."

"Wycliffe Gloom?" Elincia asked. "Who's that?"

Scarlet explained about the old sea captain."Kinda a friend of mine," she told Elincia.

"I'm nearly a hundred and I've never heard such a story in my entire life," Elincia explained. "Why did you leave your country? From what you've told me, it sounds like a nice place."

"I hate it," Scarlet spat out.

"Why?" Elincia asked.

Scarlet didn't want to bring those memories up, but they resurfaced without her permission. "My country was enslaved by Fairfalcon," she explained. Maybe it wouldn't be too hard to confide in the elf she hardly knew. "Fairfalcon is a country to the south of us. The king is the murdering tyrant who killed my father, mother and many other people. I led the last attacks on them, leaving heavy damage during the battle, but we still lost. I was disguised as a servant when the prince uncovered my disguise and I had to flee for my life. Then I met Wycliffe Gloom and got a trip over to the east. When I got here I met a dwarf and a wizard. They took me to the dwarfs' mountain and I took the rest of the way here by myself."

Scarlet stood, finished. She hadn't wanted to say all that, it just came out. It almost felt good to get it off her chest.

"An interesting story," Elincia exclaimed as her carriage drove up. "Some day you will write it in a book?"

"Perhaps, but the book won't be complete without a chapter about meeting a dragon," Scarlet explained.

They entered the carriage and sat back.

"Well, after all that adventure I'm sure my house will seem tame," Elincia told Scarlet.

"Not at all. Sometimes it's nice to have good cooking and a warm bed."

"I'm glad. But you still haven't really told me why you left your country. You fled for your life, but you could have roused up the villagers! From what you've told me, they would follow you!"

"Follow me? Never." Maybe it didn't feel good to get it off her chest.

"But why did you abandon them?"

"I didn't abandon them," Scarlet told her stubbornly. She looked out the window and hoped that Elincia wouldn't pursue the topic. What was it with people preaching at her because she left her country?

"You left them in the power of the tyrant king. That is abandoning them."

Scarlet continued to look out the window, not really listening.

"I'll take a hint," Elincia laughed. "But I still think you're wrong."

"Look at all the trees, how they grow close together and how your houses just blend right in," Scarlet began, really in awe now.

"They are pretty," Elincia admitted as she sat back. "But I never thought about it. Do trees grow in the west?"

"Yes they do. But we also have places where there is just grass and you can see for miles around," Scarlet explained.

"What does it feel like?" Elincia asked.

"Like you're the smallest thing in the world," Scarlet closed her eyes, remembering rides with her father and long walks through the silent emptiness.

"I would hate to live in a place like that," Elincia decided. "I like how the trees grow till they nearly become a part of the village."

"To every man, his home is the best," Scarlet seemed to murmur while daydreaming.

Well, Elincia thought. *I see more than I let on. She really does love her country and is longing to go back. If only something would give her that little push.* She sighed, certain this free-loving creature would never find that little push.

The carriage stopped outside a large house with a tree growing out of the middle, overshadowing the rest of it.

"Picturesque," Scarlet commented.

"Right."

Scarlet took a good look around before entering the house. She was taking notes in case she needed to leave it by the cover of darkness. *Perhaps I could leave at night and see the dragons without letting the elves know.*

They entered the house and Elincia immediately took over.

"Now dear, you just sit down there. I'll take your things and have the maid send them up to a room. I've already sent a stable boy for your horse and I'll have dinner on the table in an heartbeat."

Scarlet sat down and relaxed. *It doesn't look too bad in here, a little too green but not bad.*

She closed her eyes and felt her tense muscles relax. She was comfortable for the first time in days. Not since leaving the castle as Newle had she felt this warm, cozy and tired.

"Wake up!" Scarlet's eyes fluttered open. "It's dinner time! Come on."

Elincia was standing over her and frowning.

"Give me a moment," Scarlet asked while she stretched. "How long have I been napping?"

"An hour. I only just got dinner ready," Elincia admitted.

They walked to the table where an older elf and a child were sitting.

"Theodre? This is the Princess Scarlet. Scarlet? My husband Theodre and my son Elmir."

Elincia motioned Scarlet to a seat and they began eating.

"I heard that you want to see the dragons?" Theodre asked.

"Yes, but the king says I can't," maybe Theodre could tell her where the dragons are?

"He has reasons," Theodre nonchalantly replied.

"But are they good reasons?" Scarlet asked setting down her spoon. "The dragons will never see me, if they do I'll just tell them that I'm from the west. They would never attack you because of someone from the west! I have been waiting years to follow my dream, and now, when I'm so close, I have been turned aside by a king who will not see sense. I have my dream and I want to follow it!"

Elincia stopped eating, Scarlet had touched something in her heart. She could remember being a young girl with dreams and visions of her own. When was the last time she had dreamed of reaching the dwarven mountain? When was the last time she had dreamed of seeing the sea, even crossing it? "You raise a good point," she said at last.

"A good point?" Theodre cried setting down his fork. "It's pure folly!"

Elincia shook her head and continued eating.

"The king is right to not allow you to see the dragons," Theodre continued, "Besides the fact they are out on an island and we have no boats to reach them, your going would be folly."

Scarlet secretly grinned as Theodre went back to eating.

Island, eh? Shouldn't be too hard, she thought picking up her spoon again.

They finished dinner and Elincia led Scarlet up to her room.

"I set it up for you," Elincia told her.

She glanced around the room, never resting on a certain object, her eyes nervously scanning.

"Your things are there," she turned as if to leave but stopped, still remembering her own dreams. What did it matter if there was some danger involved? There was danger in everything!

"I ..." she hesitated, Scarlet look up expectantly. "We never lock the doors at night. Just in case." Elincia ran down the stairs, leaving Scarlet, puzzled.

Lock the door? What does she mean? Then it hit her. Scarlet packed up her things and sat on the edge of her bed till she was sure everyone was asleep. Then she grabbed her bag and tiptoed down the stairs and out the door. She circled around back to where she was sure the stables were, found her horse, mounted it and galloped off.

I'm off, she thought as she galloped away, her heart racing.

She headed south, toward the sea, thinking she could follow the coast until she found the island. Then her horse Tide could probably swim it.

"You can do it, old boy," she whispered encouragement. "I've known you long enough to know you're strong enough."

They rode the rest of the night and just as the sun was rising, they reached the sea. It was beautiful. Just like the last time she had seen it. Except this time the longing to follow it was stronger and harder to resist, though it would bring her home. The blue and green waves crashed against the gray stones that slowly faded to green grass the further inland you got.

She saw the blue sky and the bright, hot sun again. The trees in the elven kingdom had shaded and twisted the light without her even noticing it.

Scarlet stopped only a moment for breakfast and then decided to head west, hoping to see the island from the land.

At mid-morning she found a burnt village.

We're getting closer, she thought, moving her horse closer to the water's edge and straining her eyes, looking across the water forcing herself to look at the glaring blaze.

"Not quite," she muttered to herself as she continued heading west.

CHAPTER THIRTEEN

Konrad woke up the next morning, armed himself with his sword and struck camp.

They rode till lunch. Upon which they set up camp just outside Konrad's brother's forces.

"I'll take three guards and have a conference with my brother," he told captain Darien. "Perhaps you are right. I might be going into this too quickly. I will confer with my brother and hope he will reconsider before we have to openly declare war."

"Your Majesty, I will go with you," Darien offered.

"No, I need you to set up camp over there and direct the troops. I'll take volunteers for my guards."

Three men offered and they set out to the enemy's camp.

The camp was dirty and foul. The soldiers were languidly sitting around campfires, smoking and telling jokes. An air of war hung over it as in the background you could hear swords being sharpened and smiths fixing chainmail.

"We hail you in peace!" Konrad cried when he came within hearing distance.

"Who are you and why have you come?" one of the enemy soldiers called out, barely turning his head to look at his visitors.

"I am King Konrad of Hedgecliff and I wish to speak to my brother," he shouted out.

"You? King Konrad?" now the man was paying attention, though it looked like he didn't believe him.

Warriors from other parts of the camp, aroused by the commotion, meandered their way to Konrad.

"Yes, and I wish to speak to my brother," Konrad insisted. The men were making him wary.

"I'll see what I can do," the soldier walked away from the campfire and strolled up to one of the biggest, heaviest guarded tents in the camp. He spoke to one of the guards and then went in. In another moment he was out again.

"His Majesty says there is nothing to speak of. He wishes you to leave."

"But I must speak to him. He's my brother!" Konrad cried out, as his last hope fled.

The soldier grinned, leaned against a post and began to pick his teeth. "His Majesty says if you don't leave, we have full right to tie you up to this post here and leave you for dead. So scram!"

Konrad lifted his head in anger and indignation. "Right, tell my brother I am not responsible for the blood that will be shed because we have not talked over this."

He nodded to his guards and they left the camp.

"I take it your brother didn't want to negotiate?" Captain Darien observed when Konrad came back to camp.

"Yes, we will fight tomorrow," Konrad told him as he unfolded his chainmail.

"We can't possibly be ready by that time!" Darien exclaimed. "Our forces are in shambles that need to be put in order."

"Then do it tonight. Stay up all night if you have to, but I will fight tomorrow!"

"This is folly!" the captain cried, in full earnest.

"Is it any more folly than letting him take over our country, inch by inch?"

Darien bowed and left without answering.

"I take that as a no." Konrad smiled to himself as he slipped his chain mail over his head.

Scarlet saw the island at high noon. It glistened in the hot sun as she led her horse into the waves to swim to the island.

The horse fought the waves out, but before long he was smoothly growing closer and closer to the island.

"Come on," she whispered encouragement. "We're nearly there and then you can take a nice long rest while I look at the dragons."

In another moment the horse's hoofs hit the dry, sandy ground and he slowly walked up the beach onto dry ground, the wet sand sucking his legs back into the water as if reluctant to give him up.

The island was full of trees—some burnt, some not.

I'm certainly getting closer, she thought as she tied up her horse to one of the trees that hadn't been burnt down.

Her heart jumped at every sound and her heart soared knowing she was so close to what she had been dreaming about for months.

I'll just walk toward the heart of the island. It shouldn't take long to explore this place.

She slowly walked deeper into the heart of the trees, pushing back draping vines with her bare hands.

The place was overgrown with a mixture of green and burnt foliage. She would walk through a picturesque part, only to find there would be a huge burnt patch over the hill.

She closed in on the heart of the island and there came more burnt parts and the quiet grew stifling.

Where are the birds? she thought as her heart quickened. *Did the dragons eat them all? Why are there no animals?*

She felt an oppressive feeling come over her as she pushed further in. Maybe she should go back? But something kept drawing her closer and closer to the heart of the island.

She came across a small cliff and she lowered herself down by climbing on small patches of burnt grass and small, leafless trees. At the bottom of the cliff she found a small pond and a cave in the cliff. There wasn't a single green thing in the entire valley and there was a pile of bones outside the cave.

This is it, she thought as she noiselessly slid behind a rock so she could see inside the cave without being seen. *There's nothing in there. Perhaps I could just slide in a moment and see what it's like before the dragons come back.* She slid around to the front of the cave and crept inside. The floor was strewn with bones and clinking gold and silver. Scarlet picked up a shield and held it to the light that came from the opening of the cave.

It's perfect. Probably made by the elves, she slipped it into her arm and made her way toward the back of the cave. *It's enormous in here*, she thought as she turned around and looked back at the entrance to the cave. *I can still see the front though.*

She turned back to look at the treasure, but suddenly the entrance was blocked. Scarlet panicked and cried out as she fled further into the cave, tumbling over bones and gold and making a ruckus.

Scarlet tripped and lay panting on the floor, curled up and crying, as the overpowering silence of the cavern pressed against her.

Then, a slow rumbling voice came from the front of the cave. "Who has entered my domain? Kill you I shall. Feed on your flesh, if it is good. I will come after you, or you will come forth."

Her heart stopped when she heard the voice and her face turned to fear. She didn't want that dragon to come in after her, and yet she couldn't see to come to it.

The pause that filled the cave was quiet and terrible. The dark pressed Scarlet from every side and threatened to swallow her.

"Right, then," came the voice. "I'll come to you."

Scarlet scurried and pressed herself against the wall as she heard the dragon slowly making its way to her hiding place.

The slow, plodding steps of the dragon filled her with a dread she had never known before. The ever-approaching doom that stomped its way to the back of the cave took away the breath from her.

I never wanted the dragon to see me, she thought. *And even when I told the king about my plan to say I was from the west, even that was only in jest.* She quivered closer to the wall. *Funny how I could face thousands of soldiers from Fairfalcon without flinching, and yet a single dragon makes my heart melt.*

The dragon stomped to a halt right in front of her.

"Allow me to throw some light on the situation," a voice came as an overpowering heat flooded the room. Scarlet flinched, and when she opened her eyes, she found that the cave was no longer dark.

She examined the dragon. Now that she wasn't guessing in the dark, she was only a little less afraid.

The dragon looked exactly as she had thought he would, and this only added to her fear. His tall, green neck stretched up and then bent under the ceiling, his long talons dragged on the floor when he walked, sharp spikes covered his entire back and his huge wings were folded up, but still got in the way of the ugly creature. He was about the size of five horses.

"Pitiful human, you!" the dragon cried. "Match you are not for me!" the dragon blew green smoke at her and she ducked under her shield for cover.

The dragon instantly recognized it.

"Already helped yourself to my things?! How dare you!" The dragon grew visibly angrier.

The dragon slashed out at her with his long neck and without thinking, Scarlet defended herself with a blow from her sword.

The dragon roared as it reared itself up to its full height, indignant at the injury.

Scarlet, without thinking of anything but defense, drove her sword between two spikes and the dragon cried out again.

"No! It cannot end like this!" the dragon slapped its spiky tail full against her and she fell, knocked over.

"Shows you, does it not?" the dragon cried as it blew smoke at her again.

Scarlet feebly dragged herself up again, bruised and sore—her pride hurt more than her body.

"I will show you!" she cried stabbing the dragon as much as she could, blinded by her injured pride.

The dragon roared in pain. "You kill! You burn! You hate!!" his words hit her with more force than he could imagine.

He staggered back, knocking over all the torches, and stumbled toward the entrance to the cave. But he never made it.

Scarlet stood where she was. She didn't even think. The darkness pressed all around her again and seemed to accuse her.

"I killed it," she thought without feeling, its words still echoing in her head. "The beautiful creature, I killed it."

She touched the wet blade of her sword and recoiled from the acidic blood.

The darkness pulsed through her and made her feel sick. It pressed around her and accused her silently. Each moment more silent than the last.

"I killed him!" she cried out at last as she leaned against the wall. "I kill him in the name of the western countries! I kill him in the name of Hedgecliff! I kill him in the name of Fairfalcon!" The darkness was silent and Scarlet felt a strange urge to leave. "I killed him!" she repeated, almost unbelieving it.

Scarlet felt the darkness pressing around her and she gathered up her things. *I've got to get out of here*, she thought, but before she could make any steps to leave, something stopped her in her tracks.

From the back of the cave, not the front, she heard something slowly creeping forward.

"You have killed him?" came a slow smooth voice filled with hatred. "You have killed him!" Scarlet stood transfixed with fear as the steps grew faster and closer.

"I will have revenge on you! But I will have revenge on your people first!" The steps fell even faster and heavier as a second dragon stalked towards her in the dark. "I will find these westerners and they will pay for your crime!"

The dragon blew fire and smoke into the cave as she rushed out and unfolded her wings.

Scarlet, driven by the heat and smoke, coughed and tripped over the body of the first dragon as she ran out of the cave. Dazzled by the radiant sun, she stumbled back.

"I see you now, puny human! Your people will pay!" the dragon rushed up to the sky and then vanished, heading west.

Scarlet didn't even think—her people were going to die, Marja was going to die and it was all her fault. "Now what have I done?" she cried as she gazed up at the sky. "Why couldn't I have listened to the elves? Why couldn't I have listened to Grurhoum? Why can't I just listen and take people's advice?"

Suddenly, all the little things added up. She was ready to go home, she was ready to save her people.

She fell to her knees and bowed her head. "What have I done?"

Tears fell down her face, making dark spots on the red dress she hadn't bothered to change since the banquet at the dwarfs. Besides, what did it matter? She was never going back. Or was she?

Scarlet had once made a choice with her mind, blocking her heart to the cries of her people as she rushed to abandon them, now her heart fought to go back. Scarlet dried her tears as her face hardened and her heart made up her mind this time, once and for all.

I will go to them, I will save them or I will die with them, she decided as she emptied out her pack of her extra dress, her cape and the bow and arrows. *I'll travel light and make it back to the sea village before tomorrow. I'll take the first boat, I'll steal it if I have to,* she unwillingly took the dagger off her belt and set it besides the rest. *It will take the dragon a week to cross the sea and it will take me a month in good weather.* She reluctantly laid the nearly empty pack on the ground next to most of her money. It would be too heavy to take if she was going to travel light, but she would need money to pay for the trip. "I don't need that, I won't even need food. I'll only take my chain mail, it's light, and my sword."

She ran back through the woods and quickly mounted her horse.

"Come on," she whispered to him. "We'll ride all night!"

She charged the horse back into the waves but this time he could ride the waves in and they only had trouble near the end. With their feet back on solid ground, she pointed the horse to the northwest and gave him full head.

We can make it! she thought.

The sun went slowly down, tinting the woods a golden orange, but they still galloped on all night. Nothing could stop her.

Konrad woke the next morning with determination. He knew at the end of that day, he could (and most likely would) be dead.

"King?" Captain Darien greeted him. "Everything is ready. Your brother's lines are already forming. Your commands?"

"We will array ourselves the way we spoke of before. Perhaps we will last longer than you think." The captain bowed and left. Konrad stretched and pulled his helmet on. He had slept in his chainmail and his sword was already strapped into place.

He left his tent and mounted his horse with courage. They could still win this.

"Come on, men!" he called out to his ranks. "Today we fight!" the men roared. "We fight to keep our homes and families safe. We fight and die so others can live. Do not lose sight of that or you will find yourselves stumbling and growing weary before our work is done. If we work together, we will win! Have you nothing to fight for? We have a country! Is that not enough?!" The people cheered and Konrad calmed down. "We can stand side by side and win today. Though my brother's forces are vast, they fight because they are told to. We fight because we have something to gain—freedom. Are you with me?! Will we fight?!"

The ranks shouted and bashed their swords against their shields.

"Fight, fight, fight, fight, fight!" the ranks chanted. "We will fight! We will fight! We will fight! We will fight!" They shouted and bashed their swords against their shields.

Konrad turned the head of his horse to face his brother's army.

"Your Majesty?" came a panting voice. "I ran all the way from of the back of the ranks,"

"Yes?" Konrad asked, his voice turning angry at the disruption.

"I'm one of the messengers you brought. I just wanted to tell you Captain Darien delivered the message you sent. I just thought you would want to know."

"A message?" Konrad asked, his attention was grabbed.

"The message you sent to your brother. I saw him going to your brother's camp," the messenger paused. "You did send that message, right?"

Konrad's mind worked. He knew he hadn't sent any message to his brother, and he knew he certainty hadn't sent any by Darien. Quickly he decided that the last thing he should do is let the messenger know.

"That's alright," he began. "It was late last night. I must have forgotten. Thank you."

The messenger bowed and returned back to his place in the lines.

Darien went to my brother's camp right after we decided that we would fight today. Konrad's heart sank and his breath quickened. *It's suicide*, he thought. *They know our plans now. I'm leading these people to their deaths.* Konrad's heart tore within him. Continue and lead everyone to their deaths? Or call it off and look like he was cowardly and would not fight a battle he knew he would lose?

"We fight." he whispered as he tightened his scabbard around his waist and rearranged his tunic. If he was going to die today, he was going to do it with honor.

The sun was already high in the sky as he gave another glance back at his troops. Captain Darien had already left with the other half of his troops to surround the opposing army. Konrad knew they would never show up. Konrad felt betrayed. Could he trust anyone? Was there anything to do but surrender?

I'll take what troops I have, he reasoned. *We will take them down with us.* He raised his sword and called out the battle cry. Horns and trumpets picked up on his cry and slowly, the lines moved forward.

Faster and faster, beating like the heroic hearts in the breasts of the soldiers, they advanced. Each foot soldier and seasoned warrior, oblivious to the betrayal and the doom close at hand, advanced.

I can't do this, he thought as they closed in on the forces of Fairfalcon. *Not even for the kingdom.*

He knew it was too late. The two armies, one huge force on high ground, and one small one, pitifully unprotected from the rain of arrows that fell from the huge force. Each step they took was a victory. Each volley of arrows drastically diminishing their numbers.

"Charge!!" Konrad cried above the noise of death. "Get to the top!! Make a stand for it!!!!!"

People say death is a silent phantom. Stealing in and out at night, barely noticed at the time, but the void sorely felt with a passive ache. Konrad knew death was a roaring lion that eats its prey just as it eats out the hearts of the people close to the deceased. Ravenous and immoral, leaving people devastated.

Konrad's forces, encouraged by the call, rallied and pushed forward. Each step another man falling, each step crushing the bones of a fellow man who had fallen before.

Konrad's brother's forces held back, waiting until they were within only ten yards before the dam broke loose.

"For Hedgecliff and the free!!"

The two lines clashed. Konrad and his last few forces were quickly swallowed up.

The cry was picked up by Fairfalcon's army, "Down with Hedgecliff and the free!!"

The last of Konrad's forces were quickly thrown down. Konrad himself stood to the last. Each stand that his army made was a stand for freedom. Each stand they made slowly fell until all had been captured.

The next day Konrad was called into the presence of the king. Darien and a man of about seventy years old with a long haggard face and a crooked nose—Lord Grissel—were there.

"Little brother," his brother, the king spoke, in a teasing voice. "I never knew you could put up a fight like that! But now it's over, your country, *my* country shall be united under my flag."

"They will never follow you," Konrad told him, looking up in his brother's eyes and remembering everything they had been through together.

"Never? You jest! They have already invited me to the castle."

"You bullied them!" Konrad accused. Darien and Grissel shook their heads and grinned.

"Bully? Me?" the king asked in mock surprise. "I would never do that.

Now, what to do about you." The king walked toward a table and sat down in a chair. "I can't just have you wasting away, can I?"

With Konrad's head held high he glared at his brother, but his lips were sealed, pressed into a thin line.

"I see, little brother. I am above that. You do not see me acting arrogant like that. You can lose the high and mighty act on me. It won't make anything better," he called some guards in. "Take away Captain Darien and Lord Grissel and kill them. I don't care how you do it. I give in to your better judgment. I want the boy for myself."

In the back, Darien and Grissel looked up in surprise as the guards closed in around them. "But Your Majesty!" Konrad shuddered, remembering how many times those two had called him that.

"What?" Daedor, the king, asked in mock surprise.

"You promised me I would have a lordship! You promised to let me go free!" Darien struggled against the guards as they dragged him away. Grissel gave into the guards, almost as though he had been expecting things to turn out that way.

"I can't have two traitors in my employ. Can I?" Konrad's brother, Daedor, laughed a shivering, deadly laugh and then turned to his brother. "I'm sorry to have done that to you, but you did have me a little worried. With only half of your forces, you didn't prove much of a threat. But truly, I can't let it get out that I bribed a man to do that."

Konrad watched, bewildered as Captain Darien was dragged away and he was left alone with his brother.

They stared at each other, the guards now gone, the older brother looking down on his younger.

"Why are you doing this?" Konrad finally broke the silence.

The older began, his voice filling with hatred, "Our father conquered a country for you, but all I get is dismissed from his presence! I am the elder. This country, everything, belongs to me! You deserve to suffer. None of this belongs to you! You deserve to burn and cry out in pain. You deserve to have your pitiful eyes fill with tears as you see everything you love die. I want to see you ..."

"Enough!" Konrad interrupted. "You are weak! You kill without a thought! You are cruel and you hurt people for the fun of it! Is that what a king does? Is that what our father taught you?"

"Do not speak to me of our father!!" Konrad's brother cried, standing up. "He loved you! He conquered a land for you but wouldn't give it to me! The rightful heir! He hated me! He scorned me! He was better than you could ever be!" he turned and leaned against a table. "Guards!" two guards entered. "Take my brother. Tie him to the post in the middle of camp. He is not to be given any food."

The guards seized Konrad as he struggled to get free. "May this life and the next have mercy on you!" he cried.

"Don't wish on something that isn't there," his brother told him without turning around. "Instead, plead that I have mercy on you."

Konrad was dragged out of the tent.

I can't let him do this, he thought, struggling at his bonds. *The country will never survive until his twisted anger is appeased.* He closed his eyes and drew a shaking breath. *I can't let him take it from me.* With this useless plea in his mind, he stared up at the stars.

Scarlet's horse frantically galloped all through the night and reached the sea village just when the sun was rising.

The villagers stared at her, but once again she didn't care. She had a mission to take care of. Her people needed her.

She inquired after ships and found one that was leaving that day. She boarded, this time taking her horse with her.

She spent the trip on deck, not working this time. She pushed against the forward rail as if it would help her to get there sooner. The wind was favorable the entire trip and as each day passed her heart grew more anxious about her countrymen.

Will they accept me? What about Konrad's father? Will he kill me? What if they have already killed the dragon? Am I making this trip for nothing? Questions rattled around in her head, but she knew why she couldn't turn back.

If I turn back, I will never know. Father once said if I abandon my people, they will abandon me. But if I stay with them, they will never leave me. Grurhoum and Elincia were right, you can't just abandon your people and your country. You can't just leave them to their fate.

The next morning the soldiers struck camp as Konrad's brother's forces split, some taking Konrad's army as prisoners back to Fairfalcon, some escorting Konrad and his brother to the castle in Hedgecliff.

Daedor left his tent early so he could direct the striking of camp. "You, take that to the horses, the tents can go in the carts," he told one of the soldiers who was carrying supplies from one place to another.

Daedor caught sight of his brother. "I see you're not worse for the wear," Daedor told him as he knelt to where Konrad was sitting, tied to the post. "Not even your pride was hurt last night. Don't worry, we'll change that soon."

"Daedor!" Konrad called out to his brother. "Daedor, do you not wonder why our father never loved you? It's because you are cruel and your heart is full of shadow. There is still a chance for you!"

"Me? A chance? Our father is dead! He is gone! There is no chance!"

Daedor struck Konrad. “Be quiet you filthy varmint,” Daedor rose. “Your mouth won't be so quick to speak when I’ve finished with you.”

When the camp was all taken down, a guard untied Konrad from the post and dumped him in the back of one of the carts with another guard.

The caravan started at a slow pace and went only a few miles that day. They stopped outside a small town for the night.

They traveled for many days, sometimes not even leaving the camp for days. To Konrad though, the days blended into an almost-feverish dream.

Only five miles outside the castle, Daedor privately received a messenger in his tent.

“Your Majesty, your outside villages have been burnt to the ground and the people are fleeing,” the messenger explained.

“What? Why?” Daedor asked, looking angry and confused as he set down a glass of wine he had been enjoying to celebrate his victory.

“I have only heard rumors sir, nothing true I'm sure,” the messenger hesitantly explained.

“What do they say?” Daedor insisted. “Tell me.”

“They say,” the messenger hesitated and swallowed nervously. “It is a dragon.”

“Dragon?! Impossible!” Daedor cried striking out at the messenger and grabbing him by the collar, “Don't lie to me!”

“I'm not, sir! It’s true! The people have seen it! They say the dragon speaks sometimes. Something in another language.”

Daedor panicked as he spilled his glass of wine over the map he had out. “Pack up camp!” he cried. “We leave for the castle now and we will ride till we get there!!”

His panic rose and the people sprang into action.

Daedor was considered a strong warrior, though he was also known for his treachery. Now that he was faced with an enemy he could not place traitors within the reach of, his courage failed. He could face Konrad’s army without flinching, knowing full well Konrad had already lost, but he could not even look in the direction of an honest enemy, aware that his future was uncertain.

Konrad heard the cry from where he lay, nearly faint with pain and hunger. He could hardly make out what was being said, but he understood.

“Dragon!” he whispered to himself as he smiled and remembered Hedgecliff. *Maybe this will be the end? Perhaps my brother will fight it and die. It’s too late for me, but perhaps the country can still be saved.*

Deep inside he yearned to see Newle again, but he hid behind his country as an excuse. As long as he had hope for his country, he had hope for her.

He moaned as he turned over. He was sore from both beatings and travel. The guards had remembered to bring water every now and then, but they had nearly forgotten to bring food.

Guards came and dragged him up so they could walk the last five miles to the castle.

If she only came back for a few moments, he wished as he plodded forward.

CHAPTER FOURTEEN

Scarlet's voyage across the sea had only a week to go and at every delay her heart beat against it all.

If the wind blew wrong and called her back to the east, her heart cried out. For each moment of delay she aged years.

Konrad was pushed unceremoniously off to the side while Daedor gathered his forces to defend the castle instead of fighting for the villagers.

Daedor got constant updates about the dragon's progress as it destroyed first one, then ten villages—eight in Fairfalcon and two as it slowly progressed closer into Hedgecliff.

Daedor grew fearful for his life as the dragon came closer and the messengers stopped bringing hopeful news.

It only took another three days before the dragon was outside the castle and it spoke brokenly in their language, resorting to a higher tongue when their simple words encumbered it. "I have come for your king!" the dragon cried when it got outside the gates. "I will spare the villages, but I will fight the king. I have a score to settle with him!"

Daedor called in his advisors as soon as he heard the challenge. "The dragon calls for me," he told them with a smirk. "How will I not fight it?"

The advisors exchanged evil glances. "Is your majesty fearful? Do you not want to fight the dragon?"

Daedor glared at them. "No, but I know I cannot kill it myself."

"Cannot?" came the surprised voices of the advisors.

"Do you mean to say I am afraid of fighting the dragon?" Daedor cried, strangely gathering courage. "I will fight it, then! I will show I can do it!

And when I am done, you will all lose your heads! Be gone!"

The advisors smiled, bowed and whispered to themselves as they left the room. Daedor, his own act of treachery forming, called for his armor and sword.

I will fight it today! he thought. *I will show them who is scared!* King Daedor stalked out of the castle and into one of the fields to wait for the dragon. Nobles and common folk lined the towers and walls of the castle. They were waiting for the king. But he never came back.

Scarlet's ship landed that night, her horse was let off and she was gone.

She rode all night and reached the castle in the early morning. She stole a cloak off a line, and hid her horse in the woods. In this disguise, she entered the village. It was empty.

"Am I too late?" she cried, falling on her knees. "Are they gone? Where is Marja?"

She ran up to the castle and banged on the door with all her might. It was opened only an inch and she slipped in.

"Who are you?" the guard who let her in asked, pinning her to the wall with his elbow. "And what were you doing out there? Don't you know about the dragon?"

"Where is everyone?" Scarlet cried, grabbing the guard by the shoulders and pushing him off.

"They are safe here. King Daedor went to fight it last night. We are waiting for him to came back," the man explained, letting his defense down and relaxing, deciding the girl posed no threat.

"King Daedor? What happened?" she asked, confused.

"The king died, and his son Konrad became king. Konrad's brother the king of Fairfalcon conquered Hedgecliff. Don't you know?" Scarlet leaned against the wall of the castle feeling faint.

"You poor girl," the guard continued, suddenly feeling sorry for her. "Take my arm and follow me further in."

Scarlet allowed the man to lead her to one of the halls deep inside the castle.

"Wait here, I'll bring you some water," the man offered, leaving her leaning against the wall in the hall.

He ran off and Scarlet pulled herself together.

"The old king dead?" she wondered. "And Konrad king?" she took a shaky breath as she looked around, bewildered. "Except he's not. His brother has taken over." Tears streamed down her cheeks. "I'll never leave them again," she whispered. "I can't let things fall apart like this."

Scarlet quickly dashed to the kitchen, grabbed a roll that was out on the counter and slipped out of the door. Finding the dragon, killing the dragon, avenging her people and earning their trust were her only concerns.

Scarlet let herself through the castle gate, but stopped as the dragon flew into sight.

"Your king is weak," he called out brokenly. "Give me a warrior who will fight me!" he cried as he lighted upon a church building, crushing it underneath his weight.

Scarlet lay flat against the wall, trying to be invisible.

"Fight me or you will all die!!!!!" it cried.

Scarlet shook herself, took a deep breath and even though she was quaking, she cried out in the language of the west, the language of elves and dwarfs, the language that she had come to know as freedom. "*Mina arad*! My enemy! Look at me and fight!"

The people who had gathered around the towers and along the wall heard her.

"Who is he? What is he saying?" they whispered to each other as they pointed at the cloaked figure. "Will he be able to kill the dragon? Look at him! He is young!"

"I will fight you!" she cried out in the language. "I killed the first dragon! I can kill the second!"

The dragon turned to her and laughed. "You? Kill a dragon?"

"You don't remember me?" she asked with a smile in her voice as she hid in the depths of her cloak. "Perhaps you will know me now!" she tore the cloak away and the dragon recoiled in hate.

"You! You! I will fight, though you have no honor!"

The dragon reared back and blew fire at her as she lifted up her shield.

"You won't win this time!" it roared as it lashed out at her with his talons.

The dragon tore Scarlet's dress and leg as she tripped to roll out of the way.

The dragon laughed. "I have already won!" it roared.

Scarlet stabbed at the thick hide of the dragon, but her blows just glanced off his scales.

The dragon laughed again and flicked at Scarlet with its tail, wiping out at her back and then coiling around her.

"I will squeeze you the way you squeezed at my heart when you killed my mate!" the dragon declared as his grip tightened around Scarlet, compressing the air out of her lungs.

Scarlet hacked off the tail in one lop and was dropped back to the ground.

As the dragon roared, the people in the castle trembled with fear and scrambled to get under cover.

Scarlet regained her feet and took a daring move. While the dragon was rolling with pain, she climbed the spikes, tearing her dress as she went.

Clinging on for dear life, she stabbed at the unprotected flesh of his neck. The dragon reared back as if to crush her, but fell forward, motionless.

Scarlet didn't know what happened next, but while others flooded around to dance around the dragon's dead body and then carry her into the castle as a hero, she slipped away. She told herself she hadn't earned this—this happy ending wasn't for her. She told herself the bruises she had gained from the battle were what she deserved. How many similar bruises had her people sustained because of her foolishness?

"I am Princess Scarlet Elwen Silvergleam Oreldes. I am the princess," she tried to remind herself, but failed. *I left them when they needed me the most. I don't deserve to rule them.* Scarlet ran back through the familiar castle halls. She had come home, but nothing could truly ever be the same.

What have I done? she thought as she roamed. *And where is Konrad?* Scarlet stopped dead in her tracks as an overpowering dread filled her. *I must find him! He's all that Hedgecliff and Fairfalcon have left!*

Scarlet dashed to the nearest tower and went up, searching each room as she went, becoming more tired with each excruciating step. He wasn't there.

Don't give up hope, she told herself. *I'll just try the next tower.*

Scarlet searched each tower slower than the last and still didn't find him.

The dungeons, she thought with a shiver as she limped down the nearest stairs.

Her injury from the dragon was getting to her. She wasn't even sure she would be able to make it back up the stairs, but she went through every chamber, each one darker than the last, each one filled with more terrible devices than the last.

Scarlet reached the last torture chamber and leaning heavily, pushed the door open.

Inside there was a guard standing watch over the closed and dark doors.

"Good sir," she asked as pleasantly as she could, eying his weapons carefully. "Do you know where they are holding Prince Konrad?"

"Prince Konrad?" the guard said, staring at her. "Aye, I do. And what's that to you?"

"I know him," she cautiously answered as her heart quickened.

"Know him or know of him?" the guard laughed a hollow laugh.

"I know him. We were friends."

"Were?" the guard laughed again.

"Look! You are trying my patience, where is he?" Scarlet asked, getting angry.

"Oh the poor little girl," he continued to laugh.

Scarlet, impatient and angry, drew her sword and pointed the blade at the man. "I'm only going to ask this once so try to pay attention. Where is he?"

The guard stopped in surprise and fear. "He's in that cell right there," he pointed across the chamber.

"The keys," Scarlet demanded, holding out her hand.

"Here," he pulled out the bunch from his pocket.

Scarlet opened the door back up the stairs and motioned for the man to leave. He answered in confusion, unable to understand what was going on.

"The dragon has attacked the castle. I have been sent down here with orders from the king to make sure every guard joins him in defending the castle," she assured him with a hasty glance around. She didn't stand a chance if he put up a fight. Thankfully there seemed to be a commotion going on upstairs and seemed to be evidence of a dragon. "Go! Save your country. They need you more than you are needed to guard an already-locked in prisoner!"

"Dragon?!" the man rushed up the stairs without a backward glance, his sword already drawn. Scarlet was only too glad.

The moment he was gone she locked the door and rushed over to the one he had indicated, unlocked it and dashed inside.

The cell was dirty and moldy. The floor was bare and the corner a dark shape paced.

She examined him from where she stood—his clothes were torn and blood stained his shirt in more than one place. His lips were cracked and dry, his hair was filled with grit and filth and stood up on end from the many times he had run his fingers through them.

"Konrad!" she cried when she laid eyes on him, words failing to give voice to the emotions that fought within her. She was unsure if he still wanted her, unsure if she should leave.

Konrad turned. "Newle? You're back?"

There was still distance between them, both physical, mental and emotional. Neither one knew how to close it.

"Yes!" Scarlet cried, mindlessly answering to her servant name. "It's me."

Just those simple words were enough for both of them, and in a moment they had met in the middle and embraced.

Scarlet felt like everything was right again.

Konrad held her back at arm's length to examine her. "You're alright? You're not hurt?"

The weight of the miles and her frantic search suddenly seemed to catch up with her and as she fell and Konrad caught her.

"You're injured," he finally noted the large gash on her leg.

"I'm fine. It's only a scratch I got when I killed the dragon." Scarlet tried to walk away but Konrad scooped her up and began carrying her back the way she had come.

Neither one said anything as he passed through the cell door and unlocked the door to the stairs. Konrad kept stealing glances of her, making sure she was comfortable and not just a figment of his imagination. Scarlet, too tired even to keep her eyes open, nodded off. She was home—all the weight she had been carrying was gone. She was accepted. Her pain was over.

Konrad took the stairs two at a time, closing in on the noise coming from upstairs, barging through the doors at the top and taking huge strides down the hall.

The hall was empty, which was strange considering how loud things were, but at the end of the hall, a young woman (smaller than Scarlet) stood in the shadows, her black hair and pale skin contrasting with each other. She was a refugee from the dragon. She had fled from her home to the safety of the castle. She started when she saw the prince charging toward her and she curtsied, her face hidden in the shadows. As she rose she stole a glance at the prince and his burden, her face changing in recognition.

"Lady," Konrad began, halting in front of her. "Find the physicians, this woman needs help!"

But the only answer he got was a startled cry of pain.

"Scarlet!" the woman called out, reaching for the motionless bundle in his arms.

"Who are you?" Konrad recoiled from the unknown woman's touch.

"No time to explain," the young woman began, unable to take her eyes off the form. "She needs help. Come this way!"

The young woman took off at speeds Konrad thought the frail form unable to obtain, and he struggled to keep up.

"Who are you?" he asked again when he had caught up with her.

"No time," she repeated again, almost nervous.

He didn't press her any more and they continued their journey in silence.

The woman slowed down outside a room. "This is hers," she told him. "Leave her in there. I will get the physicians."

The woman took off again and Konrad was left to open the door and place Scarlet on the bed. Before he had even finished, the young woman was back with the physicians, all crowding around the bed and blocking Konrad from the circle around her.

He slipped out. She was back. His part here was done. He only just heard what was being said inside, he only just heard a young voice call out: "Scarlet! It's me, Marja!"

Konrad turned from the door. He was no longer needed here. But what was all the noise? And why was it getting louder?

He turned around and watched, startled, as a group of people stormed around the corner, Daedor heading the group.

"What is this?" Daedor cried out in surprise.

"I believe I should be the one asking that question," Konrad replied, unsure of what this even was himself.

"The people are celebrating *my* victory over the dragon," Daedor snickered.

Konrad stood, taken aback. "But Newl-" he caught himself, "Scarlet killed the dragon!"

Suddenly, everyone was silenced and all eyes were on him.

"Brother," Daedor let out a hesitant laugh. "You do not know what you are talking about."

But Daedor was pushed off to the side as the crowed gathered in around Konrad.

"Scarlet is back?" someone whispered.

"Yes, she is back," he replied.

"Where is she?"

"In her room. She sustained injuries from the dragon that must be treated."

Slowly, every eye turned back to Daedor who was trying to escape the crowd.

"And what do you have to say for yourself?" Konrad began angrily. "Steeling her victory and lying about it?"

"Yea," another one began. "Didn't you go off to fight the dragon yourself? Why are you not dead? Why have you returned to us alive without killing the dragon?"

Konrad drew his sword, storming at his brother.

"It's a misunderstanding!" Daedor began, stumbling back and drawing his own sword to defend himself.

But Daedor never had the chance. Konrad attacked with such force that Daedor could do nothing to defend himself and was injured with the first blow.

Daedor regained his composure and pulled himself together. He didn't think of what the people would do if he won. The only thing that mattered was the fight at hand.

Konrad attacked again, but Daedor was ready this time and deflected the blow.

They traded on and off for a few blows when Konrad, his anger rekindled, tried something desperate.

He took a step forward and gave his sword a little twist that he had only seen once before. Daedor's sword slipped off to the right and clattered to a halt.

"In the name of the free and true, in the name of all that is good on this earth, in the name of every living thing, in the name of Hedgecliff, I bid you begone!" Konrad forcefully spoke.

Daedor's cowardice showed finally showed through, "Brother," he began with a fake smile. "I submit to your authority."

Konrad pushed on, closing the ground between them. "You submit to no authority," he accused. "You are too proud and sinful to submit to anyone other than yourself."

Daedor dashed to where his sword had fallen. People were flocking out of his way. He picked it up and pointed it at his heart.

"Stop and listen to me!" he cried out as Konrad took a step forward. "You have dishonored me. There is nothing to live for if you are in authority. Goodbye brother!" Daedor fell on his sword, pinned all the way through.

Konrad dropped Scarlet's sword in horror and rushed over to Daedor to gently turn him over. There was no mistaking it. Daedor was dead. His face a tortured mass of evil pride, cowardice, and hate. Konrad let Daedor's head fall back to the ground so he wouldn't have to see it.

As Konrad turned from his brother, the people gathered around him, cheering him on the way they had cheered for his brother, but louder this time. Their princess was back.

CHAPTER FIFTEEN

Scarlet was standing on a pleasantly cold white balcony, the summer night's stars shifting through a silver gray cloth that had been lifted to let the cool breeze in.

"Daughter?" Scarlet's father whispered as she walked towards the railing, "You came back,"

"Yes," she admitted, "I'm sorry I left."

"You left for what you thought was a good reason. You came back for what was an even better one."

"Father, should I have left?" she asked, searching his face.

"Should you have left?"

"Yes, what if I hadn't left?"

Her father gave a low laugh, "You know that I cannot tell you what if. You know that no one can tell you what if."

She smiled, remembering how Crovprix had said something similar.

"But I want to know. What if?" she insisted, catching his hand.

"What if I had never died? What if you had never left? What if the dragon was not stopped? Daughter, because you left, you were safe. You were alive and able to come back when they needed you."

"They only needed me because I left them," she argued, "Because I went to find a dragon,"

"Perhaps it was better this way. Perhaps something worse and unstoppable would have happened if none of this had ever happened," her father embraced her and pulled a lock of hair out of her eyes.

"I can only tell you what is. You are back. Your people want you again. Konrad has a country that is broken. They need him. You have a country that is broken. They need you. Perhaps you were meant for this,"

"Meant for it?" Scarlet clutched at her father as she felt him fading away, "But wait!"

He was gone.

Scarlet woke up and shook the dream away. She glanced around the room. It was richly furnished and there was a fire burning in a grate. Her chainmail and sword were laid across a chair along with the red dress she had been wearing. The dress was spread out so you could see the tear that the dragon had ripped in it, still covered in blood. The dress had not been washed.

Scarlet lay propped up by pillows, her leg wrapped in white strips of cloth. She had been changed into a soft green dress and she could tell her face had been washed.

Her eyes closed and when she opened them again, someone was bending over her.

"Getting along?" the person asked.

Scarlet nodded, not exactly sure what that would mean,

"You gave us quite a scare, Your Majesty. After Konrad brought you in, we were very worried for a while."

"Majesty?" she asked, a little dazed,

"Yes, Queen of all Hedgecliff and Fairfalcon," the man smiled.

Scarlet sat back and tried not to think about it.

The man went on, "I've been to see you eight times a day since then. I dressed your wounds and made sure you were getting the right care. Would you like something to eat?"

Scarlet nodded.

"Good, I'll have the cook bring something up and if you're not too tired, perhaps her son could come with her. He has been dying to see you."

"Himdir?" Scarlet smiled as she remembered the little boy, "Let him come up,"

"Good, then I'll send for them. There is also a young woman who has refused to leave your door. She says her name is Marja."

Scarlet started—she was alive!

"Send them in all at once!" she cried.

The physician smiled and told her he would send them in together.

He left the room and Scarlet waited patiently for something to eat, but more so for the company of her friends.

Before long, there was knocking at the door. "Come in," Scarlet called out.

The door opened and Samantha walked in with Himdir behind her.

"Morning, Miss," Samantha smiled.

"Morning," Scarlet's face fell. Where was Marja?

Himdir stood by the door staring.

"Hello, Himdir," she greeted him.

"Did you really see dwarfs?" he asked, skipping the formal greeting,

"Yes," Scarlet laughed sadly.

"And elves?"

"Yes."

Himdir's eyes grew round.

"And you killed two dragons?"

"Yes."

Himdir rushed to the chair and climbed on it, "Is this your sword?" he asked reverently touching it.

"Yes it is. I got it from a sea captain."

"And the chainmail?"

"Grurhoum Greatbrow made it for me out of Ijeslum. It is rare, light, beautiful and strong."

"Is this tear where the dragon hurt you?" Himdir asked.

"Yes," Scarlet replied absently, watching as a shadow grew in the door and materialized.

Marja stood there, as timid as Scarlet had remembered.

Scarlet, smiling, opened her arms and enveloped Marja.

Marja and Scarlet didn't know where to start, but soon the words came tumbling out head over heels.

"Come now," Samantha laughed setting down the tray she had brought in. "The doctor told us not to make her talk. She is too tired for that just now."

Marja stopped talking and just sat on the edge of Scarlet's bed.

"Alright," Himdir sat down and continued to stare at the things on the chair while Scarlet ate some bread and stew Samantha had brought up.

"I heard Konrad can't wait to see you," Samantha told Scarlet. "He's up and about organizing things. He should come by for a visit soon."

"He would have been by sooner, but he wanted to make sure everything was in place for you to step into power when you're better," Himdir explained. "I have been by, but only to bring him updates as to how you are doing. He told me to talk to you for him. He even thought about sending a note for a while."

Scarlet gave a feeble smile as her heart sank a little. "What did the doctor mean when said that I was queen?" she asked Samantha. Scarlet already knew the answer, but she needed to be sure, she needed conformation.

"The people remember everything you have done for them and they would like you to rule them," she explained.

"But what about Konrad?" she asked.

"Konrad is still only from Fairfalcon. The people don't want him,"

"The doctor said I was Queen of Fairfalcon too. What did he mean?"

"Konrad's brother, Daedor, attacked Hedgecliff and he took it over. He combined Hedgecliff and Fairfalcon into one country. Then Konrad killed him."

Scarlet didn't feel like debating with her and so she let the matter drop.

"Himdir? Tell me what you've been doing,"

Himdir launched into a detailed account of the last month of winter and the beginning of spring.

"I went sledding! I wanted to go horseback riding, but Konrad never asked me after you left. Is it true?"

"Is what true?" Scarlet laughed.

"That you're the princess?"

"I guess," Scarlet replied vaguely, turning to look at Marja who had been silent during all of this.

"Why didn't you ever tell me?" Himdir asked.

"Because I couldn't trust anyone to not kill me," Scarlet blushed. "Then Konrad saw the ring that meant I was the princess and I ran away. I don't even know if he wants to be my friend after I lied to him like that."

"Come Himdir," Samantha called. "That's enough. Scarlet needs her rest. Goodbye!"

Scarlet snuggled back down and carefully turned onto her side as Samantha and Himdir left.

Marja stayed behind, still sitting on the edge of the bed.

"How are you?" Scarlet asked, turning to her friend with watchful eyes.

"I'm wonderful. Everything is just the way it's supposed to be," she replied, her voice as content as it could sound.

"I'm glad," Scarlet smiled, also content. She was back, Marja was here and the kingdom was hers again.

Queen, she thought, enjoying the blissful comfort. *Not really what I wanted to be. I wonder if I could convince them to let Konrad rule while I go back out east.*

Scarlet knew in her heart they would never let her do that. And thankfully, she would never let herself do it either.

Konrad, wrapped up in helping people move out of the castle among other things, waited impatiently for Himdir to come back with information. So far he had only been told she had her leg cut open and was unconscious.

Himdir slipped in next to him.

"How is she?" Konrad asked expectantly, still directing people.

"She was awake. She told me all about her armor and her sword," Himdir cried, his eyes shining.

"Is she alright?" Konrad asked anxiously, helping a woman lift her things into her cart.

"Mum gave her some food, and she heard some news. Her sword is really cool. She fought a sea captain for it!" Himdir exclaimed, still caught up with excitement.

Konrad smiled. How could he trust a little boy to bring him the news he really needed?

"And the armor? I've never seen anything like it before! Somebody made it for her out of some precious metal,"

"And what about her condition?" Konrad asked, setting the box down in the cart and leaning back.

Himdir instantly calmed down and his tone grew quiet for a boy his age, "Her leg was neglected. She should have had it looked at when the cut was made."

"Nothing too serious?" Konrad asked quietly,

"No, but she killed two dragons!" Himdir told him, unable to contain his excitement. "She fought a dwarf and won! She saw the elves and lived with them!"

Himdir continued to go over the entire story again. His childlike excitement showing through with every word.

That's Scarlet, Konrad thought, smiling. *She can take care of herself, though now that she's queen, the people will take care of her. She doesn't need me.* He sighed and asked Himdir when the doctor said she could get up again.

"I don't remember," Himdir told him.

Konrad smiled. "Send a message to the physician and ask if I could eat with Scarlet. She should be able to stand it and we have something we need to talk over now that she is back and her kingdom is hers again,"

"The doctor was just leaving her," Himdir told him, standing up and heading for the castle gates. "I'll bring him over and you can ask him yourself."

Himdir slipped out of the castle and pounded down the road in chase of the physician. In another minute he was back with him.

"Well? I heard you wanted to talk to me?" the physician asked when he re-entered the courtyard.

"I was wondering if perhaps the queen is able to have visitors for dinner, just me and maybe her cousin, Marja."

"She should be glad of the company," he explained, "As I won't be seeing you before then, there are a few things that you should keep in mind. First, don't mention her travels or why she left. She might not even know why yet. Second, try not to help her. She's very independent and won't like it. And finally, don't talk too much. She is tired and she won't be able to stand it for long. I'll have Samantha set up a table and chair for you next to her bed. Good day!"

The physician bowed and left with Himdir, who was strangely interested in the man and what he did.

Konrad turned back to his work of helping the people. He needed to be done in time to invite Marja to have dinner with him. He was no longer king, here or anywhere, but the people submitted to his authority, if only because he was better than Daedor, but also because the princess—their princess—approved of him.

Scarlet was woken up for lunch but went back to sleep before long.

The shadows outside the castle grew longer and longer as rumors began to spread.

"Princess Scarlet killed five dragons!"

"She befriended the spirits of the trees while she was gone."

"You know that beautiful armor she had on? She stole it from the dead bodies of her enemies."

"That sword was stolen from dragon's treasure."

"She went east to find a demon to help her kill the dragon."

No one paid any attention to the more ridiculous rumors, but they were out there all the same.

The butcher she had known was the center of the more pure gossip. He told them everything Samantha had told him when she was there getting meat for dinner.

"She's weak as a sapling," he told them. "But she's proud as a peacock! They say she's having dinner with the prince tonight. She'll banish him or have him killed no doubt!"

People gathered around as he wound his story the way he wound the twine around the packages of meat.

"She's killed two dragons and has fought sea captains, dwarfs and elves! She had trinkets of each battle. The chain mail from the dwarf, the sword from the sea captain, her shield from the first dragon and her wounds from the second one!"

The romantic tale spread throughout the city and before dinner, everyone had heard it, or at least some version of it.

Scarlet lay awake when Samantha came in with her dinner. Scarlet had noticed a table and two chairs had been set up, but she didn't say anything.

"Afternoon, Scarlet," Samantha greeted her with a smile. "Konrad offered to eat with you tonight. The physician said he could and Konrad invited Marja to join you too. I'll get him right now."

Scarlet nodded. She felt a little nervous and worried. The last time she had had a real conversation with him, she had yelled at him. But she didn't have much time to think about that.

Marja appeared at the door. Scarlet waved her in to join her and Marja sat on the edge of the bed again.

"Konrad invited me to join the two of you for dinner," she began. "I've hardly spoken to him since I got here."

Marja looked at Scarlet expectantly.

"Well," she began. "I think you'll like him."

The door opened unexpectedly and Konrad walked in. Marja stood up and curtsied.

"Good evening," he smiled as he bowed first to Marja and then to Scarlet.

"Hello," she smiled, turning from Marja.

"Sit down," she told them, trying to be casual. "Samantha has already served everything."

Konrad pulled out a chair for Marja and waited until she was seated before he sat down himself. They felt the tension in the air and the constraint inside them. The physician had basically told them not to talk about so many things, there wasn't much left to talk about.

After a few more moments of silence, Konrad gave in.

"How are your injuries?" he asked as he set her plate on the tray on her lap.

"Thank you. I haven't been up yet, but I hope I will be up soon," she calmly replied, awkwardly trying to continue the conversation. "What happened while I was gone? One of the servants gave me a little history, but not really details."

Konrad brought her up to date.

"And what about you? What did you do in the east?" he asked when he was done.

"I really never should have left," she admitted avoiding his glance, "If I had never left none of this would be happening right now."

Konrad avoided the topic for the moment. "What are you going to do as queen?"

"I don't know," silence fell over the room when she asked. "I don't want Fairfalcon. It's not rightfully mine. Will you take it?"

Marja looked up, surprised.

"It belongs to you now. It was united with Hedgecliff under my brother's rule," Konrad reminded her.

"Your brother Daedor?" she asked, searching her memory.

"Yes, that one," Konrad continued. "Your country needs healing."

"And so does Fairfalcon," she explained. "I can't help them both at the same time. I insist that you take Fairfalcon. It's not mine!"

"But my country was supposed to be Hedgecliff after my father ruled, I never wanted it."

"Then take Fairfalcon!" Scarlet pressed, "It will be just the way it was before. Your father's line will continue to rule Fairfalcon, and my father's line will rule Hedgecliff."

"But it's not mine, it's yours," Konrad insisted.

Scarlet hurriedly searched her mind for some way to convince him and she blurted out, "You can't just abandon your country!"

Konrad slowly agreed. "Alright, when you put it like that."

Marja smiled, "Now, we are dying to know what you did in the east. Can you not tell us finally?"

Konrad admitted he too was curious and Scarlet told them everything.

"I'm almost envious," Konrad told her when she was done. "You had quite a trip,"

Marja looked shocked. Why would anyone want any of that happening to them?

"I really didn't even stay down there that long. Most of the trip I was on a boat."

"You still saw quite a lot. Dragons, dwarfs, elves, wizards!" Marja interjected.

"I only saw one," she corrected her.

"One what?" Marja asked.

"One wizard," Scarlet clarified.

"But you traveled with him. You should be an expert on wizards now." Konrad continued to debate her.

"Expert? I don't think anyone could become an expert on anything. There's just too much to know. I want to go back though. I want to explore the rest of the place and have more adventures."

The room grew silent and Scarlet attempted to shift herself, but ultimately ended up cringing in pain.

"What's wrong Scarlet?" Marja asked, standing up and crossing the few steps to her bed. Konrad stood up too.

Scarlet turned her face so they couldn't see how much agony she was in.

"Does it hurt now?" Konrad asked.

"Only a little," she replied, still looking away.

Marja helped her into a more comfortable position and Scarlet flopped back on the pillows, emotionally and physically empty.

"Never mind," she told him, wiping the single tear from her face and pushing the tray away, "I'm tired,"

"Goodnight then," Konrad said understandingly. "I'll take the tray down to Samantha."

"Thank you," her voice quivered as he left.

Marja sat down on the edge of the bed and rubbed Scarlet's hand.

"I love him just as much as the day I left," Scarlet whispered when the door had closed. "Maybe even more. How am I ever going to go back to living normally?" Scarlet looked up at Marja and burst into tears. "Too many scars that will never heal are making sure that doesn't happen. Every day I will be reminded of my stupidity—how I abandoned those I loved, how I will never live up to the love I have for Konrad. How could he still love me after all I have done to him? After he found out I lied, after he watched me abandon my country, after all that I had done to him." Tears rolled down her face as Marja sat there, a comforting presence, knowing the pain Scarlet was going through. Hadn't she experienced this exact thing when she had lost Stefan?

Scarlet slept fitfully that night and the physician ordered her to sleep and not bother with anything.

All day she was in constant pain and she suffered it without a word. Only the cool night brought her peace.

CHAPTER SIXTEEN

Scarlet took weeks to recover. Himdir took messages between Konrad and the queen and slowly she came to terms with her wounds and with the fact that she would never be worthy of Konrad. They had two separate countries. Their paths were different. Her heart broke a hundred times in those weeks. She figured eventually she would become immune to it, but how she longed for that day with a fearful dread. How could she ever become senseless to the pure love she had in her heart?

One day, the doctor handed Scarlet a walking stick and she left the confinement of her room.

Konrad was leaving for Fairfalcon that day and she went to see him off.

"Goodbye Scarlet!"

"Goodbye Konrad!" she called back, showing no emotion.

"When our countries have been pulled back in order, perhaps you will come see me?" he asked hopefully, bending over her hand and kissing it.

"Of course Konrad," she smiled, pain coursing not only through her wounds, but through her heart. However, she hid what she felt and put on a smile for him.

"We can have the ball that my father planned. You did promise to come with me," he reminded her.

"I also promised to go riding with you," she reminded him, scrambling for any chance to be close to him, but at the same time, feeling repulsed, knowing she would only grow fonder of him.

"I'm sure that will have to wait a little bit while you get steady on your legs," he told at her.

"It won't be that long," she smiled.

"And remember, that day when we slid down the banister? Remember how I said I would have to have a talk with you? Nothing has changed. I still have something to talk to you about when you have the time," he finally hinted, looking down at her from his steed.

Scarlet looked away, unable to look in his eyes and read into every line as much as she could. He couldn't mean it, could he?

"Your country still needs you and I'm not ready yet," she told him finally.

Konrad nodded slowly. "Goodbye!" he called back as his caravan pulled away.

"Goodbye Konrad!" she cried.

She watched as his small caravan disappeared into the village and her heart sank.

I will wait till he comes back, she thought. *Or when he calls for me to come to him.*

She slowly limped back into the castle.

Scarlet and her country slowly healed together.

Each burnt village built back up from scratch, each small wound turning to scar. It took nearly an entire year before the villages were built back and Scarlet could walk without a staff. She still limped when she was tired, and had a huge scar that would never go away, but adventures come with a cost and she would never regret anything that had happened to her.

It was then that a messenger arrived at the castle, his foreign insignia starting rumors throughout the villages he passed through.

"I have come for an audience with Her Majesty, the queen," the messenger told the guards outside the throne room. "I have an important message from His Majesty Konrad, King of Fairfalcon."

The guard led the messenger into the throne room.

The young queen, only seventeen, sat upon her throne conversing with her cousin, the beauty of the kingdom. The queen's young head was held high under the weight of the gold crown, but she didn't resent it. Her scarlet dress set off her beautiful green eyes and jet-black hair.

She had been a jewel in her country before everything, but now, with all her trials, her hard work, her endurance, and her resolution—her failures even— she was more than a jewel, more than just a credit to her family. She was becoming stronger, and even if no one noticed, she was becoming more beautiful as more than just the air of a princess shone through. Something deeper, something better than all the jewels and credits could ever become.

Her attention moved when the Fairfalcon messenger entered the room. Her eyes sparkled and her lips smiled.

"I am Sidwell, royal messenger to His Majesty Konrad, King of Fairfalcon." the messenger bowed.

"Proceed," the queen told him, tremors in her voice as her cousin clutched her hand in excitement.

"His Majesty has sent you an invitation," the messenger held out a scroll with another bow.

The queen came down from her throne with a whirl of skirts and took the scroll from him. "Thank you. If you will stay here for a moment I will write a reply to take back with you."

The messenger bowed as the queen and her cousin left the room, their eyes sparkling with girlish delight.

> To Her Majesty Scarlet Elwen Silvergleam Oreldes, Queen of Hedgecliff and Adventurer of the East.
>
> My Dear Queen,
> I have the honor to invite you on behalf of Fairfalcon to a summer ball the 15th day in the 6th month of the year. We will celebrate with dancing, food and stories.
> You may extend this invitation to any and all noblemen and lords.
> Thank you for considering and I madly await your reply,
>
> His Majesty, Konrad, King of Fairfalcon.

Scarlet's heart pounded as she wrote out an answer. Accepting it.

> To His Majesty Konrad Thurindir Starseed Faervel, King of Fairfalcon and peacemaker of nations.
>
> Dear King,
> Thank you for inviting me, my nobles and my lords to your ball. We gladly accept your invitation and await the event with anticipation.
> Thank you again and we will see you on the 13th.
>
> Her Majesty, Scarlet, Queen of Hedgecliff.

Scarlet sealed the letter and ran back to the throne room.

"Here is my reply," she told the messenger when she reentered. "Tell his majesty I'm dying to catch up with him,"

"His majesty will be pleased," the messenger smiled with a bow. "I will tell him."

"Thank you."

The messenger bowed and left the room while Scarlet went back up to her throne, the scroll still in her hand.

"Lord Edmund?" she hailed a passerby. "Please have this invitation circulated among the noblemen and lords."

"Your majesty," Lord Edmund bowed. "I will have my messenger take it out immediately."

Edmund took the invitation and left.

Time passed and the day grew closer until only a week was left. Scarlet left the castle so she could head down to the seaport.

"Well, Miss," the innkeeper had told her. "If you ever come home again, look me up."

Scarlet smiled, remembering those words.

Well I'm back, she thought. *It's time to look you up again.*

Scarlet and Marja started out on a rainy day. She was with seven of her nobles and lords and a small company of servants.

They headed toward the seaport. It took three days this time because she was not riding day and night for her life.

They reached the inn around nightfall of the last day.

"This is it, friends," she told them leaping from her saddle. "Order rooms and food for the night. We are staying here." The nobles and lords dismounted as the servants unloaded the horses and led them to the stables.

Scarlet entered the inn, her nobles and lords following her.

"Your Majesty," the innkeeper murmured bowing. "We did not expect you. I will have rooms and food ready for you in just a moment."

Scarlet smiled, "Innkeeper, do you not remember me?"

"Your Majesty? How could I!" the innkeeper was astonished. "You must have remembered someone else."

"No, it was you innkeeper. Do you not remember? Only a little more than a year ago I came riding in, nearly faint with hunger and you fed me and exchanged my money for Chrono Tluapee. You advised me against going with the sea captain Wycliffe Gloom. I'll tell you that you were right."

"That was you, Your Majesty?" the innkeeper cried in surprise, examining her closely.

"Yes, it was me and I have come to repay you," she turned to one of the servants. "Bring forth the title."

The servant brought forth a scroll and handed it to the queen.

"Innkeeper? What is your name?" she asked curiously.

"Wardell Gower," he replied, confused as to why this great lady would need his name.

Scarlet wrote something on the scroll and then told Wardell to kneel.

"In the name of all authority that is in heaven, or on earth, I christen thee, Wardell Gower, knight of Her Majesty the queen. Rise."

The knight rose and bowed, "Your Majesty, how can I ever repay you?"

"Repay me?" Scarlet smiled. "I am repaying you. Your advice was invaluable," she changed the subject. "When is the next ship going to the east? I have something to put on it."

"In three days Your Majesty," the baron bowed again.

"I will be sending a servant with another title to Grurhoum Greatbrow, the dwarf. I am afraid that Crovprix the wizard is long gone by now."

She stayed up till the dawn was in the east telling Wardell about her adventures. He frowned when he heard about how he was right about Wycliffe Gloom, and smiled when she told him about Grurhoum and the armor.

"You found then, what you were looking for?" he asked when she was finished.

Scarlet was thoughtful for a moment. She looked out at the sunrise and relived everything she had been through. "I found adventure if that's what you mean," she said at last. "But sometimes, I wonder if what I was looking for, I was really running away from."

The baron smiled, "I remember you were worried about having burnt all your bridges behind you."

"All but one," Scarlet replied. "And that's why I'm here,"

They rode off in the morning leaving a servant with the title for Grurhoum. She had invited the innkeeper to the ball, but he refused. He wasn't quite ready for that just yet.

They rode all day for another three days. Each day covering more, and new territory as they ventured deeper into Fairfalcon. On the last day they reached the castle.

It was a magnificent structure that seemed to reach toward the setting sun. Its white-gray stones glittered in the reflection of the moat and except for the lack of trees, it had a nearly elvish air. Dark green ivy trailed up the walls and the loose pieces blew about in the breeze.

The drawbridge was lowered and they entered the stronghold to the sound of trumpets.

"Queen Scarlet!" someone cried out.

Scarlet knew that voice anywhere. "Your Majesty!" she replied her heart soaring.

Konrad knelt besides the horse and offered his hand to help her down, just like he had helped her up only two years ago.

"Traveled far today?" Konrad asked when she was safely down so he could offer his left arm.

"Reasonably," she smiled accepting it with her right arm as he led her into the castle,

"My servants will take care of the horses, if the rest of you will just follow me," he led the way slowly through corridors, being considerate of Scarlet. "The city is having a festival tomorrow and in the evening we will have the ball. Right now we will have dinner," he led the way into the dining room and settled Scarlet in a chair at his right hand before sitting down himself. The lords, ladies and noblemen each sat down.

The first course was brought in, "Just like the time when my father invited you to have dinner with us. Right?" Konrad smiled down at Scarlet.

"Yes, except back then I was only a scullery maid who taught Himdir."

"If you remember anything I said," he reminded her, "You would know I thought of you, and still think of you, as much more than a scullery maid or even a queen."

Scarlet smiled, tears in her eyes. "Give me a little while longer," she told him picking up her fork. "There are some things that we must get used to first."

"Alright," he agreed, looking a little sad.

The lords and ladies were having a delightful time. There were jokes and singing, and the prospect of a ball tomorrow was over their heads.

The second course was brought in and the conversation between Scarlet and Konrad dropped dead.

At the end of dessert, Konrad rose, glass in hand.

The room instantly grew quiet.

"Thank you," Konrad exclaimed, looking around. "It is now time to propose a toast. From the moment I met this girl, her ideals and higher way of life have made me strive to become worthy of her friendship. Her flaws only make her more beautiful and dear in the eyes of her friends, though she would hate to admit it," he looked down at where she was sitting and she blushed. "To Scarlet! I wish her long life, I wish her road to be smooth, I wish her country to be a blessing and not a burden, I wish for her happiness. May she find it in whatever form it comes to her by!"

The guests rose and cried. "To Scarlet! May she find her happiness in whatever form it comes to her by!"

"Thank you," she replied, her eyes shining as the people drank and slowly left the table, the dinner over.

Morning came all too soon for Scarlet. Breakfast was served in the dining room and again she sat at Konrad's right hand.

When breakfast was over, they got horses and rode into town for the festival.

Konrad offered to show his guests around. The two slowly made their way to a play as the crowds parted ways before them.

"Come up here," he led the way to the balcony. They sat down and watched as a funny drama was played out before them.

All that day they walked around observing things until Scarlet could walk no more and Konrad had to send for her horse.

"I'm sure you'll want to dance tonight," he told her bringing it to her and offering her a hand up. "I'll take you back to the castle and you can rest before the ball."

They slowly cantered back up to the castle where Konrad dropped Scarlet off at the gate, promising to come back to escort her to the ball later on.

Scarlet gave a sigh of relief, but felt so alone when Konrad was gone.

She carefully flopped herself down on her bed and curled up with the pain in her leg and in her heart.

I can bear it, she thought, closing her eyes and squeezing out a tear while trying to convince herself. *It's not that bad.*

Carefully she uncurled herself and lay flat out on the bed.

He can never love me, she thought nonchalantly. *I left my country and ran away for my own selfish desires. How could he ever love me when all I have given him was strife and hardship?* Something deeper in her heart cried out, *He loved you when you were but a scullery maid in his eyes, he alone was your friend when your family was killed by his father, and he alone stood by you and helped you. How could he not love you? You helped him. Your heart showed through with every time you helped another friend in need.*

Her mind spoke again. *His father killed your father! How can you let him love you? He didn't trust you after you lied to him, he shouted at you when he finally found out that you were a princess and worthy of his love.* Her heart cried out again. *But he still loves you! Did you not hear what he said at the toast? 'May she find her happiness in whatever form it comes to her by.' He means himself.*

Scarlet rose late in the afternoon, missing the midday meal, so she headed down to where she thought the kitchen would be.

"Good afternoon, miss," the cook smiled up at her. "His Majesty said you might be coming down. He was worried when you missed the meal."

"Worried?" she sat down at the table as the cook set a plate in front of her,

"He was hoping that you weren't in trouble," the cook answered.

"Oh," Scarlet laughed. "It's not that. I was just so tired."

"Wait," the cook set down her dishcloth. "You're not the princess who ran away to the east and killed two dragons?"

Scarlet stammered.

"Don't even say it, it wasn't you! You went gallivanting off to the east to find adventure! You're the one who killed the dragons! The king's told me a lot about you."

"I'm sure it's all exaggerated," she told the cook modestly.

The cook smiled. "His majesty said you should have enough time to head up to your room to freshen up and change before the ball. He was also wondering if you would want a maid to help you. "

Scarlet felt indignant and disagreed that a maid would be helpful before she went up to take a look at the ballroom.

She carefully entered the room and scanned it before she was noticed. The room was empty except for Konrad. He was standing alone in the back, his head bowed and his hands behind his back.

Scarlet turned away, not wanting him to know she was there, and went back to her room to change.

Scarlet brought out a dark green gown that matched her eyes and had gold trim on it. She carefully let her hair down and smoothed it out. She decided not to put it up because she would have to wear her crown and it wouldn't look right. She slipped the dress over her head and arranged the folds. The dress hugged her waist and then flared out in pleats. She passed a gold belt around her waist and tied it again in the front. Her draping sleeves came most of the way down her arms before flaring out to show a gold lining.

The last thing she did was settle her thin, gold crown (not much more than a circlet) on her black hair.

Just as it was settled, there was a knock on the door. Scarlet opened it.

"Scarlet?" came a voice. "Are you ready?"

She smiled, "Ready."

Konrad stood there, waiting for her. His gold hair and brown eyes exactly the way she remembered them the first time she had seen him, the night she shared her bread with him before she knew he was a prince.

Konrad's long sleeve, light blue tunic peaked out from underneath his short, dark blue quilted doublet. The trim on both was gold. His sword was hung from his belt and the tops of his black boots were folded over to allow his knees to move freely. His simple gold crown pressed down on his blond hair and he bowed, offering her his arm.

They silently walked down the corridor and entered the bright ballroom as the sea of people parted, bowing and curtsying on each side.

"Remember the last time you walked into a banquet on my arm?" Konrad asked, smiling down at her as she surveyed the room from his arm.

"I do," she replied. Her heart almost too full.

They moved to the front of the room and sat down.

"Will you take the first dance with me?" he asked as Scarlet's heart flew to highest heaven.

"Yes," Scarlet replied simply, she couldn't look at Konrad. "If you insist." She carefully took his hand and they slowly made their way to the dance floor.

Konrad carefully held her hand. Scarlet gathered up her skirt in her left hand and they slowly began to move to the waltz. They moved gracefully but Konrad and Scarlet didn't think of that, their hearts soaring above the world.

They didn't say anything, everyone watching them as they spun around the room. The dance ended and Konrad bowed to her and took her hand as he led her to the front of the room.

Another dance started and Scarlet was pleased to see Marja accept an offer from Konrad.

The dancing passed away with smiles and laughter, and as people were beginning to migrate to the diner table, Konrad pulled Scarlet into one of the adjoining halls.

They could still hear the music through a cracked door, but no one was around to bother them.

They spoke of their countries, their efforts to clean them up after everything that had happened in the past year and Scarlet spoke of the pains of having to get used to everything.

Konrad looked anxious, his answers were curt and to the point, but after a few minutes he finally divulged his true purpose.

"Scarlet," he turned to her and took up her hand. "I love you! There is nothing to get used to! You are shoving me aside because you are not used to yourself yet. Yes, you came back from the east different and you think I will regret this, or I'll shun you because you are different now. Scarlet! How could you be so wrong!"

Konrad got down on his knee and pulled a ring out of his pocket. "This is for you. Whether you take it or not is for you to decide. If you refuse it, I can only hope that you are not quite ready yet. I can only hope that you will take it at some point."

Scarlet looked down at Konrad, hardly understanding the words he said because her heart was full. "I'll take it, Konrad," she whispered her eyes shining down at his. "I'll take it."

Konrad took her left hand and slipped the ring onto her finger.

"Are you sure?" he asked, searching her eyes.

"I'm sure," she leaned over and kissed him. "I don't know what I would have done without you, I might even be dead! You ... I love you."

Konrad stood up and enveloped her in a hug and a kiss. "Scarlet, my Scarlet."

"Oh Konrad!" she whispered into his jacket. "All these years, looking for something that was right under my nose."

"Sometimes you need to back away to see the big picture, that's all,"

Konrad assured her.

They stood in the hall a long time. Scarlet twirled the ring around her finger and looked up at Konrad. Konrad looking down at Scarlet, knew he had something he would always protect, something that he would die for.

"Come," Konrad said at last. "Dinner will be on in a minute and they'll want us to do the honors. Come in with me?"

"Oh Konrad, on your arm? In front of everyone?" she asked frantically.

"Why not?" Konrad smiled. "You didn't mind before."

"I guess you're right. Could we not tell them for a while?"

"What are you afraid of?"

"Nothing," Scarlet blushed. "I just think I would like to keep it a secret from them for a while."

"Alright, just don't take the ring off," he told her.

"But it's on my left hand! Everyone will see it!" Scarlet protested.

"Then slip it on your right hand for the moment. No one will notice," he assured her.

Scarlet slipped the ring off carefully and put it on her right hand, "There, is that better?"

"If you really want the answer, no," he smiled at her as he led her to the door. "But I think you might be right. We both need time, even the people need time, before we can say anything about this."

Scarlet smiled from the haven of Konrad's arm as he led the way to the dinner table. He seated her at his right hand and then sat down. Everyone followed.

Scarlet didn't know what happened to the night. She remembered staring up into Konrad's eyes most of the time through a distant whirl of gaiety and laughter produced by the guests.

Toasts were offered but they didn't remember any of them. They didn't need to. They were living their own romantic dream, one that passes only once in a lifetime.

After dinner Scarlet didn't need any urging to dance. She felt confidence in front of everyone. People stared as Scarlet and Konrad tripped across the dance floor, too happy to care about rhythm. They were not graceful, far from it. Scarlet laughed as she tripped over Konrad's feet, and Konrad smiled, carefully righting her and steering her to safer waters.

The night passed too quickly. When the guests had departed, Scarlet and Konrad moved out to the balcony.

"Look at the stars," Scarlet told him. "I recognize all of them."

"Were they different in the east?" Konrad asked, grasping her hand.

"Magnificent," she whispered. "The stars there glowed like nothing here. Perhaps one day I can take you there."

“Our honeymoon?” Konrad asked.

“If Fairfalcon and Hedgecliff can spare us,” she assured him.

“Did you slip the ring back to your left hand?” Konrad asked.

“It’s right here,” she held it up to the light.

“It’s pretty,” he said touching it. “Don't ever move it again. Promise?”

“I promise.”

EPILOGUE

Before a week was over, the entire country of Fairfalcon knew about the engagement. Before the end of two, Hedgecliff also knew.

Queen Scarlet went back to her country and the next thing anyone knew, she was married to King Konrad. The two countries were joined at the wedding and it began a new history and age of prosperity.

Queen Scarlet and King Konrad had two children, a boy and a girl to pass on the family name.

King Konrad and Queen Scarlet never went on their honeymoon, but when they were old they left the country in charge of their children and they went to the east.

Messages came back and forth. The last one that was received was about being reunited with Grurhoum Greatbrow, knight and lord to her majesty Queen Scarlet. He had met with the messenger Queen Scarlet had sent over years before, and had rejoiced when he heard she had gone back to her country. The king and queen died years later after having made lasting bonds with the other nations.

Their son, King Daedor, named after its uncle who had passed away, became king not long after that. His sister never married. She stayed by his side, his strength in time of trouble. Her ideals and higher way of life led Daedor from trouble many times. Her name was Newle.

The End.

ABOUT THE AUTHOR

Erika is a promising young author from the Cleveland area. Combining an active imagination with enthusiasm for outdoor adventures, she enticingly creates worlds of fiction that draw you into her stories. These range from conversations with a ladybug to exploring entire kingdoms full of elves, dwarves, dragons and wizards, sword fights and battles that decide the fate of kingdoms.

She is a cat aficionado and wishes that her hometown would allow her to have more than two.

Find out more about Erika at www.teragram.ink

CPSIA information can be obtained
at www.ICGtesting.com
Printed in the USA
LVOW12s1629121216
516922LV00006B/1414/P